"What's supp
a Christmas n

"Two things. First,
will come true. Sec_____ ____ best, it's said
that if a couple kisses under a Christmas moon,
they'll be together forever." Liberty smiled. "Kind
of sweet, don't you think?"

Jake shrugged that off. "Sweet is in the eye of
the beholder," he murmured.

"Come on. You can't be that jaded about
Christmas and romance, can you?"

He was silent, then said, "I've never been a
romantic."

"Of course, men hate to admit being romantic."

He exhaled. "Believe it."

"You don't date or anything?"

"I do. But I've got my career, and with it being a
questionable one, I don't drag anyone into it."

"I guess if you think you're dragging someone
into your life, it wouldn't be very romantic, would
it?"

Jake studied Liberty. "You have enough
romance in you to make up for the lack in me."

Dear Reader,

To most of us, family is everything. It's our center in a sometimes chaotic world, having loved ones who care about us no matter what happens. It's that safe place when nothing makes sense. It's all ours, and we love it beyond measure. But the definition of family is what we make it.

In my new series, Eclipse Ridge Ranch, *family* is a group of three men who as teenagers were sent to a ranch in northern Wyoming when it was a group home for foster kids, run by Maggie and Sarge Caine. For Jake Bishop, Seth Reagan and Ben Arias, they found hope and acceptance, and it was the only time in their lives when they knew the meaning of family.

Under a Christmas Moon is the story of Jake Bishop and Liberty Connor—two people on seemingly different trajectories in their well-planned lives. They find that love can come without warning... especially if a couple kisses under a Christmas moon. The legend has it that, if that happens, the couple will be together for forever.

I hope you enjoy Jake and Liberty's story, and remember that love comes in the most unexpected ways and at the most unexpected times.

Happy holidays!

Mary Anne Wilson

HEARTWARMING

Under a Christmas Moon

—

Mary Anne Wilson

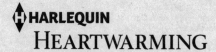

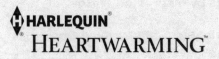

HARLEQUIN®
HEARTWARMING™

ISBN-13: 978-1-335-88999-7

Under a Christmas Moon

Copyright © 2020 by Mary Anne Wilson

Recycling programs
for this product may
not exist in your area.

This edition published by arrangement with Harlequin Books S.A.

For questions and comments about the quality of this book, please contact us at CustomerService@Harlequin.com.

Harlequin Enterprises ULC
22 Adelaide St. West, 40th Floor
Toronto, Ontario M5H 4E3, Canada
www.Harlequin.com

Printed in U.S.A.

Mary Anne Wilson is a Canadian transplanted to California, where her life changed dramatically. She found her happily-ever-after with her husband, Tom, and their three children. She always loved writing, reading and has a passion for anything Jane Austen. She's had around fifty novels published, been nominated for a RITA® Award, won Reviewers' Choice Awards and received RWA's Career Achievement Award in Romantic Suspense.

Books by Mary Anne Wilson

Harlequin Heartwarming

Unspoken Words
For the Love of Hayley
Undercover Father
A Question of Honor
Flying Home

Visit the Author Profile page
at Harlequin.com for more titles.

Tom,

With every beat of my heart, I still think of you.

I will love you forever.

PROLOGUE

Arizona, September

IT LOOKED LIKE a road to nowhere, but Jake Bishop knew better. After a mile of driving on the cracked asphalt that turned off the highway north into the desert, it ended at a set of massive metal gates. The ten-foot-tall barrier bore no logos or company names. There was no explanation for it or the imposing security fencing that ran into the distance both east and west with a spiraling razor wire topping it.

Jake had been here three months ago on a job and knew exactly what was behind all that security. He brought his dusty black pickup to a stop and lowered his window to gain access to a call box on a heavy support post. As furnace-like air hit him, he grimaced. In the second week of September, the Arizona sun was relentless. His black T-shirt and jeans, which he wore with tooled leather boots, felt too heavy and too confining. Even wearing sunglasses, he had to squint to see the call button before he pressed it.

A surveillance camera swiveled around to aim at him. "Hey, right on time." He recognized the voice of Simon Fox, the head of security for Madison Development, when it came over the speaker.

"The man said 1200 hours. I'm here."

"Well, come on up."

The call ended as the gates swung slowly back to give Jake access to the sprawling compound. He drove through and up a well-paved access road for about half a mile toward the central core of the business buildings, a group of low-roofed stone-and-wood structures. He drove past them, then turned onto a gravel road that ran parallel to a runway large enough to accommodate most commercial-sized jets.

He drove up to a single Quonset hut a good distance from the main buildings. Painted a chalky white, it was only recognizable as Security because two Jeeps parked right by it had *M.D. SECURITY* lettered in red on their doors. Jake stopped and pressed his truck's horn.

His cell rang and he answered it immediately. "I'm waiting out here."

"Sorry," Simon Fox said in his ear. "Change of plans. Madison isn't wheels-down until 1400 hours." Victor Madison, who oversaw everything from the first ideas to the final product of his cutting-edge private jet development company, had been precise when Jake had talked to him two days ago. *Two days, 1200 hours. I'll be waiting for you*, the man had said. Now Jake was the one waiting.

Simon gave Jake the code for the access door to the hut, then added, "Go on in and cool off." The call ended.

Jake stared at the security building. Two hours. He hated delays and wasting time, especially when he was more than up for an emergency retest on the MT-007 prototype, which was why he was here. He wanted to find out what he must have missed on the first flight test, as much as he wanted to check out the plane.

When he got out of the truck into the smothering heat, the desert wind caught at his hair, which was in real need of a trim. He raked it back with his fingers, then grabbed his cell and swung the door shut. He didn't even think about going into the Quonset hut. Instead, he walked the football-field length to the runway, then stepped up onto the tarmac and headed east.

By the time he reached the closest of the two massive hangars, his clothes were sticking to his skin, and his hair was clinging damply to his neck. He walked over to the bank of independently operating, thirty-foot-high doors that made up the front of the oxidized green building. Grabbing a thick leather strap on the closest door and avoiding contact with the hot metal, he pulled the door open. There was a groan of metal on metal, then he had a wide enough gap to get out of the heat and sun.

The outward appearance of the buildings in the compound were deceiving. They looked old, dusty, sunbaked and totally unremarkable. But inside, the setups were cutting-edge in every way. That included total climate control, and the cool air felt great as Jake took off his aviator sunglasses to hook them on his T-shirt.

As his eyes adjusted, he saw his target right in the middle of the vast space: the prototype MT-007. She was incredible, her lines elegant yet fierce. The slightly downward wing thrust and high angle of the tail by the double engines enhanced that feeling of movement even when she was sitting still. There was none of the showy paint or logos and chrome that would eventually be added, but even the dull black finish didn't diminish her.

"Flawed, but beautiful," he breathed as he strode across the concrete toward the eight-passenger jet. He made it to within ten feet of it before he heard the shout he'd expected but thought would take longer to come.

"Stop right there!" He turned toward Simon Fox, who was little more than a dark silhouette against the brilliance of the sun behind him in the doorway.

"Your timing sucks, Simon," Jake called.

"I've got perfect timing," the man said as he took a couple of steps into the hangar and motioned Jake over to him.

The security man was about as tall as Jake but not as lean, and maybe five years older than Jake. With dark buzzed hair, he looked annoyingly cool in jeans, a white shirt and lugged boots. The only sign he was on duty was his black shoulder holster.

Jake slowly jogged back to within three

feet of Simon. "I just wanted to have a look at her."

Simon shook his head. "When I got the alarm, I knew you were faster than I thought you'd be in this heat."

Jake ignored that and asked, "What came up with her?"

"Don't know, but if I did and told you, I'd have to eliminate you and then myself."

He shrugged. "I'm just curious about what was so important that a new test had to be run so expeditiously."

Simon exhaled. "It's not in my job description to know anything about that." He shook his head before his deep brown eyes met Jake's. "You need to chill, literally and figuratively."

"No, I need to figure out what I missed the first time."

"The boss was right about you. No nerves, no hesitation. He knows you press it to the limit as if you have nothing to lose or as if you have some special lucky charm."

Jake reached into the watch pocket of his jeans and took out something he'd carried with him for fifteen years. He caught it between his thumb and forefinger and held it up to show Simon.

The man squinted at a gold medal about the size of a silver dollar. It wasn't quite a true circle and had mellowed in color. It had once been engraved, but that was long gone due to the fingers that had worried it over the years.

"So, that's your lucky charm?" Simon asked.

Jake closed his hand around it as he drew it back. "I got this from my foster dad, a retired marine. We all called him Sarge. When I was heading to boot camp, he gave this to me. It's a Distinguished Service Medal he was awarded in Vietnam. He told me it was to help me remember I make my own destiny, and to own it." Sarge—whose real name was Jim Caine—and his wife, Maggie, had opened up their ranch in Eclipse, Wyoming, to run a foster care group home. Jake had moved there at fifteen. He didn't know if he'd told anyone this before, but Sarge had been on his mind a lot lately.

"You figure this is your destiny?" Simon asked as he motioned to the plane behind him.

Jake pushed the medal back into his pocket. "Until I drive back out the gates and head to Florida for my next contract."

When Jake had been released from the foster system at eighteen, he'd left the ranch and shaped his own destiny as much as he could. But he always kept in touch with Sarge as well as with Seth Reagan and Ben Arias, his best friends on the ranch. They were all living their own lives now, the way Jake was living his.

"Sarge sounds like a good guy," Simon said.

"Yes, he was and is." In a flash of memory the man came to him—six foot five with imposingly broad shoulders, big hands and a big voice. *You are part of this place now if you want to be*, Sarge had boomed at Jake, a teenager whom everyone else had written off as a lost cause. "He told me if I did right, he'd do right by me," Jake said. "He meant it."

If Jake had downtime between this retest and his next contract, he would go up to the ranch and see if Ben and Seth could meet him there. He'd been away far too long this time.

"Smart, too. Now let's get you out of here," Simon said, and stepped back out into glaring sun and heat.

Jake started to follow. He was about to step over the threshold when he heard a double-clicking sound echo behind him. In a single heartbeat, there was a massive roar accompanied by a rush of fiery air.

Jake instantly knew it was an explosion, and it hit hard and fast with a force that lifted him off his feet. He was hurled up and out into the brilliant light of day. For one surreal moment, he was flying. The next moment, pain beyond endurance came along with a crushing pressure that targeted his chest and head. No air. No way to breathe or stop his momentum as the sky and tarmac reversed places, and in that single moment, Jake knew he'd run out of time.

He'd never see Seth, Ben or Sarge again. This was the destiny he'd designed by his own actions.

CHAPTER ONE

"TWENTY-ONE DAYS until Christmas, and I'm stuck," Libby Connor called out to her assistant in the reception area just outside her open office door.

"Twenty-one days? Are you sure?" Wendy Davis called back.

Libby pushed her chair away from the desk and the oversize monitor that showed the architectural repurposing she'd been working on. She stretched her arms to ease the tightness in her neck and shoulders. She'd been in the Brant Chase Architecture and Design offices in Seattle since early morning. It was a Friday, nearing six o'clock. Libby hadn't had any meetings today, so she'd dressed down in jeans, sneakers and a T-shirt from her college days.

At five foot two, she was often called petite but persistent. When she wanted to do something, she was determined. Right now, she was very determined to figure out how to give a stubborn client what they wanted so she could get home before dark. Wendy, a slender woman who had just turned fifty, came to the door to peek in. "I'm heading out. Anything else you need?"

"Not unless you have a great idea how I can give Swanson a full luxury exercise area for the tenants in the new lofts without him agreeing to give up any existing space for it."

"You're the adaptive reuse expert for redoing buildings in the city, and you're a brilliant architect and designer, so wave your magic wand and give him his space."

Libby laughed at that. "I forgot about that wand."

"When does Roger get back?" Wendy said.

"Monday."

"How long's he been gone this time?"

Wendy had been with Libby through all her fiancé's comings and goings for work as head of his family's charity foundation, The Montgomery-Thomas Water Initiative Group. "Three months in west Africa, near Mali. But he'll be here for our first Christmas and New Year's together. Then we have a ton to do for the wedding."

She just had to finish with her final client of the year. Roger would be here in two days, and then her focus was all about spending the holidays with him and planning their big day. Libby had waited her whole life for this, and she wanted it to be all theirs. Now she was finding it difficult fighting off his mother's daily suggestions for the wedding without him here. Offending his family was the last thing she ever wanted to do.

"You're lucky. He's got money and looks, and runs all over the world helping people get, what is it, clean water?"

"Yes, and now he's doing most of the on-site work."

Wendy waved to Libby. "Well, I'm gone."

"Have a good weekend."

Libby turned to the large monitor and saw an incoming call. She smiled at the caller username GeekPro and accepted the call. A moment later Seth Reagan, a good friend of hers, came on the screen.

She could tell he was at his corporate headquarters in the city, no more than five minutes away by car, maybe ten by bike. She greeted him with, "You had to call instead of coming to visit in person, didn't you?"

"Hey, you're at work and there's Friday afternoon traffic out there."

"I'd like to see you in person once in a while. You're the only tech geek who can make me understand why my computer hates me so much."

"Oh, am I interrupting something between you and your computer?"

"Yes, you are," she said, and smiled. "Thank you so much."

Seth laughed, looking like some college grad in a T-shirt with his company logo on it, his thick brown hair mussed from raking his fingers through it. No one would mistake him for being the founder and CEO of a very successful tech company dedicated to developing cybersecurity. He also didn't look incredibly wealthy, but he was. "What's going on?" he asked.

"I have this client who's driving me nuts."

"You've got enough pressure getting married to the golden boy of the Montgomery family without client problems."

"Hey, I'm okay with whatever I have to do to make it easier for Roger. But his parents just keep pushing their ideas for the wedding. They're giving me suggestions that are incredibly formal and not what I want." She sighed heavily. "But it's what they want. Three months to go and they want it held in some new place that extends out over the Sound. Can you believe that?" She wasn't going to fall into a self-pity role, no matter what happened. She knew she was marrying into the Montgomery family, one of the most powerful families in the city and state. She'd fit in with them and make Roger happy. She just had to figure out how to fit in and still get the wedding she wanted without offending anyone.

"Of course I believe it. But you're tough. You can keep them at bay."

Seth and Roger hadn't exactly hit it off when they first met. Libby had wanted her best friend to get along with her future husband, but a nice lunch at a restaurant on the Sound had turned into an awkward hour of finding out the only thing the men had in common was her. Seth never spoke badly about Roger, but he'd never asked for a second lunch, either. "Did you call for a valid reason?"

"Yes, and I'm sorry to make your life more complicated, but since you specialize in repurposing places, I need to run something past you."

She put her elbows on the desk and rested her chin on her clasped hands. "Okay. Go for it."

Seth spoke quickly and succinctly, laying out a plan he wanted to put into action as soon as possible. She began to understand why he'd called her and just how his request was going to complicate her life even more than he knew. He finally finished, "That's it. I need to know if you'll come on board through your firm?"

Libby sat back in the chair as she considered how to do what he needed and still plan her wedding, which was set for March. She knew redesigning the ranch where Seth had grown up and making a summer camp for foster kids on it was doable. But the job was way out of Seattle, in northern Wyoming, and it would be a long-term commitment for her and the firm.

"Come on," Seth finally said impatiently. "Tell me you can do it."

She turned her diamond engagement ring around and around on her finger, then nodded. "I love the whole idea. I think it's incredible." Libby knew Seth adored the ranch he'd lived on with Sarge and the whole area around Eclipse, Wyoming. "To give kids time out of impossible situations, to get them temporarily away from their lives that are pretty ripped up, is a wonderful gift...but it's a lot to take on."

"I know," he confessed. "Just tell me it's doable."

"Of course it is."

Seth let out a long sigh. "Thank goodness. I got to thinking I was crazy or close to it."

"Far from it," she said. "I get why you want to do it." She got it because she'd been in foster care, too. She and Seth had a lot of common ground. They'd first connected when her firm had sent her as a representative to a charity event in the city and they'd been seated at the same table. They'd bonded over their pasts after he'd mentioned he'd been in the foster care system. A cup of coffee later that evening had stretched to hours of conversation.

"The financing's going to be in place through a private foundation I'm in the process of setting up, so the funds will be available by the new year," Seth said.

"You understand it can't happen overnight? You're talking repurposing existing outbuildings and laying out the camping areas, and that's not to mention the safety codes and requirements for minors. Just because Sarge and Maggie had the group home there doesn't mean it's a slam dunk. This is totally different. I'd say you're looking at two years to completion."

"Okay, it's up to you to figure out how to do it faster."

She almost rolled her eyes at the simplicity of his statement. "You want super speed, and my client wants me to design, to use his words, 'a sublime spa and gym experience' in a building that doesn't have any space for it. My mind is going numb."

He chuckled. "Sorry. I'm anxious to get this off the ground. What building are you working on?"

"We're doing a loft split in the old Swanson building."

"I know that place. It's been empty for ages."

"Well, no more. But there isn't any room for what Swanson's son wants without giving up one of the units. He won't do that, because of the loss of future revenue."

"The roof."

"What?"

"Do it on the roof. That place used to have a helipad. When we moved in here, I could see the helicopters coming and going. That was seven years ago, so it has to be structurally sound or require very few updates for load and stress and whatever else you have to do for code. But it could be doable."

She grinned at him. "And here I thought your genius was limited to computers. That's perfect. Thanks."

"What about the ranch? You will do it, won't you?"

She didn't hesitate. "Absolutely. Count me in."

"Then let's get on it right now. The ranch is empty, so there wouldn't be any distractions."

"Isn't Sarge there?"

He frowned and raked his fingers through his unruly hair. "No, he's in the hospital in Casper. He fell and broke his leg. The ranch has been downsizing since Maggie died, but now it's shut down until I can figure things out."

"Oh, I'm sorry. He's going back there to live?"

Seth leaned closer to the screen. "Yes, I hope he will. That's why I wanted you to start with a design on the main floor of the ranch house for a suite where he can live and be safe, with a live-in caregiver factored in." He hesitated. "There's something else that makes timing important. Sarge was diagnosed with Alzheimer's a year ago and never told us."

"Oh, Seth, that's awful."

He brushed that aside. "He doesn't have unlimited time to understand what we're doing for him. He and Maggie wanted to transition from the group home to the summer camp as they got older, but now she's gone, and he just let it all go."

She hurt for Seth. Ben and Jake, who Seth had once described as his foster brothers, and Sarge, who he loved like a father, were the only family he'd ever known.

"If you can pull this off, I think Sarge would have a reason to be engaged in things there, and that might be good for him." He paused. "Since the ranch is empty and Roger's going to be home for Christmas, maybe you and him could go up there and get a break from his parents. You could look over the main house to get an idea of the layout and begin putting the plans together for Sarge's space. And you and Roger would have some time together without his family."

She smiled at him. "Are you trying to bribe me?"

"If it's working, I am."

She laughed as she felt things fall into place. She was starting a new family, *her* family, and she wanted it to be perfect, especially for the holidays this year. The Christmas she was eight years old, she'd finally found her own family when she'd been adopted. It had been the best Christmas of her life. She wanted the same thing, another "best Christmas" in her life when she and Roger became a family. "Consider me bribed," she said.

He was grinning now. "Thank you so much."

If Sarge only knew what Seth was doing for him, for a week or a day or just for a moment, she would do whatever she could to make it happen. "My pleasure."

"Okay," he said. "I'll let Ben know."

"What about Jake?" she asked.

"He's been out of touch for a few months. He's probably in a high-security situation, but he'll call." She and Seth finished discussing details—Libby would head up to the ranch next week and stay there until after New Year's to enjoy the holidays and get some groundwork done. With their plan set, her friend signed off just as she received a text from Roger.

Sorry, another opportunity came up west of here. I have to nail it down and set the crew up. Not sure how long it will take but will call as soon as it's set. Love you.

Libby was stunned. She had not seen that coming, not after Roger had promised he'd be here in two days. This year was going to be their first Christmas of their new life together. Roger hadn't made it home last year. She bit her bottom lip to stop the silly tears building behind her eyes. She sat staring at her reflection in the blank monitor and could see the defeat written all over her face. It hurt, but she pushed it away. Roger was good at what he did, and she trusted that he'd make sure to be back before Christmas. There was time, and meanwhile, she could go to the ranch and take care of the preliminaries before he got there.

Right then an email notification popped up on the screen, and she recognized the sender. She'd seen it so often since the engagement: Roger's mother. She ignored it, putting off reading it until she got home. Instead, she wrote an email to Roger. She laid out everything she'd just discussed with Seth and asked him to please call her as soon as possible so they could plan the holidays. With that settled in her mind, she felt a bit better. She'd get as much work out of the way as she could before he showed up, and then her time would be all his.

"Merry Christmas," she whispered to herself.

JAKE LAY COMPLETELY still as he slowly drifted out of another night of broken dreams and broken sleep. The noise in his ears, a combination of muffled whining and ringing overlaid by a blanket of numbing pressure, had been a constant in his life since he'd regained consciousness after the explosion almost three months ago. At first, the sum total of the other pains in his body had made it almost possible to ignore the damage to his ears.

But as he recovered, it had become obvious that most of the body pain would fade away. The damage to his ears was a different story. He accepted the fact that he'd have to wait longer to see if he could win his battle to get his hearing back and be able to fly again.

Now, he woke to the noise every morning, and he dealt with it every day. The only time he could hear was in his dreams, and some of that wasn't what he wanted to hear. The damage robbed him of any ability to actually hear beyond the persistent noise that blotted out any and all outer sounds.

He opened his eyes slowly to thin morning light streaming into his room on the top floor of a sprawling Malibu beach house. He had his privacy thanks to Victor Madison, so he could keep healing after leaving the private hospital Madison had also paid for, without anyone knowing what had happened to him. It was nice, but he ignored the view of the ocean through the glass doors. He'd learned the hard way not to move too quickly after he'd fallen facedown at the hospital one day, when vertigo had hit with a vengeance. Now he carefully moved to sit up on the side of the bed.

He was staring down at the black marble floor of the bedroom when he sensed he wasn't alone. "You're early this morning," Jake said without looking behind him. He had no idea if Cal Harris said anything before he came around to stand between him and the view.

Cal was a solidly built man with a shaved head who had traded the uniform he'd worn as a physical therapist at the private hospital for high-end casual clothes. He was Jake's personal support system, having agreed to accompany him to Madison's Malibu house to see him through the obstacles of being deaf... for now. Cal held a red-and-white Christmas stocking in his hand. "Did you sleep?" he read on the man's lips.

He'd been losing the sleep battle for too long. "Some."

Cal was a blessing in a lot of ways, and Jake knew he'd been lucky to become friends with him while recovering. As the son of a deaf mother, Cal had realized that Jake had a natural ability for lip-reading and had worked with him on it. "Read my lips," he said with a smile. "I know you can do it."

"Just tell me why you're smiling."

"First of all, your back's looking good."

Jake doubted that. His back had taken the brunt of the impact from the explosion. The burns and lacerations from flying shrapnel had left an ugly pattern where they'd struck him. "Sure," he said with undisguised sarcasm. "My back makes a pretty impressive connect-the-scars game."

"I've heard that some women think scars are sexy."

"The same way some women think a broken nose, a collapsed lung, a broken collarbone and a dislocated shoulder are sexy."

Cal shook his head. "Yeah, women love that."

Jake didn't laugh at the man's sarcastic humor. "I need a shower."

"You need a haircut and shave, too. Hippies aren't in style anymore. But before you head to the shower, I've got some good news and an early Christmas present."

Jake exhaled. "Give me the good news and forget the present."

"Simon Fox is back to work, and the lowdown is, his wife still thinks he's hot."

Jake was relieved to hear that. "I'm glad Simon's okay."

Cal held out the stocking. "This is for you."

Jake took it and felt its weight, then tipped it upside down over the bed. A cell phone just like the one he'd had before it was destroyed in the explosion slid out. He looked at Cal. "What's this?"

"A cell phone, duh, and I did a bit of digging and put your most important numbers in the contacts."

"Appreciated," Jake said, but didn't pick it up.

Cal looked slightly deflated by Jake's response. "I thought you'd be anxious to make use of it. Sarge's number is in there, along with Seth's and Ben's—also Madison's direct line and my cell."

Jake was anxious to connect with all the family he'd ever had, more than Cal could know, but he couldn't. "You know I can't contact anyone." He raked his hair straight back from his face as Cal stared at him. "I can't do it, Cal."

"Listen to me," the man said.

"Can't do that, but I'll watch."

This time Cal gave Jake a "get over yourself" look as he said, "Hey, you know this ear damage could be temporary—you could heal up from it. We know there's a 25 percent chance you'll heal naturally, and that window could be bigger than we're aware of. So quit feeling sorry for yourself."

The chance of natural healing was all Jake held on to. Without that, he'd lose everything he'd made of his life. If he had surgery, he'd have to inform any prospective client, and they wouldn't hire him as a test pilot. It was why he'd elected not to operate right away. If he could heal on his own, he'd be able to go back to work and no one would be the wiser. The odds of healing naturally without intervention were low, but he'd wait to do anything else until he knew one way or the other where his luck landed. "Yeah, okay," he murmured.

"You need to get back to living. You need to contact Ben or Seth or Sarge."

Jake exhaled heavily. "I signed the mother of all nondisclosure agreements. I did it willingly because I like what I do and want to keep doing it. But I can't tell anyone about what happened from the moment I was under contract to Madison, until, well, forever."

Cal shook his head. "It's a tough agreement, but those guys are your family. They can't be off-limits."

"They are, and so is the doctor who delivered me, if there was one."

"Madison told me you're free to go where you want, do what you want. Just keep quiet about what happened out in Arizona. I mean, I don't even know what happened, but he seems to think if it gets out, he's going to take a hit to his business image. But I'm here to help you if you need it, or even go with you, if you want me to."

Of course Jake was free to do what he wanted, but the agreement was clear. "If I violate that agreement, Cal, I'll lose all the money I've been paid for a contract that I'll never finish, along with the total medical care I'm receiving, and the nice package Madison gave me. But the biggie is, if it gets out that I have ear damage, everything's over for me, and I'm in the dust heap. It's a lose-lose, forever kind of thing. I can't take that chance."

"Jake, this is your life, like it or not, but you need to live it, not endure it."

"It is what it is," Jake whispered to himself as he looked down at his hands pressed to his knees. A tap on the top of his head got him to look up. "I can't lie to Sarge, for heaven's sake, or to Seth or Ben. I won't. It's easier to be here without them knowing anything until I know how this all falls out. I'll gradually see if I can contact them in the future."

"You've got temporary ear troubles, and you're working on it. You don't have to say much more than that. You'd lose everything. I get that, and I'd say you have more at stake than Madison. That's your incentive to not mess up."

It did come down to his own risk, and he missed Ben and Seth and Sarge. He really missed them, and he actually started to think about what he might be able to do to keep his word to Madison and still see the only family he'd ever had. "Maybe it could work," Jake conceded as he closed his eyes for a moment. There was a glimmer of hope, if he played it right. He wouldn't be looking for sympathy, but he needed the contact. He felt a heaviness in him tentatively ease. Cal tapped his head again. "Stop doing that," Jake said as he looked up.

"Okay but do whatever you have to do so you can connect with your family."

Jake couldn't fly, either as pilot or passenger for now, and anyone he wanted to see wasn't local. He'd thought about texting people before but had passed on it. Maybe now was the time to take that step. He exhaled, picked up the phone and pressed the power button. Images of music notes flowed across the screen, then icons appeared. He hit the one for contacts and touched the message icon for Seth's cell.

Quickly, he thumbed in: Hey, how're you doing? Been a long time, and life gets busy. Let me know what's going on with you and the others. He sent it, then looked up at Cal. "Done."

Cal seemed pleased. "I have it set to vibrate when it's receiving. Calls are a steady vibration. Messages are a double beat," he said.

As if the man's words caused it, the phone started to vibrate steadily in Jake's hand. He checked and turned the screen toward Cal. "This was your big idea. Seth's calling."

Cal took the phone just as it stilled. "You want me to call back and take a message or just ignore?"

Before Jake could answer, Cal frowned and

looked down at the phone then back at Jake. "Voice mail," he said. "Want me to check it?"

"Please."

He watched Cal listening to the message for what seemed like forever. When Cal put the phone down by Jake, he looked grim. "Okay, not good news, but you need to know." Cal told him about an accident, and about Sarge in the hospital in Casper with a broken leg. He'd been asking for Jake, and Jake felt as if someone had punched him in his gut. Cal added something about doing restructuring at the ranch, setting up some kind of camp for kids, but all Jake could think of was Sarge.

He saw Cal say, "Oh, man, I'm so sorry. What do you want to do?"

Jake wanted to be able to hear so he could call Seth and talk to him. He wanted to be the person he used to be, and be there for Sarge, who had virtually saved his life when he was a teenager. He wanted to see Sarge. He didn't hesitate to reach for his phone and quickly text Seth. What hospital is Sarge in? Where are you and Ben? Tell Sarge I'll be there as soon as I can. For now, use texts. Easier for me to get. Let you know when I'm on my way.

He sent it, then looked up at Cal. "I need your help."

Cal nodded. "Name it."

CHAPTER TWO

Two DAYS LATER, Jake spotted the welcome sign for the town of Eclipse almost five hours after crossing from Utah into Wyoming.

Welcome to ECLIPSE, WYOMING. Pop: 2,001. Elevation: 4,952'. THE WEST AT ITS BEST.

When he passed it and took the turn off the highway, he was twenty miles from the only place he'd called home in his life—the Eclipse Ridge Ranch.

According to the welcome sign, the town's population had doubled since he'd lived in the area. He drove his black pickup along the main street, Clayton Drive, more than aware how the population growth had affected the small town. Stores that were a lot more up-scale than in the old days lined the raised-plank walkways. Gift shops catering to the town's unique offering of the best locations to see solar and lunar eclipses had sprung up everywhere. They were intermingled with determinedly Western-themed stores that fed into the other reason people came here—an Old West experience at dude ranches.

Jake was relieved when he looked ahead and spotted at least one piece from his past that had survived seemingly intact. He slowed the large pickup and eased into a parking space directly in front of Garret's General Store. It was still the same warehouse-sized barn where Jake had worked as a teenager. It was done in wood and bricks, both honestly weathered over the years.

When Jake walked inside the store, it could have been fifteen years ago. Packed shelves and racks held everything a person could want from guns to boots to Western clothes. A space in the back area, where townspeople gathered for coffee, doughnuts and gossip, was still there. The sweet scent of fresh pine came from a huge Christmas tree in the center of it all. The Garrets had always put up the biggest and best tree in town. Obviously, they had kept that going to the present day, down to a spectacular moon-shaped tree-topper that glowed gold.

Jake scanned the rows of merchandise, then

spotted what he'd come in for. His leather aviator jacket and jeans were no match for the cold that arrived on penetrating winds in this part of Wyoming. He needed serious winter clothes. As he approached the rack of heavy denim jackets lined and collared with shirred fleece, he was startled by a tap on his shoulder.

He exhaled, then turned and faced his past. The man was at least thirty pounds heavier and fifteen years older, but Jake recognized him immediately. Farley Garret, the owner of the place, didn't seem to recognize him. Jake, at thirty-two years old, was a huge change from the gangly youth he'd been. Farley was different in other ways, too. His flannels and denim had been changed up for flashy Western clothes in varying shades of blue and silver. A Santa hat didn't completely hide his thinning gray hair.

Jake picked up the man's words in the middle of a sentence. "...called out, but this Christmas music is too darn loud." Jake remembered how the Christmas music had annoyed him as a teenager, but right then, he would have welcomed being able to hear it. "I was looking for a jacket," he said.

"We've got the best."

Jake reached for the one he wanted from the rack and turned to Farley. "I'll be needing one of these."

Farley's eyes narrowed, then recognition hit. "No. Jake Bishop?"

"Yes, sir."

"Wow!" Farley said, then unexpectedly pulled Jake into a bear hug and thudded his shoulder. When he let go, he was in the middle of saying something. "...sooner or later, and I was right."

"Sorry, what?" Jake asked.

"I knew you'd show up sooner or later." He looked around, then back at Jake. "Where's the crew?"

He understood. "Ben and Seth aren't with me. I'm here to check on the ranch, then I'm heading down to Casper to see Sarge."

The man's expression sobered. "I was real sorry to hear about the accident." He held up a hand, and Jake read, "One sec," before Farley turned in the direction of the entrance.

Jake looked over at the door and saw the bell over it swinging frantically, announcing customers arriving. Farley waved a welcome to two older women before turning back to

Jake. His dark eyes narrowed. "You okay, kid? You didn't hear something bad from the hospital, did you?"

"No, it was just a long trip." He changed the subject. "How did you recognize me?"

That brought Farley's smile back. "You're still that kid, just a bit older and a heck of a lot taller. But the giveaway was that." He pointed to the jacket. "Sarge always got those for you boys when you first arrived. Are you here to get the ranch up and running again?"

"I don't know yet."

"Dwight Stockard was the only hand left, and he's moved on down to help his cousin, Sonny, near the Wind River Rez." Farley looked back to the entrance again and said something that Jake didn't catch before the man headed in that direction.

Jake stayed put when he saw a woman wearing a puffy white jacket smiling up at Farley by the door. Measured alongside the man at five foot ten or so, the newcomer wouldn't top five two. Her deep red hair was brilliant. It fell against the white of her jacket in loose ringlets, framing a delicate face that was flushed from the cold.

What really caught Jake's attention was the

combination of her smile and what he read as she spoke. "Sir, I know I shouldn't come into your store to ask you about another store, but I need to find a place that has cold-weather clothes for women."

"Smart girl," Jake murmured to himself as he kept watching.

"I'm really not into Western gear. I need clothes that I can wear here and when I go back home to the city."

Jake guessed her giant marshmallow coat wasn't a bad image for her to project in the city. Then her smile grew as Farley spoke, and she responded, "That sounds perfect. Just point me to it."

Farley motioned to the north and the woman said, "Thank you so much." She turned to a display rack by the register and reached for a pair of bright red gloves paired with a matching knit beanie. "I'll give you a sale, at least," she said.

Farley was nodding as she handed him some cash, then she pushed the hat and gloves into the pockets of her jacket. After taking her change, she said, "I've never been here before. The man at the gas station was telling me about the eclipses."

She listened intently to what Farley was saying. "You might just see me back here when that happens. One more question. Where's the best coffee around?" When Farley pointed to the back area of the store, she looked pleased. "Then I'm in the right place, after all," she said, and went in the direction of the visiting area.

Jake turned away as she disappeared deeper into the store and finally went in search of what else he'd come to buy. In fifteen minutes, he was checking out at the register with the jacket, flannel shirts, collarless thermal shirts and warm boots.

Farley rang up his purchases and spoke as he took Jake's credit card. All Jake caught was "…came in?"

"I'm sorry. What did you say?"

"You're not used the altitude around here anymore, are you?"

"No, I am not," he agreed gladly.

"I asked if you saw that pretty little lady come in."

"The one with red hair wearing a marshmallow jacket?"

Farley guffawed. "Yeah, that would be the

one. Sure hope she gets a good jacket at Bailey's shop."

Jake agreed, then said his goodbyes before heading out into the cold with his items. He got in the truck, tossed his bags over by his duffel on the passenger seat, then started the engine. Sitting back, he closed his eyes for a minute, breathing in and out evenly. It had gone well with Farley, no big slip-ups, and the man had handed him a generic excuse when he'd missed what he'd said to him.

He exhaled. The driving was wearing him out. Despite the truck being upgraded with every conceivable aid for the hearing impaired, he still felt strange driving it. So far, he hadn't had a problem. Another twenty miles and he could get some sleep and he wouldn't have to worry about hearing or not hearing another person, until he went to see Sarge. He opened his eyes and exhaled.

Putting the truck in Reverse, he started to back out of the parking spot, but before he'd gone more than a few feet, the truck slammed to a bone-jarring stop. His bags tumbled to the floor, and when he looked at the rear-camera view on the screen in the dash, he saw the reason for the stop. Quickly, he looked over his shoulders at a road-dirty blue Jeep barely inches from the truck's tailgate. The automatic emergency braking system had stopped a disaster.

When he saw the driver, he grimaced. Even through the tinted rear window, he could clearly see a takeout cup in her right hand. It was probably empty, because what looked like coffee was now a brown stain all over her white puffer jacket.

Her face was almost as red as her hair when she looked toward him. There was no great smile now as he easily read her lips. "What a stupid jerk!" With a swipe at her face, she shook her head, then drove off.

"Tourists," Jake muttered to himself as the Jeep disappeared up the street to the north. Too bad Eclipse wasn't like the old days, when Clayton Drive was used by people riding horses or driving trucks, and the people smiled and waved if they saw you. Now it was angry strangers who called you names.

LIBBY WAS FRUSTRATED. She had almost collided with a local in a massively oversize truck about an hour ago and ruined her jacket with spilled coffee. She didn't mourn the coat, just the fact that she'd paid so much for it back in Seattle. At Snow Dreams, the store the flamboyant cowboy back at the general store had recommended, she had found a thermal-lined green jacket with a hood and had worn it out of the shop. She'd also bought what the owner had suggested—some flannel shirts and thermals along with boots that were lined with soft faux fur. Her new white puffer jacket would have to be dry-cleaned to save it from the trash can.

She knew she'd taken too much time shopping in town before heading to the ranch. Daylight was starting to fail, and she turned on the headlights. Finally, she heard the female voice come over the GPS. "In two miles take exit 91 and continue west on County Road 27 for 3.4 miles. Your destination will be on your right."

The woman's voice had barely stopped when her phone rang. A quick check showed her it was Seth, and she accepted the call through Bluetooth. "Hey there, Seth," she said.

"Are you at the ranch yet?" His voice came through the car speaker.

"No, but I'm close."

"Great. No problems on the drive?"

"I made it." She wouldn't go into the incident with the black truck in town. "You said that there are two rocks that mark the entrance to the ranch. Any signs or anything else?"

"No, but the rocks are boulders and at least ten feet high and just as wide. Go right between them on the gravel drive, and that takes you up to the house. It's set back a good ways from the road."

The female GPS voice cut in, "In two hundred feet, take Exit 91 and travel west for 3.4 miles. Your destination will be on your right." She saw the exit, then Seth was back on the line. "…and I don't know if it's locked up."

"I have the keys you gave me," she said, assuming he was talking about the house. "I'm just going onto the county road."

Seth's response broke up. "…to…drive… no reason to…"

The female voice spoke again. "Signal lost."

"Great," Libby muttered, but kept going until she saw the huge boulders caught in the glow of her headlights. They really were massive. She slowed and turned between them and drove onto the six-thousand-plus acres of ranch property. The Jeep's tires crunched on the gravel as she headed up the drive.

When she topped a low rise, she could make out the hulking form of a building in the distance. Although the growing dusk hid details, she knew from the plans she'd studied before the trip that it was the main house. The center section was the two-story original log construction topped by a metal roof. Two single-story wings, also made of log, had been added years later on the east and west sides. The house looked dark, with no lights coming from it, except for reflected flashes from her headlights bouncing off the first-floor windows.

As she drove closer, she realized that the light wasn't totally from the windows but had been bouncing off a huge dark pickup truck. It was parked directly in front of steps that led up to a wraparound porch and entry. It actually looked like the truck that had almost backed into her in town.

Seth had assured her no one was at the ranch, but obviously some wires had been crossed in the information chain. She pulled to a stop by the pickup, turned off the Jeep, then looked at her useless phone with its no-service icon on the screen. It wasn't a hard decision to make to go back and find a signal, then call Seth to find out what was going on.

But when she turned the key in the ignition, the headlights she'd left on dimmed as the engine started to turn over. Then they died away, followed by a series of clicks. She flipped the headlight switch to off, then tried the key again, but there was only a grinding sound and more clicks.

"Shoot," she muttered, and tried to turn the headlights back on. There was no glow from them, and darkness was everywhere. Without the motor running, there was no way to use the heater, and if she stayed in the Jeep to wait for someone to show up, she was certain sooner or later she'd freeze to death.

She had to go inside. She reached in her purse to find the keys, along with a slender canister of pepper spray she'd never used before. Quickly, she got out of the car, then hurried up to the porch as she zipped up her new coat and pulled the hood up to keep out the cold.

She hesitated at the door when she realized there was a dim yellow glow in the two tall, narrow windows on either side of the door. She gripped the pepper spray cylinder and pushed the keys into her jacket pocket, then moved to her right to look cautiously through the window. She could barely make out anything in the dim interior light, but there didn't seem to be movement inside.

She knocked on the door. Nothing happened. She knocked again without getting an answer. She tried one last time. When no one showed up, she gripped the pepper spray in her right hand and the ice-cold door handle with her left and turned it. It clicked and the door started to swing back, when a gust of wind came up behind her and snatched the door knob out of her hand. The door flew back and slammed violently against the log wall inside. She hurried in, fumbled and dropped the canister as she turned to fight the wind and get the door shut.

When it was closed, she picked up her pepper spray and stood still, listening and trying to catch her breath as she looked around. The dim light came from a huge wagon wheel chandelier that hung from a coved ceiling high above the two-story space. Only four bulbs of maybe ten were lit, but she could

see the worn stone floor, the cheesy Western decorations and a cowhide bench beside
the wide archway. The great room, which she
knew lie beyond foyer, was dark.

Nothing was moving. No one was coming
down the staircase to her right. No one was
coming out of the hallways used to access
the east and west wings of the house. No one
stepped through the archway from the great
room. She was beginning to think the house
was empty. Maybe someone had parked the
truck, then taken off. Or maybe they broke
into the house and had passed out or were
drunk or on drugs.

Surely the crashing of the door against
the wall would've made the dead sit up and
take notice. Ignoring a mounted animal head
snarling down at her from the log wall to her
left, she cleared her throat and called, "Hello!
Hello! Is someone here?" Nothing.

She waited a moment longer, then yelled
as loudly as she could, "I'm in the house, and
I don't mean any harm." The only noise she
could hear was the moan of the wind outside,
and she shivered. Slowly, Libby crossed the
stone floor and took the single step down into
the great room. She kept talking loudly as she

went. "I'm going down into the great room. Now I'm looking for the light switch."

Shadows blurred everything in front of her, and she shifted her pepper spray to her left hand and reached with her right to see if she could find the switches on the wall. She never felt it because someone's hand was already on it—a large hand. She jerked away, barely stopping a scream, and stumbled backward into the room.

The overhead lights flashed on, blinding her momentarily. She jerked the pepper spray up in front of her, ready to use it as she blinked rapidly trying to focus. With false bravado, she spoke to the tall blur of someone in the archway. "I'll use this if I have to." She only knew how stupid those words were when her eyes finally adjusted, and she saw a man on the step facing her.

While she might have had him within spraying distance, he had a double-barreled shotgun pointed right at her. "Hey, no, no, don't," Libby sputtered, trying to back up more, but stopped abruptly when his eyes narrowed on the pepper spray. She quickly let it fall to the floor with a clatter, then raised her hands, which were embarrassingly unsteady. "Please, don't do anything stupid," she said, not beyond begging. "I'm supposed to be here, I really am. I promise." She just stopped herself before she crossed her heart. She certainly didn't hope to die.

The tall, rangy man didn't move. His ash-blond hair was almost shoulder length and mussed, and a few days of beard darkened a strong jaw. He was planted firmly on the step down to the great room.

"If you'll just listen…" Her voice trailed off at the intensity in his eyes that she could see now were a deep blue. "I won't move. I won't." She didn't even think of running. He towered over her by maybe a foot in height and outweighed her by way too much. Thankfully, he slowly lowered the shotgun to point it at the flagstone floor.

He looked kind of sick, or maybe he was drunk or hungover or had taken drugs or something. Whatever he was or wasn't, she knew she had to get some control. When she saw him frown, she decided to play the sympathy card. "Are you okay? Is there some way I can help you?" He didn't respond. "I'd be more than glad to help in any way I can."

"No," he said abruptly.

So much for sympathy. Maybe a good apology would work. "I'm really sorry for coming in like I did. I didn't mean to scare you, honestly. I knocked and knocked and it's freezing out there. The door wasn't locked. I mean, I didn't break in or anything. I actually have the house keys in my pocket, and I…" She let her words fade away when he stepped onto the flagstone floor and came closer to where she stood just past an old green couch.

She inched backward, but he veered toward the couch that faced the back wall. He never took his eyes off her as he sank down on the sagging cushions to face her. Thankfully, he laid the rifle by him on the seat.

Her stomach was knotting. "Thank you," she said. "I…I really do hate guns. I mean, I've never even touched one, not that they're bad." She knew she was babbling but couldn't stop. "I know around here you probably have a lot of guns, and you have every right to have those guns. But thank you for putting that down."

He took a deep breath, exhaled, then said, "Pull one of the chairs over here to face me."

His voice was low and edged with roughness. She didn't have to be told twice and turned to the four pub chairs that formed a half circle in front of the stone fireplace. She motioned with her head toward the closest one and asked, "Is that one okay?"

"Great," he said as he leaned to rest his forearms on his knees. He looked lean and hard in a rumpled black T-shirt that covered wide shoulders but exposed muscled biceps, and his worn jeans molded to strong thighs.

She pulled the chair across the flagstone and positioned it to face him. She sat, shaking her hands to try to ease the tingling in them, and she couldn't believe the action sent her engagement ring flying off her finger and through the air, right at the man. It barely missed his shoulder to fall onto the cushions by the rifle. She knew it had to be resized but hadn't had a chance… She didn't think it was that loose.

He reached to picked up her ring and held it between his thumb and forefinger to study it. She wanted to jump up and snatch it back, but she made herself stay in the chair. "It's impressive," he said, but didn't offer to return it to her. He closed his hand around it and kept staring at her.

It was cool in the room, but nothing close

to the cold outside. "I'm going to unzip my jacket."

He made a vague movement with his hand, and she undid it, then flipped her hood off and shook her hair out. She sat back and met those blue eyes again. *What a mess.* She clasped her hands tightly in her lap. "Can we start again and pretend this never happened?"

He frowned at that. "What are you doing in here?"

"What are *you* doing here?" she countered and couldn't believe she'd done that.

"I asked you first," he said without any sign of annoyance.

"We'll be here forever and never learn anything if one of us doesn't break down and explain things."

CHAPTER THREE

JAKE STARED AT the woman across from him as he kept his hand closed around the biggest diamond he'd ever seen. There was no more marshmallow jacket stained with coffee, but the same coppery red hair in loose ringlets fell around her shoulders. The woman who had called him a stupid jerk had eyes that were a true green. She pushed back into the chair and took a quick glance at his hand holding the ring. Then she fixed her eyes on him, just the way his were on her. This was turning into an old-fashioned stare-down.

If he hadn't gone into the east wing to look for some more blankets for his makeshift bed on the couch, Jake knew he never would have known someone was there until it was too late. Even so, he'd almost stepped out into the entry and right into her when she'd been going down into the great room. With her back to him, he'd grabbed the shotgun off the wall right by the east wing hallway, then moved to the archway to reach in for the light switch just before she had.

He was trying to figure out what in the heck she'd been up to when he'd stumbled on her. No one should be here, but maybe it had gotten around that Sarge was gone and the house was empty. Squatters weren't unknown in the area. If she broke in to stay here, how could she own a ring that could choke a horse? Maybe she'd taken it from another house that had been conveniently unlocked and empty. Or maybe he was overthinking everything and getting overprotective of Sarge and the ranch.

"You know what, this is stupid," he watched her say. "I'll start."

She looked less afraid now, but her nervousness showed in the way she bit her lip. "First, I came here because I was asked to come here."

That didn't make sense at all. "Who asked you to?"

"Seth Reagan."

The name hung between them. "Seth Reagan?" Jake repeated back to her, not certain he'd read her right.

"Yes, and he's coming here soon, very soon." A blush of color rose in her cheeks, and freckles he hadn't noticed before showed up in a light dusting across her nose. "He's pretty busy, but he'll be here."

"So, you're engaged to Seth Reagan?"

He could see that startled her, and she quickly looked at his hand as he opened it and exposed the ring lying on his palm. "That's cubic zirconium. It just looks really expensive," she said in a rush.

Now she thought he might rob her. That was almost laughable. He'd never thought Seth would find anyone after a monumentally painful experience with romance over two years ago. But life obviously had changed while Jake had been out of contact. "I don't care if it's real or glass." He looked down at the round-cut diamond in its overly ornate gold setting. He was quite sure it was very real. What he wondered was how such a tiny hand could support that oversize display of bling. "Here," he said, and carefully tossed it to her.

It sailed through the air, and she caught it. Quickly, she put it back on her finger, then looked at him.

Seth wasn't the kind to flaunt his wealth like that, but maybe love had made him stupid. "So, you're Seth's fiancée?"

She slowly put her right hand over the ring to hide it in her lap. "Seth is a dear friend, but that's all."

That took him aback. "Then you're a dear friend who's here to do what exactly?"

She worried her bottom lip, and she said, "I can't tell you that. I don't know you. For all I know, you broke in before I got here."

"No need to break in. They never lock the front door," he said. "I used to live here, a long time ago, and Seth is *my* very good friend."

As he spoke, she frowned, then smiled suddenly. "Oh, my gosh," he saw her say. "Are you Jake Bishop?"

That was *not* expected. "How do you know who I am?"

"We've never met, but Seth has a picture of you and Ben, although it's maybe five or six years old. The beard and hair…" She shrugged. "I'm sorry it took so long for me recognize you."

Jake knew he'd never seen her. She'd have

been memorable. "Seth never showed me a picture of you," he murmured.

"No reason he would." She hesitated. "Seth told me you'd contacted him and were heading to Casper to be with Sarge. He never mentioned you'd be here."

"I decided to come here first, and I didn't tell him."

Her smile started to come back. "I'm so relieved you found me here and not some wacko."

He couldn't say he was relieved. She was messing up his plan to be here alone, and to be close enough to visit Sarge when he was moved to Cody for rehabilitation after being released from the hospital. "No, I don't want…" he started to say with a shake of his head, but he never got to finish.

Dizziness overtook him as his world went out of control, then he was falling forward with no way to stop himself from landing facedown on the old braided rug. The smell of dust and age invaded every breath he took as his world kept spinning.

Gradually he realized that he was being tugged over onto his back, and he had no ability to resist. The woman was a blur over him, patting his cheek. He closed his eyes to block out everything. But that didn't stop the motion. She was so close now that he felt her hair brushing his face. He wondered if she was screaming at him.

Slowly, the dizzy spell receded, and he eased his eyes open. As he began to focus, he saw her on her knees beside him, and he could read her lips. "Good, good, just stay still, and I'll get help," he could see her say. "I'll call—no, shoot, I can't. My cell has no signal." She was scrambling to her feet now and extending her hand down to him. "I'll get you up and drive you to an ER."

"No," he managed. "Don't. I must...have stood too fast."

She frowned down at him. "You weren't standing up. You just sort of shook your head and fell onto the floor."

He commandeered the excuse Farley had handed to him. "The altitude, I'm not...not used to it anymore and got dizzy."

She drew her hand back and tucked her hair behind her ears. "You're a test pilot, and you can't take altitudes?"

She was right, and he was starting to get uneasy lying on his back with her standing over him. "Equipment. Oxygen. Pressurization. This is temporary…and… I'll adjust."

She didn't push back at that but held out her hand to him again. "Let's get you up off the floor and see how you are."

There was no way he could leverage his weight against hers, and he ignored her offer as he slowly maneuvered into a sitting position without any dizziness attacking him. "I'm okay," he said, and hoped he could get to his feet. He cautiously pushed and was finally standing without his stability being affected.

When he looked at her, she still seemed concerned. "I can take you to see a doctor or to a hospital. I don't know what's around here, though."

"No," he said more abruptly than he'd intended, and tried to soften it. "Thanks, but I'm okay. It's over."

With them both standing now, he was very aware that despite the fact that he had the upper hand in height and weight, the advantage was still hers. He needed to sit down. He tried to be casual about getting back onto the couch and was thankful when he made it without an incident.

She came closer, and he looked up at her as she spoke. "You drove that huge truck here?"

"I didn't walk."

"How could you drive if you're having dizzy spells?"

He had a gut feeling that she wasn't going to be easy about anything. The sooner she left, the better. "That's my first spell." A total lie. It was more like his first spell in a month.

She shrugged off her jacket and tossed it onto the chair she'd sat in earlier. When she turned back to him, she was speaking, and he caught her words partway into a statement. "…being pushy, but before you drive out of here, whenever that is, you need to see a doctor."

With the jacket gone, he could see she was wearing a pink sweater with slim jeans. Despite the old adage he'd heard about red hair and pink not mixing, it looked good on her. "I appreciate your advice, especially after I pulled a shotgun on you, but I know what I should or shouldn't do. You don't know me, and I don't know you. No offense meant."

She didn't take offense but agreed. "Okay, that's fair."

"Please, sit down. You're making my neck hurt."

She smiled easily at that. "Sure," she said, but instead of retaking the chair, she sat down on the couch to his left, far away from where he'd put the rifle. That forced him to reposition himself so he could see her lips. "Now, what do you want to know about me?" she asked.

He rested his left arm on the back of the couch. "Who are you, and why are you here, other than to meet Seth sometime soon?"

"I'm Liberty Connor. I'm here to figure out how to make this place into a summer camp for middle school and high school boys in the foster care system."

He didn't mind keeping her talking so he could have some time to gather himself. "You work for Seth? I thought you said you're friends?"

"Both. I'm from Seattle and do architecture and design for adaptive reuse of existing buildings."

An architect from Seattle. He would have never guessed that in a thousand years, but then again, he'd never met one before. He felt like a fool pulling a weapon on her. "Sorry for the gun. If it makes you feel any better, it's not loaded. It never has been as far as I know."

She waved that away without the huge diamond leaving her finger this time. "Forget it. I kind of thought you were a drunk, or a burglar."

"Okay, that's a wash," he said. "Now you're an architect who does adaptive reuse or whatever you said?"

"I specialize in redoing older structures to update and repurpose them, sort of change them without leveling them first. That's why Seth asked me to come here and stay, so I can see the place and start drawing up plans for the changes he wants."

He vaguely remembered Cal telling him something about a camp, but he'd been too concerned about Sarge to really pay attention at the time. Now this woman who was small enough for him to restrain her with one arm was explaining it to him. He sat there feeling like a jerk for treating her the way he had at first. Then he realized what she was saying about her plans to stay at the ranch. That did not work for him. "How long does that take, to size up things and get a feel for the place?"

"I'll be here until the first week in January."

And he'd lost this place as a refuge to heal for the foreseeable future. "You're here to do exactly what?"

"I'm supposed to start in the house, redoing part of the west wing as a suite for Sarge when he comes home. That's my goal this time, to get things going on that and get it done as quickly as possible."

"And that will take until next year?"

She smiled at that. "Oh, that makes it sound long, you know. I'll be here for about a month, to get the plans finalized and approved. Codes and things. Seth knows a contractor he trusts around here who will take over when I leave."

Jake would definitely have to make new plans, and he hated that. He wanted to be here, where he'd found healing as a teenager, but her being here wouldn't work. "You're forgoing the holidays to do this?"

"Oh, no, of course not. Christmas? Never. I'm big on Christmas and honestly, I've never had a real white Christmas, so if it snows here, I'm very happy."

"Until you get snowed in," he said.

She still smiled. "Oh, that would be absolutely perfect."

There was obviously no way to dampen her enthusiasm, so he gave up on that. "I'm impressed by your dedication, coming up here for a Christmas by yourself to do this for Seth."

A hint of color in her cheeks brought out her freckles again. "Well, the alone part was a last-minute change and it's not permanent. I was going to come with my fiancé, but he can't come right now. I talked to him just before I left Seattle, and he promised he'd definitely be here before Christmas."

He wanted to ask what was wrong with the guy that he'd let her come here alone, but he didn't. "You've got your work to do, so I'll take off as soon as I can."

"No, you can't."

"Excuse me?"

"I'm sorry, but it wouldn't be smart to take to the road after you fainted."

He corrected her. "I didn't faint. I was dizzy."

"I was almost hit by a truck like yours today and could have been really hurt."

"You're exaggerating," he said without thinking first.

She looked offended. "For your information, I don't usually exaggerate much of anything. Besides, how would you know if I'm exaggerating or not?"

He weighed his options, then decided truth was the best policy. It wasn't worth lying to her, so he came clean. "I'm the one who almost backed my truck into your Jeep at Garret's."

Her green eyes widened. "That was you?"

"That was me," he said, then thought better of leaving. He was rethinking that after her comments about him driving. "I really wanted to head out tomorrow to see Sarge, but you're right that I can't drive, at least for a few days." He'd started to feel more whole after he'd left Malibu, but now he wasn't certain of anything about himself. "But I will leave you to your work as soon as I can."

"Okay." She seemed fine with that, then skipped to another subject. "Now we need heat. It's getting colder in here."

"You can forget about that."

"Please don't tell me the furnace doesn't work."

"It probably does. But it's part of a full system for here and the buildings near the house. The thing is, the controls to get it primed and going are in a side room in the hay barn."

"Okay. How do I get to the hay barn?"

"You don't. You don't know the system, and I'm not going out tonight to do it."

She looked over at the massive stone hearth, then back to Jake. "It looks like you had a fire going before."

He'd made it poorly and it had died down too quickly. "Yes, and there's plenty of wood."

She got up. "You take the couch and I'll take one of the chairs. You need the length, I don't."

The last thing he wanted was to share space with her for the night. He wanted to be alone and think. He also didn't want her around if he got dizzy again. "I'll get the fireplace going in the master bedroom upstairs for you."

"What about you?"

"I'd rather stay on the couch," he said as he carefully got to his feet without any light-headedness. "I'll get the fire going down here first, then I'll do it upstairs."

"No, you rest. I can do that."

When she started across to the fireplace, he called after her. "Liberty?"

She turned. "It's Libby."

"You need to get your things out of the Jeep now, especially anything that can freeze."

"Okay, but you sit down. I've got this."

He almost laughed at her giving the orders and thinking he'd follow without pushback. "You're good at telling people what to do."

She shrugged. "I'll take that as a compliment," she said with good humor.

"And I'll get the fires going while you get your things out of the car."

"Okay. I'm not that good at making fires, anyway." She crossed to pick up her jacket on the chair. As she headed toward the entry, Jake picked up the useless rifle and put it back on the wall, then went to the fireplace. He laid a decent fire this time, and when he got it blazing, he eased to stand up. He turned and saw Liberty coming back inside. She had a laptop in one hand and two bright pink shopping bags in the other. A large suitcase was already sitting in the archway with two boxes stacked by it. He watched her kick the door shut before she looked at him as he came toward her.

"Done," she said.

"You've got everything that can freeze, right?"

"Oh, shoot, my phone. I'll be right back."

LIBBY SPOTTED HER cell phone on the car seat and pushed it in her pocket. Then she ran back to the door to get inside and out of the wind and cold. Before she could reach for the knob, Jake was opening it for her.

"Thanks," she said. The scent of wood burning was in the air now, along with a touch of warmth as Jake closed the door on the night.

He crossed to pick up her suitcase and shopping bags. "I'll take these up and start the fire," he tossed over his shoulder as he took the stairs.

Libby quickly shed her jacket and boots, leaving them at the cowhide bench, then hurried after him. She knew the floor plan of the original section on the second level. One large bedroom to the left across a walkway with a half wall that overlooked the entry. A similar one to the right, then the master bedroom took up the whole middle of the upstairs area. It was a smaller version of the great room below.

The double doors to the master suite were both open, and soft yellow light fell out onto the plank flooring. When she went inside, past closets that lined a short hallway, she saw Jake crouched with his back to her at the stone fireplace across the room. It was half the size of the one in the great room. There were windows on either side, instead of the glass doors she'd noticed framing the down-stairs hearth.

The bedroom layout on the blueprints was nothing compared to standing in it. A huge four-poster bed that looked as if it had been carved from tree trunks faced the fireplace and the view. Equally large pieces of furniture lined the log walls. An open door on the opposite wall showed the shadowed bathroom, and she knew a large walk-in closet was accessed through it.

It was cozy yet impressive, too. Sarge and Maggie had clearly put a lot of thought into it when they'd built the original house. She moved closer to Jake as the wood he laid in the fireplace caught and flamed. "That feels wonderful," she said as heat started to flow into the space around her.

Slowly, Jake stood and turned. He looked startled to find her behind him. "What in the…?"

She'd thought he knew she was there after she'd spoken, but maybe he was just a person who had the ability to totally block out the rest of the world. "Sorry, I was going to say, you did that so fast. Can you show me how to make a really good fire like that before you leave?"

"Matches, logs and kindling," he said. "It's that simple."

She looked toward the massive bed as she said, "Simple is as simple does." When she glanced back at Jake, he didn't respond. "You never saw the movie, did you?"

He looked totally confused. "What movie?"

"That was my version of an iconic line in *Forrest Gump*. I changed it a bit, from 'stupid is as stupid does.'"

Jake shrugged slightly. "Oh, sure. I'll show you how to build a fire in the morning."

"Thank you, that would be great." Then she motioned to the stripped mattress. "Where's the bedding?"

"In the closet," he said.

She turned to go to the closets in the hallway, but she stopped when Jake said her name. "Liberty."

She faced him and almost repeated that she answered to Libby, but she kind of liked him calling her Liberty. "I can get it." She didn't want him moving a lot until she was sure he wouldn't topple over again. That had scared her far too much. It had seemed like more than just a dizzy spell to her, and she didn't want it to happen again.

"Just wait there." He turned and went into the walk-in closet beyond the bathroom, then came back a few minutes later carrying folded linens topped by a brilliantly colored quit. He laid them on a wooden chest at the foot of the massive bed. "They're custom made," he said.

Libby faced him across the bare mattress. "I always thought just the rich and really picky had custom-made bedding."

"Sarge designed the bed to fit his size, and he made it out of the logs that were being used for the house and the other buildings. It's not regulation size at all. He actually made it as a gift for Maggie."

She reached to slowly run her forefinger over the satiny wood of the closest poster. "He did beautiful work. Did they ever have children?"

"I don't think they could. Maybe that's why they started taking in kids one by one when they'd only been married a couple of years. They filled this original part of the house, then added both wings to make room for more kids."

"Where was your room?"

"To the right across the walkway outside the double doors." He reached for a sheet and shook it out with a sharp snap to open it and let it drift down onto the mattress. Libby pulled it toward her side, and they worked in silence making the bed. A few minutes later it was done. The handmade quilt on top, with a design of flaring circles in gold, red, green and blue splashed color into the room. With the pillows in fresh cases, Jake tossed them up against the headboard.

Libby stood back and smiled at him. "Boy, you sure know how to make a bed and with no fitted sheets or anything."

"I do have some skills, thanks to Sarge and the army."

She could hear the wind blowing outside, a loud unsettling sound, but Jake seemed to be ignoring it. She tucked her hair back behind her ears. "Apparently you do." Then she looked around the room before she met his eyes again as the sound outside got louder . "Is that just the wind?" she asked him. "It sounds almost like a tornado or something."

"Yeah, once it blew with such force that it felt like an earthquake."

"I hate the wind. I hope that doesn't happen much while I'm here."

Crossing over to the window to the left of the fireplace, Jake pressed his hand on the cold pane of glass. "It's really blowing hard."

She moved over to stand beside him and copied him by pressing her left hand on the window below where he had. Almost immediately she jerked back and looked at him. "You're right. It's so strong."

"This house has been around for over fifty years and gone through storms you couldn't even imagine. It's still here."

"Let's hope that luck holds up," she said before turning to go and sit down on the just-made bed. She took a deep breath slowly, trying to calm herself and keep bad memories at bay.

"Hey," he said as he crossed to stand in front of her. "It'll be over before you know it."

"I've never liked wind. Thunder, that's okay, but wind just feels so overwhelming."

He seemed to sense something else was going on with her, and offered her comfort. He smiled at her slightly. "Sarge told me once that he built this house as a fortress against the world, and no measly windstorm was strong enough to harm it or anyone inside it."

"Did you believe him?"

"I did. I trusted him."

She exhaled. "Okay, then… I'll trust you."

CHAPTER FOUR

LIBBY TRIED TO ignore the unsettled feeling that wind and the rattling sound of glass being tested gave her. "I'll add some more wood to the fire," Jake said, and went back to the hearth.

He reached for the poker off a rack of tools that was fastened to the stone facade of the fireplace. Then he crouched to push the burning logs farther back into the firebox. She turned to get her suitcase by the bed, but a loud crash startled her. She spun around, afraid that something had been pushed over by the storm or that that Jake had fallen again. But he was hunkered down in front of the growing fire, seemingly mesmerized by the leaping flames.

Then she saw the source of the cacophony. The rack that had held the fire tools had fallen, scattering the metal objects onto the raised hearth and the floor. "Jake?" she said.

He didn't respond. She took two steps to get closer to him. "Jake?" She saw his shoulders strain against the confines of the black T-shirt as he reached for another log to his left. Three feet of space separated them, and when he put the log on the fire, she heard the wood thud, the fire hiss and sparks snap. "Jake, are you all right?" she said, louder now. Still nothing.

She tapped him on the shoulder lightly, and he took a beat too long to shift and look up at her. His eyes went to her lips immediately, and her stomach sank. No wonder he hadn't responded to any noise she'd made coming into the house earlier, not even the door smashing against the wall.

"I'm finished here," he said, slowly getting up and looking at her, but not quite directly in her eyes. It was as if he was looking somewhere in the middle of her face. "It should last a while." He glanced as if to look back at the fire, but he hesitated when he saw the scattered tools. He sighed before he crouched down to collect them. Then he laid them together with the rack on the hearth.

She waited until he stood again and looked at her. "What's going on?" she asked him.

Jake hesitated, as if he expected the question and was still trying to come up with an answer. Seth had never suggested Jake had a hearing problem, but he obviously did. She had no idea why he'd hide it. He stared at her, then took the offensive. "What do you mean?"

She couldn't let it go. "You didn't hear the fire tools falling, did you?"

"I didn't jump out of my skin, if that's what you expected."

She bit her lip, then finally said, "You didn't answer me when I spoke to you, either."

Now she could see she was annoying him. "Sorry," he said. "Now get some sleep."

He ducked his head and started to go past her. She didn't expect to do it, but she reached out and grabbed him by his upper arm. He stopped, then drew back from her hold and looked straight at her. "What?"

It worried her that Seth had never mentioned Jake had a problem. He had to know, and she suspected it wasn't just some simple problem, either. But she had no right to press Jake. "Nothing. Thanks for the fire."

He turned and walked away.

JAKE FOUGHT THE urge to run out of the room and keep going. He hurried down the stairs, but when he stepped onto the stone floor in the entry, Liberty was right there behind him. She passed by him and went over to where she'd left the rest of her things. She picked up her laptop but left the boxes, then came back to where he stood.

He hoped she'd just keep going back up to the master bedroom. But she stopped and looked him right in the eye. "I just needed this," he watched her say. Then she went upstairs and out of view.

Jake sank down on the second step of the staircase and buried his face in his hands. He was trapped. She was right about the dizziness, so he couldn't leave. He accepted that. But that didn't mean he wanted to have someone around worrying about him. He didn't want someone hovering over him or asking questions he wouldn't have answers for. He'd been sloppy, obviously, and she was bright enough to catch on. All he wanted was his solitude, to gather strength for what was ahead of him with Sarge. But that had been taken from him by a woman who saw too much and asked too many questions.

Running both hands over his face, he slowly got up, then put his boots and jacket on to retrieve his duffel and new clothes from the truck. A biting cold driven by the growing wind pushed hard at him as he made his way outside, and he wondered how Liberty could have stayed on her feet in this weather. He hurried back to the door once he had his things and barely turned the handle before he lost his grip and the wind sent the door flying violently inward.

That's when he saw Liberty jerking back as if she'd barely escaped being hit. He tossed his things off to one side and grabbed the door to force it shut. Then he turned to her. He wished he could muster up some anger at her being there, but with her looking so stunned, anger was nowhere to be found. However, frustration was there in spades. "That door could have hit you right in the face and knocked you into kingdom come!"

He watched her as she backed up to put even more space between them. Then he saw her speaking slowly and deliberately. "I heard the door open and close. I thought you might have left." He just bet she was talking louder than normal, too. "I wanted to find out."

He read her lips and knew what she was doing. Slow and easy so he didn't miss one word. "Please, don't do that," he said trying to control himself.

"I didn't know if—"

He cut that off by turning away from her and took his time removing his jacket and boots. He set them by hers before he turned to her again. "Don't yell when you speak to me or go very, very slowly with exaggerated enunciation. Neither is needed. I have a slight, temporary hearing problem. Just look at me when you talk. I'll understand."

"Okay," she said.

"Good night," he said, and he didn't give her a chance to say anything as he walked toward the great room with his bags. He felt a vague breathlessness that had nothing to do with his ear damage as he passed Liberty and inhaled the soft scent of something, maybe flowers. He turned off the lights and dropped his stuff by the couch, then lay down and pulled the blankets over himself.

Errant thoughts were annoying to him. Liberty Connor was attractive, he'd give her that, and she seemed smart, maybe too smart. Despite her annoying curiosity about him—and the fact that she wasn't his type at all—she nudged at him for some reason. He wondered why in the heck Seth hadn't dated her. Or maybe they had dated before she'd found her fiancé. One thing he knew, whoever that fiancé was, the man had his hands full. He almost felt sorry for the poor guy.

As JAKE SLOWLY drifted out of sleep, he felt warmth on his face, then inhaled and caught the aroma of coffee brewing. He opened his eyes to the cool light of morning that was filtering in through the glass doors on either side of the fireplace. He figured he'd missed dawn by a minimum of two hours. Disengaging his legs from the tangle of blankets, he slowly pushed to a sitting position. The world was steady, and he felt hungry, not nauseated. A fire was roaring as it sent its heat into the room and its sparks flew up the chimney. It seemed Liberty knew how to lay a fire, after all.

Jake looked toward the kitchen and that's when he saw her at the stove. Her hair was caught back in a clip low on her neck, and she was wearing pink again, a thermal top she'd matched with faded jeans. She moved to her left and disappeared inside the combination pantry and storage room by the old refrigerator on the back wall of the kitchen. She came back out carrying a bottle of something.

She stopped when she saw he was awake. "Good morning," he saw her say with an uncertain smile. "Pancakes in two minutes." With that she went over to the stove.

He stood cautiously, but he was still good. Maybe last night had been his last episode. He crossed to the long dining table between the kitchen and the great room where he'd sat for so many meals years ago. Plates and flatware were laid out for two on the end near the back wall, closest to the heat from the fire.

Liberty came over carrying a plate of pancakes in one hand and a bottle of syrup in the other. "Are you hungry?" she asked, making sure he was looking at her before she glanced down to put the food on the table halfway between their plates. When she looked back at him, there was no smile as he kept his silence. When she said, "Well, are you hungry?" very slowly, he knew she was not happy with him.

He couldn't blame her. He knew he definitely owed her an apology for being abrupt with her last night. She was only trying to help him. "I am," he said.

She went back to the kitchen and returned

carrying two large mugs, and steam curled up from them. Making eye contact with him, she said, "Please, sit down."

He took the chair with its back to the kitchen and she went around to sit opposite him. She put the mugs down and nudged one closer to him. "Coffee. No milk, sorry. It was spoiled. This place is stocked with enough staples for the whole town to survive for a year, yet no bottled or even powdered creamer." As he reached for his mug, she added, "But there's sugar if you want it."

"Black's fine," he said as he cupped the mug in both hands.

She motioned to the pancakes. "I need to be honest and tell you that I'm a terrible cook. But I can do two things quite well. I can brew coffee and make pancakes. At Christmas I make green pancakes. The red ones looked awful, so I stopped doing them."

He knew he should make polite small talk to prove he wasn't some ogre, maybe even make a joke about red and green pancakes to lighten the tension between them, but he didn't know what to say. Instead, he helped himself to a couple of the pancakes before he got up and headed to the pantry. He came back with an unopened jar of peanut butter and sat back down. After he removed the lid, he took his time spreading the chunky mixture on the pancakes.

When Liberty reached over to tap his hand, it surprised him, and he dropped his knife in the process. He looked up to see her say, "I'm sorry." He was getting fed up with himself. There she was cooking for him and apologizing to him because he obviously hadn't responded to something she'd said. He didn't deserve her apology.

"No, I'm sorry," he said. "I'm not very good at dealing with people sometimes."

She frowned. "You're 'dealing' with me?"

"No, I meant, I was rude last night, and you cooked breakfast for me this morning. You're a saint."

She laughed at that. "I'm no saint."

It hit him how much he missed hearing laughter. "I beg to disagree. I know I'm not the easiest person in the world to deal with."

She was still smiling. "Now I'm dealing with you?"

"Yes, you are, and I apologize for you having to do that."

She reached for the syrup bottle. "Apology

accepted," she said, then drowned her stack of pancakes in the liquid.

It was that easy to appease her. "Thank you."

She put the bottle down. "I need to explain something about me to you. I know some people don't like to be touched. I was a non-toucher before, but..." She hesitated for a fleeting moment, then finished with a shrug, "I'm a toucher now. Still, I'll be careful about it while you're here, unless it's necessary."

She'd nailed him on that. He'd never been a toucher and actually wondered how a person went from disliking it to allowing it. "Okay."

"I have to say, the reason I touched you was, I started to say something to you, and I needed to get your attention first."

There it was, the elephant in the room, and she wasn't afraid to put a spotlight on it. He tried to ease the glare. "Sorry, spreading peanut butter on pancakes is a sacred ritual to me."

"Okay, but I have to just throw this out there. No offense intended, which I always thought was stupid to say, because that usually means what's going to be said will be offensive."

Jake braced himself for the worst. "Just say it."

Liberty exhaled. "Either your taste buds are dead, or you have serious problems with food." She motioned to his plate and grimaced. "That's the worst concoction I have ever seen."

He was relieved she was offended by his peanut butter and pancakes. That didn't matter at all to him, and he smiled at her. "It would look a heck of a lot worse if you'd made these pancakes green or red," he said.

She laughed. "You're right."

"How about putting peanut butter *and* cottage cheese on pancakes?"

She looked disgusted. "That's sick."

He didn't blame her for being put off by the idea. "Ben had me taste pancakes after he'd filled them with cottage cheese and topped them with peanut butter."

Her eyes widened. "Oh, my gosh, did you throw up?"

"I actually ate a bit after I smothered it all in syrup. I think Ben had it at one of his foster homes before he came here. He also put warm water on his cereal. Figure that out."

"I guess we all have our quirks and do weird things because of our pasts." She offered him the syrup bottle. "This might help those."

He took it, but just set it down on the table between them. "So, do you have quirks? Are you weird?"

"Pretty much," she said after chewing and swallowing a bite of her food. "I don't like palm trees, those big date palms. I don't know why, but I would walk a mile out of my way just to avoid getting close to one. Crazy, but true."

"No, that's understandable. It's all those killer monkeys hiding in them," he teased.

She gave him an exaggerated eye roll. "Oh, Dr. Bishop has solved my weirdness. How much do I owe you?"

He chuckled at that, and he felt a very foreign sense of normalcy in that moment. "I'll send you a bill," he promised, then got to work on the food.

Last night he'd been tied up in knots by Liberty and worrying about what she'd think or do today. He'd been rude to her, too. Now they were eating and laughing together. He knew this wouldn't last, but he'd take it for now. Besides, the pancakes were actually good, and before he knew it, his plate was empty.

When he looked up, Liberty was watching him. She had half a pancake left, but she'd obviously finished eating. "So, how did I do?" she asked.

"The best I've had in a long time. But I haven't actually had pancakes in years."

"Very honest of you," she said with a nod, and reached for her mug. "No polite pretending. I like that."

"I'm not good at that. So I try to do as little of it as possible," he said, and reached for his mug to drain the last of the now tepid coffee. Over the rim, he saw Liberty's eyes were fixed on him. "What?" he asked as he set his cup down by his plate.

"Honesty is good," she said, then caught him off guard. "So I need to explain something else to you. The truth is, I have a hard time giving up on things or letting them go if I'm curious or worried. I think that's how I'm weird, but I'll try not to let that happen too often."

"Okay," he said as he stood up. He wondered if he should tell her he'd already figured that out about her, but he kept silent as he gathered his dishes along with hers. He took them into the kitchen and the sink in the island that overlooked the great room. He rinsed them and put them in the old dishwasher. It gave him time as he struggled with the feeling that he needed to explain just a bit more to Liberty so she wouldn't feel uncomfortable around him because of his hearing. That was a foreign idea to him, trying to appease someone who worried about him.

Liberty brushed past. Out of the corner of his eye, he caught her disappearing into the pantry and coming back out almost immediately. He concentrated on closing the dishwasher and inhaled that light sweetness of flowers right before he felt her touch on his shoulder. He couldn't help tensing, but he made himself not jerk away. After all these years since he'd been in the foster care system, he still couldn't bear touching unless he saw it coming and wanted it. A terrible by-product of a past he tried to ignore.

Slowly, he turned to her as she drew her hand back. "Sorry," she said as she took half a step back to put more space between them. "You aren't leaving today, are you?"

Jake was sensing the elephant getting bigger and the room shrinking. "Can we sit down for a minute?" he asked her.

"Sure," she said and didn't hesitate following him over to the couch. He pushed away his rumpled blankets, then sat, and he wasn't surprised when she came to sit beside him again. So much for distance.

As Liberty clasped her hands in her lap, he spoke before she could. "I should have explained things a bit more to you last night."

"No, I was being pushy," she said.

He waved off that piece of truth with a vague motion of his hand. "I'll say this simply. I was exposed to noises a few months ago that were way off the decibel safety scale. It hurt my ears."

"Like a heavy-metal rock star?" he saw her ask.

"What?"

"You know, you hear about heavy-metal rockers being nearly deaf by the time they're forty because of the loud music they surround themselves with."

"No, well, maybe it's the same type of

thing. I just know that it hurt my ears and the healing is slow."

"That's it?"

He looked away and out the glass door to the right of the hearth. Grayness was permeating everything outside as heavy clouds gathered above. He'd given her a simple explanation and hoped it would satisfy her curiosity. "That's all there is," he said, dancing on a thin ledge around the truth. He wasn't about to tell her about the explosion that had nothing to do with being a Rockstar. "The vertigo happened at first, but I've been fine until last night." He looked back at her.

"Seth doesn't know about this, does he?" he saw her ask.

She really was way too smart. "No, and I don't want Ben or Sarge to know, either. They have a lot on them, and the last thing they need is more of a burden."

"I won't say anything," she said without hesitation.

That had been easier than he'd expected. She didn't attack with more questions, so he shifted to look more directly at her as he rested his arm along the back of the couch. "I appreciate that."

She shrugged. "It's your call," she said. "Whatever you want."

None of this was what he wanted, and he was done sharing more with a relative stranger than anyone else he knew, besides Cal. "Okay." He held her eyes with his. "That's it."

Then the hesitation came before she finally nodded. He saw the look of sympathy in her eyes, maybe concern, and he hated that he'd shared anything with her at all. His sharing days were over. She pitied him and he didn't want that from anyone, especially Liberty Connor.

LATER THAT MORNING, Libby explored the west wing while Jake headed out to start the furnace. He'd made it very clear that he didn't want her tagging along, despite her wanting to see how the furnace worked. He'd insisted she stay inside to keep warm and do her work. The idea of fighting him on it came and went. She had a feeling he just plain wanted to be alone, so she'd backed off and decided to check out the rooms Seth wanted to be used for Sarge's suite when he returned.

The spaces she entered were all icy cold

and had obviously been closed up for some time. When the wind started rattling the windows, she went back to the great room. Libby stood in front of the fire and held her hands out to its warmth, thinking back on the morning. She wasn't at all good about keeping Jake's hearing problem from Seth, but she'd do it. That's what Jake wanted. He'd said loud noises caused it. Maybe from the jets he flew or something like that. She wouldn't ask him for specifics. She'd found out the hard way that the man wouldn't be pushed for answers. He just gave them when he felt like it, and she figured that explaining anything was a rare occurrence for him.

She heard the front door open and close with a slam. Turning to look toward the entry, she waited, heard boots drop on the floor, then Jake was in the archway. His jacket was off, but he was still wearing the red beanie she'd lent him with his gray thermal shirt and jeans. "It's done," he said. "Now I'll go and set the thermostat to get the house warmed up." He tugged the beanie off and flipped it over onto the couch. "Thanks for the loan." Then he was gone.

She rubbed her hands together but stopped

and looked down at her left hand. Her ring finger was bare. Frantically she looked around at the floor and the hearth, trying to remember the last time she'd noticed the ring on her finger. "Jake!" she yelled instinctively, then caught herself and ran after him. She found him in the east wing adjusting a small box on the wall in the hallway.

She touched his shoulder, and he jerked around. "Hold on. I'm trying to—"

She cut him off as she held up her left hand, which was shaking. "My...my ring," she said, "It's gone. I lost it. I must've dropped it or something."

She didn't expect him to take her by her shoulders the way he did, nor did she expect the softness in his voice when he spoke. "Hey, calm down. It's okay. It has to be here. Try to think about where you remember seeing it last."

"I don't know." She closed her eyes tightly. "I think it was on my finger after getting the things out of the Jeep and maybe when I went up to bed." She opened her eyes to find Jake was watching her intently while still holding her shoulders. "I don't know, maybe I didn't have it then, but I think I did."

"You had it upstairs. I saw it when you touched the window in the master bedroom last night." He let go of her. "Retrace your steps and go everywhere you did since going upstairs last night. I'll check around down here."

"Okay," she said, and ducked past him to hurry out of the hallway and up the stairs to the bedroom.

She couldn't believe she'd lost it like that. She should have never worn it after the fiasco when it had flown off her finger, almost hitting Jake. Now it was gone. How could she explain that to Roger, no, worse yet, to Roger's mother. A family heirloom, and she hadn't even felt it leave her finger the way she had last night. Frantically, she tore the bed apart, looked under it, then headed into the bathroom. Nothing. She went back downstairs a lot more slowly than she'd gone up. When she stepped down into the great room, Jake was coming toward her.

"You didn't find it?" Jake asked when they met in the middle of the room.

She shook her head.

"Where else were you?"

She took a breath. "The west wing, I was

looking around in there. I redid the fire here, and I was in the kitchen and the pantry making breakfast earlier." She shivered. "I don't know what else to do."

"You did the fire?"

"Oh, yes, but I…" She remembered something. "I had to straighten it on my finger after I put the poker back."

"Great, that narrows it down a lot."

"I'll recheck the pantry," she said. "Could you look around in the kitchen?"

Minutes later, they were face-to-face by the kitchen island. She shook her head as Jake kept insisting, "It has to be here."

Do not cry, Libby told herself over and over again.

"It's insured, isn't it?"

That was a logical question, but it made her even more upset. "Yes, but that's not it. It's tradition, family and history. I can't call Roger and tell him I lost it. He was so proud to give it to me. This is horrible." It was beyond that, but she stopped talking before she really did embarrass herself. If she couldn't find it, her chance of ever being good enough in the eyes of the Montgomery family was in jeopardy. He came closer. "Sorry, that was a stupid question."

No, he was being rational. "I just need to think and remember. How could it have come off without me feeling it."

"It was loose," he pointed out.

"I know, but I'd see it if it flew off again."

Jake glanced past her, then said, "Wait a minute." He moved around her to go to the counter by the stove. She was right with him and watched him pick up one of the oven mitts laying there and push his hand into it. He tugged it off and turned toward her with the ring lying on his open palm.

"Jake, oh…" she gasped, grabbing it, but shook as she put it back on her finger and looked up at him. "Thank you, thank you, thank you," she said, and before she knew it, she was hugging him tightly.

She felt her heart settle as she inhaled the scent of soap and felt body heat around her. The rumble of his voice was against her cheek when he said, "You're very welcome." Then she realized he was standing motionless. He wasn't hugging her back.

CHAPTER FIVE

LIBBY LET JAKE go and moved away. "I'm so sorry for that. I really am. No touching, I know that, but I'm so grateful to you. I never would have looked in the mitt."

She couldn't tell if he was mad or not, but he didn't acknowledge her apology. "It was caught on the lining. You need to put it away."

"I know. I'm always afraid that I'll hurt it some way."

"Or hit someone with it," he said with the shadow of a smile.

"Sorry." She clasped her hands together, so the ring was hidden. "I hate to think what would happen if I'd lost it. It was Roger's great-grandmother's on his father's side. I should have had it resized right away." It hit her that she'd never been comfortable wearing it. "I mean, I didn't wear it to work or anything." She shrugged. "I'm so thankful you found it."

Jake waved that away. "Roger's wealthy, I take it?"

"He's the only heir to the Montgomery-Thomas money, not that Roger wants it. I mean, he only wants it to help others. He heads his family foundation that gets safe water to as many people as possible in third-world countries."

"Impressive."

She wasn't sure if he was being sarcastic or not. "He's really good at what he does for the foundation."

"Paperwork and fundraising in a tuxedo?"

It wasn't sarcasm, but she felt as if Jake was being judgmental about what Roger did. That bothered her. He'd never even met Roger. "Some," she said. "But he's also there with the workers on every site for the setup and the testing. He's been on three continents in the past two years."

He seemed to let the subject go and changed direction completely. "I need to find out where Sarge is. Last I heard, he was in Casper, but was going to be transferred to Cody for rehab soon, which is pretty close to here."

"I'd tell you to call Seth and find out, but

my cell is totally without service out here. Is there a landline?"

"There used to be," he said, and headed across the great room past a pool table protected by a dust sheet. He opened a door on the far wall, and Libby followed him into a space lined with floor-to-ceiling bookshelves on two walls and filing cabinets stacked to the left of the door she'd just stepped through. A large window at the back gave a northern view from a massive wooden desk that held an old-fashioned rotary phone.

Jake sat down in the desk chair, reached for the receiver and handed it to Libby. He gave her the name of the hospital in Casper, and she felt him watching her as she called the operator to get the number. They connected her and she spoke to the patient liaison, then put the receiver back in the cradle.

"They moved him to the Wicker Pines Therapy & Rehabilitation Center in Cody. yesterday."

"Good," Jake said as Libby reached for a wooden chair to sit across from him. "I probably should stay here another day or two, so I've got a proposition for you."

She sat down. "What is it?"

"You drive me to Cody so I can see Sarge, and I won't be on the road in that truck."

She'd love to meet Sarge. "That sounds like a good idea, but the Jeep is stone-cold dead. I need to get a battery for it. I can't remember the last time I had it replaced."

"Okay, we can get you a battery in Cody, and I can see Sarge."

"I can drive your truck?"

"Sure," he said. "As long as you can reach the pedals." He ran a hand roughly over his jaw before he looked her right in the eye. "First, call Wicker Pines and ask if Sarge can have visitors."

As she reached for the receiver, she tried to ignore the rattling of the windowpanes as the wind pressed in on them. She listened but didn't hear a dial tone. There was nothing. She jiggled the disconnect button in the cradle, then slowly put the receiver down. "Good thing we called about Sarge when we did, because the phone's dead."

LIBERTY ALMOST CAME up short on reaching the pedals in the truck until she got her seat as far forward as it could go and put two pillows she'd retrieved from the house between the seat and her lower back. She finally made good contact with the pedals, and as they left the ranch, having decided to head to Cody anyway, Jake watched her get more comfortable in the driver's seat. She was easy on the speed and careful on the blind curve when they neared the highway.

She wore jeans but had put a red flannel shirt over her thermal, then her green jacket over that. The hood was down, and her hair was skimmed back in a low knot. The severity of the style only exposed a certain delicateness in her features. He found he kind of like the dusting of freckles across her nose.

What he didn't like was the way she seemed to wear her emotions on her sleeve. That wasn't easy for him to be around. She kept taking him by surprise. The hug earlier had been spontaneous; he knew that. But the feeling of her pressed up against him, even only for a few moments, had set off something in him that he didn't want to deal with. He had to take a mental step back. Maybe two or three steps back would be required until he could leave the ranch.

They were halfway to Cody when Liberty darted a look at Jake, then back to the road.

She was a good driver, and he'd started re-laxing, but something was wrong. "What's going on?" he asked.

She was sitting straight up, looking franti-cally at the gauges in the dash, then slowed to pull over onto the gravel shoulder. Turning to him, he saw her say, "The seat is vibrat-ing! I didn't touch a thing, I swear I didn't. Now it's stopped."

He was pretty sure he knew what had hap-pened. "It's okay. The seat does that when you're drifting too close to the lane next to you. It lets you know which lane by where it vibrates. I should have told you about that."

"Well, why don't you go ahead and tell me what else you should have told me about the truck. I can listen and drive," she said, then returned to the almost-empty highway.

He quickly briefed her on all of the cus-tomizations to the pickup. It wasn't until he ended with "It's specially equipped for the deaf" that he'd realized how that sounded.

She slowed again as she glanced over at him. "You got this truck customized for the deaf after you told me it's temporary and you just need time to heal?"

"Watch the road," he said, and she did. But

she wasn't giving up. Without turning back to him she held out her right hand and made the "give me more" motion with her fingers. She darted him a look. "Explain," she said.

He wanted to ignore her, but he couldn't because she just didn't stop. "Call it an abundance of caution. I need it so I won't plow over a dirty blue Jeep when I'm backing up."

She pulled over onto the shoulder again. "What now?" he asked as she came to a stop.

She turned in her seat to look right at him. "We need to talk, and you have to be looking at me. So I stopped to get something straight."

He couldn't think when she looked at him so intently, and if this was another staredown, he didn't see himself winning. "Okay."

She was blunt. "How bad is your hearing?"

He didn't want any part of this. "Why?"

"I'm going in with you when you see Sarge, so I really do need to understand how it's all going to go down."

She was right. When they got to the facility, he knew he might need some backup with the doctors to make sure he got things straight. "I don't know," he said truthfully.

She made no move to get back on the highway. "How bad is it?" she persisted.

He almost admired her determination, but not when he was the one in her line of fire. "This is just between you and me. Right? Not even Seth."

She didn't hesitate. "Absolutely."

"Okay, it feels like the worst case of your ears being plugged at high altitudes, but with continuous noises under it all. If I might be able to hear anything, it's voided out by the noises right now." He added with weak sarcasm. "Before you ask, I can't pop it away by holding my nose, closing my mouth and blowing." That was true. "Not much pain at all, but it's annoying." That was really minimizing something that dominated his life.

"How did it really happen? Was it an accident or…?" She waited, nudging him to fill in the blanks.

He found himself being truthful to a point but knowing it would take her in a totally different direction than the truth he couldn't tell her. "I woke up one day about three months ago with the noises and a lot of pain. The pain's over, but the pressure and the noises stayed."

"What did they say caused it?"

"Decibels, a super-high level. Now, can we get going?"

That actually worked. She put the truck in gear and drove back onto the highway. He thought he'd been able to read her pretty well before. But right then, he didn't know if she'd simply given up—which he wouldn't bet on—or if his explanation had been enough. Either way, she'd gotten a lot more out of him than he'd ever intended to give anyone. In some way he felt real relief that she knew as much as she did, and that he wasn't going to see Sarge alone. He wasn't certain he could carry that off without Liberty there.

He looked ahead at the increasingly dark gray of the cloud-heavy sky. "Snow's coming," he said as he reached in his jacket pocket for his cell phone and checked it. He saw three bars. "I've got a strong signal," he said right as a text from Seth popped up. He opened it and read it to Liberty as she drove. "'Sarge is at rehab at Wicker Pines in Cody. In New York for a week. Where are you?'"

Jake quickly responded. Nearing Cody. Be there soon.

He felt the phone vibrate almost immediately. Let me know what's going on.

You got it, he texted, then sat back and glanced at Liberty. "So, Seth won't be here soon, after all."

She pulled over again, and it was getting annoying. "I told you that to make you think I wasn't alone, you know."

"Yeah, I know."

"Now, can you let him know I got to the ranch safely? I was talking to him when I lost cell signal."

He did as she asked, and his phone vibrated a minute later. He read the text out loud. "'Glad Libby got there okay and you're with her. Was worried about her. Take care of her. Call me after you've seen Sarge.'"

"You don't have to take care of me," Liberty assured him. He put his phone away.

"Thanks for telling me," he said.

"Now, what are you going to tell Sarge?"

"Whatever I have to, so he won't be worried about me or anything else. He needs to concentrate on his own healing." That was the absolute truth.

"Okay," she agreed, but hesitated this time before cutting to the chase. "So, you don't want people around here to know you're having trouble with your hearing?"

Liberty Connor had been a stranger before yesterday, but he'd spoken more about his situation to her than anyone but Cal. And now she'd got him. He never wanted to be an object of sympathy for anyone. He could take care of himself. But Liberty was different and that worried him. "Yes, I'd appreciate you not telling anyone."

"It's totally up to you who you tell or don't tell," she said, and drove back onto the highway.

When she pointed ahead after a long stretch of silence in the truck, he looked up to see the sign for Cody on the right. The traffic was heavier as they drove nearer to the city, then swung off the highway and into town.

Jake saw a few streetlights coming on as more and more daylight was lost because of the heavy clouds from the coming storm. He could barely make out the mountains in the distance that were shrouded by more dark clouds.

He'd been in the position he was in right then a lot of times in his life—jumping into the unknown to see what he'd find. But with Sarge, he was very uneasy about the unknown factor. Sarge no longer had Maggie by his side, and those five years since she passed had changed so much in every way.

He hadn't even seen Sarge in a couple years. Everything had changed, including the Alzheimer's diagnosis that Sarge hadn't shared with anyone. That hurt. Sarge had kept it from them, but he understood. Jake was doing the same thing with his condition, not selfishly, but to keep those around him from sharing that burden. Now, Jake didn't even know if the man would recognize him. He braced himself as Liberty turned off the street and onto one less traveled. Then Wicker Court came into sight. Before he could say anything, Liberty turned onto the narrow street lined with an assortment of small brick and wood houses. She slowed and took the curve at the end, and the entrance was right there.

Jake looked up at an arched sign suspended between two substantial brick pillars. *Wicker Pines* was in fancy script, giving no indication to just what the place was.

As big as the pines that seemed to encircle the property's perimeter were, the wind was bending them with its force. Following a wide drive, they pulled into a cobbled clearing protected by a ring of even more trees. The space was dominated by a large two-story colonial-style brick building. It was fronted by a circular parking area marked FOR OUR GUESTS. Liberty parked nose-in near the entrance.

When she shut off the truck, she turned to Jake. "You said that you want as little stress as possible for Sarge. So if you find yourself with any problems, such as missing a statement, or not understanding what's being said, or if you just need to leave, you can give me a high sign. I promise I'll do anything I can to protect Sarge and make things easier."

She surprised him by her generous offer, and he must have taken too long answering, because she spoke quickly. "I'm sorry. I didn't mean to say you couldn't handle it, but I just—"

"What kind of sign?"

He couldn't hear it, but he saw a relieved sigh when her shoulders dipped. "Just say something that isn't going to make someone wonder why you said it. Especially nothing Sarge would be uncomfortable with. But it has to be something you wouldn't accidentally say in a normal conversation, either."

Something came to him that he hadn't

thought about for years. "Moon Dance. That's the first horse I had at the ranch."

"Okay, say anything about Moon Dance, and I'll be all over it," she said with such earnestness that Jake smiled.

"I bet you will be," he said as he turned to get out. He walked across the cobbles with Liberty beside him, the huge pines buffering the wind. Taking a step up to the wide entry door that held a large Christmas wreath wound with gold ribbon and red berries, he spotted a call box to the right. Liberty pushed the button.

She looked at Jake as she spoke. "Jake Bishop to see James Caine." He saw her nod at him as she moved back. "They'll buzz us in."

After a few seconds, Liberty pointed to the door and he reached for the latch. The barrier swung back, and they stepped out of the cold into the balmy warmth of a reception area that looked like an English library. It was all dark wood and leather. The touch of Christmas in the space was elegant—a perfect tree with twinkling lights and red and gold ornaments. The scent of fresh pine lingered in the air.

There was a large desk near the back with easy chairs and low tables grouped by it. A blonde woman wearing a Santa hat came out of a side door. She appeared to be in her early thirties, tall and slender. She wore a pastel blue shirt, jeans and neon-blue sneakers, and she had a fantastic smile when she held out her hand to Jake.

"Welcome, Mr. Bishop. I'm Julia Weston, nurse and case coordinator for Mr. Caine." She glanced at Liberty, and Jake saw her say, "Welcome, Mrs. Bishop."

Liberty had obviously corrected her when Julia quickly responded, "Oh, I do apologize, Ms. Connor, but you aren't on the approved visitors list. I'll have to check before you can see Mr. Caine. Give me a minute," she said, and exited back through the side door.

Jake looked at Liberty. "I didn't think he'd have a restricted visitors list."

"It's probably just part of their services. I'm sure it's really expensive here, and heavy security for the patients tends to come with big money being paid." She smiled. "You know, like a rock star who comes here and wants total privacy. No one will ever know he's here."

Julia came back smiling again. "As long as you vouch for Ms. Connor, Mr. Bishop, she's cleared."

"Thanks."

"Now, we ask that you please make your visit as brief and calm as possible. He's a bit confused because of the move, which is normal, and he needs rest to get reoriented."

They signed a leather-bound guest book Julia had laid open for them, then she guided them through double doors at the back of the room and into a wide corridor. They went to the right, passing pictures that had been wrapped to look like presents, hanging on pale green walls. Julia led them into a short hallway with only two doors that faced each other across a waiting area that offered upholstered bench seating. Julia went to the door on their right and pushed it open.

"There's a call button by the bed," she said. "Enjoy your visit."

"Thank you," Jake said, and stepped into a spacious room, comfortable and homey in some ways, but still obviously a medical service space. He looked across at the only bed and saw Sarge for the first time in what seemed like forever. He was in a modified reclining position with a blue blanket up to his waist. Jake had to make himself keep walking toward the bed.

The giant of a man Jake had known looked older and less imposing. His hair was thinner, almost white, his weathered face tinged with paleness. When he got to the right side of the bed, Jake looked into the man's faded blue eyes, and there wasn't a spark of recognition there.

He glanced at Liberty, who had gone to stand on the other side of the bed to face him. She seemed to understand right away what was wrong, and she mouthed, *Call him by his name.*

"Hey, there, Sarge," Jake said, and wondered if his voice sounded as tight as it felt.

Sarge frowned. "Hey," he said.

"I told you I'd be back, and here I am."

The man looked confused. "You told me? You sure?" Sarge asked.

Jake walked that back quickly. "Oh, no, I didn't tell you. Not really, but I hope it's okay that I came?"

Sarge's pale eyes seemed to clear when he took a sharp breath. "You... Jake, boy, it's you!" He reached to grab Jake's hand where he was holding on to the safety rail attached to the bed.

Jake felt the roughness of calluses and some strength in the contact as he bent closer to Sarge. "I'm sorry for taking so long to get here, sir. I'm really sorry."

Jake straightened and was shaken when he saw tears brightening the man's eyes. "But you came. That's good. You came. You hear me, boy, it's good."

Jake wished he could hear him. "Yes, sir," he said. "But I don't salute marines, you know."

Jake knew without hearing that Sarge responded with that low rumbling chuckle he remembered from so long ago. "That army ruined you, boy." His eyes narrowed. "You look thin."

"I'm lean," Jake countered, then pulled a chair closer to the bed. He glanced at Liberty as he sat down and motioned toward her. "You're ignoring the lady," he said. "Liberty Connor. She's a good friend of Seth's."

As the older man glanced at Liberty, Jake angled his chair so he could see what was being said by both people. "So, you and Seth, huh?" Sarge asked her with a smile.

"We're just good friends." She held up her hand with the ring on it. "But I am engaged."

Sarge glanced back at Jake, and his smile grew bigger, bringing a bit of color to his face. "Jake, finally? I never thought you'd settle down. Me and Maggie sure wanted you to."

Jake stopped that right away. "Hey, hold on. Liberty's engaged to a really rich guy who's off saving the world."

He glanced at her and smiled as she mouthed, *Not funny.*

He rephrased that. "He's a good man."

Sarge nodded. "I'd say good enough to give her that ring."

"I did say he's rich, didn't I?"

Liberty spoke to Sarge. "The ring is a family heirloom from my fiancé's great-grandmother."

"Well, it's big. My Maggie, she didn't get a ring right away, and when she did, she wouldn't let me get a big one." Sarge frowned, and his large hand pulled away from Jake's to start worrying the hem of the blue blanket. "It was small, so small, but she really loved it."

Jake touched his arm to get his attention. "Now, tell me what's happening with you."

Instead of answering Jake, Sarge asked his

own question. "You still testing them fancy million-dollar jets?"

"Add a lot more millions to that and yes, I do it once or twice a year."

"You should have gone into the air force, not the army, then you could've done it there and had regular work."

Jake had joined the army right out of high school, and he'd only done that to figure out what he wanted to do in life. It hadn't been his goal to stay in the military longer than he had to. "I do what I want to do, when I want to do it," Jake said with a familiar ease that he knew smacked of a teenage boy who'd been cocky sometimes.

"Like you always did," Sarge said on a sigh. "No ties, no bonds."

"And no need to be told what to do, either."

There wasn't the expected smile from the man that should've come with the banter. Instead, Sarge turned to Liberty. "You know him well?"

She glanced at Jake, then leaned toward Sarge as if sharing a secret with him. "I'm getting to."

"Let me tell you something about Jake. Same old, same old," he said. "Jake stays with

Jake. He's on his own. He should have been a marine and learned to be a team player."

"So, Jake's a loner?" she asked with a smile.

But Sarge frowned. "Most of the boys are. It's hard for them to trust anyone, you know. They never learned how. Me and Maggie tried, but it's hard for them."

Jake touched the man's arm, but once again, the contact was ignored. "What's your name?" Sarge asked Liberty, despite the fact that they'd just been introduced.

"Libby."

"No, no, the other one."

"Liberty?"

"Liberty, yes. That means freedom," he said, looking pleased with himself. "Maybe you can help Jake get free."

She gave Jake a look he couldn't read at all and said, "Jake's very free."

"No, no," Sarge said, shaking his head, slowly at first, then a bit faster as he turned to Jake. "You never listen to me, son, never. I told you, you need a Maggie in your life. Someone to be with, to…" He looked sad suddenly. "To make you not alone."

Jake was holding the metal safety rail so

tightly his hands were tingling. He felt tight in the chest, too, and just wanted to breathe cold air. Before he knew he was going to say it, he asked Sarge, "Whatever happened to Moon Dance?"

CHAPTER SIX

LIBBY LOOKED AT JAKE, and there was no doubt he hadn't missed anything Sarge had said, nor was he confused by what was said. He wanted to leave. His face was taut, and his hands looked as if they would crush the metal railing he was gripping. "We should let you get some rest," she said to Sarge. Unexpectedly, the man reached toward her and took her hand in his. She was stunned by his next words and the tight grip he had on her. "Maggie, please don't go."

She tried to think what to do. But one glance at Jake watching the big man with clear pain in his eyes told her she was on her own. Taking a breath, she prayed she was doing the right thing. "I never want to leave you," she said. "You know that."

Sarge spoke in a shaky whisper. "I just get so lonely sometimes, Maggie."

Her heart ached. "You'll always have me,"

she promised with absolutely nothing to back that up. "But you need to rest. You need to get better." She squeezed his hand gently. "Will you do that for me?"

He sighed. "Okay, I'll try."

"Thank you," she said as she heard the door open. She turned to see a gray-haired man in casual slacks and a short-sleeved blue shirt coming into the room. He had a sprig of holly clipped to a gold name tag on the breast pocket of his shirt that read Dr. Clayton Miller, Director.

"Hey, Sarge, what's going on?" the doctor asked as he approached the bed on Libby's side.

Sarge let go of her, and Libby moved back to give Dr. Miller space. "Doc, you…?" Sarge screwed up his face with an intensity that came from nowhere. "I just…don't know."

In a soothing tone, the doctor said, "That's okay. I'm not here for more tests. I'm here to get your order for dinner. We have great beef stew tonight or roast chicken."

Suddenly Sarge was talking about what he wanted to eat and didn't seem to notice Libby moving farther away. She glanced over at Jake and mouthed, *We need to talk to the doctor before we leave.* Then she spoke to the doctor. "Dr. Miller?"

He glanced up at her, and she didn't have to ask her question. "I'll meet you in the hallway in a few minutes," he said.

Immediately Jake spoke to Sarge. "Sarge, I'll be back soon."

"Okay," the big man said without looking up from the laminated menu the doctor had handed him.

Jake started across to the door with Libby following him, but they didn't make their exit before Sarge spoke up. "Real sorry you went tail-over-head trying to get on that horse, Jake."

Libby quickly touched Jake's back to stop him, and when he turned to look at her, she mouthed what Sarge had just said. He understood and looked past her at Sarge. "Hey, you were the one who told me to push and pull as hard as I could."

Sarge looked up at him with a slight smile. "Yeah, I did, son, but it was still pretty darn funny. You should have told me you'd never ridden anything but a bike before. Lies can bite your back end sometimes."

"Yeah, they sure can. Now, I'll be back

after you get some rest," Jake said, and turned to head out of the room.

Libby nodded to the doctor and stepped into the hallway after Jake. A few minutes later, Dr. Miller came out, and he didn't say anything until the door was shut behind him. Libby made sure that she was facing Jake when Dr. Miller spoke. "He's doing well, considering his other issue, but right now, he's tired from the transfer and needs rest. His leg is healing faster than expected, so we're getting him into physical therapy after he settles in."

"He's confused and thought I was his wife, Maggie," Libby said. "I let him believe it. I hope that wasn't wrong."

"Indulging him to make him calmer and feel better is never wrong."

"Thank you."

Jake finally spoke up. "I'll be back to see him in a few days."

"He needs rest, so call before you come to see how things are, but it will do him good to see familiar faces. If you have any questions, feel free to call me or Julia."

When the doctor went back into Sarge's room, Jake and Libby headed to the reception area, then stepped out into the wind and cold. Jake went directly to the passenger door of the truck and got in while Libby went around to get behind the wheel. When she started the engine and heat began to flow into the cab, she reached to pick up her cell phone off the console. One glance at the screen and she saw a text from Roger's mother. She ignored it the way she had the other two she'd noticed earlier. She wasn't in the mood to talk about wedding plans, not after this visit. She'd do it later. She tapped Jake's arm to get his attention.

"Do you want me to call Seth, maybe do a video call so you can talk to him?"

He took out his own cell and quickly wrote a text, sent it, then looked back at her. "Just messaged him," he said, then asked, "Where do we go for the car battery?"

She put in a search on her phone and found an auto supply store they must have passed coming to see Sarge. When she glanced up, Jake was looking at her. "Found one," she said. "It's right on the way back to the highway."

"Okay," he said. "Let's go."

Putting her phone back in her jacket pocket,

she glanced at Jake and could see him taking slow, measured breaths. His head was back against the headrest, and his eyes were closed. She reached across the console to tap his arm. As he opened his eyes and slowly turned toward her, she asked, "Are you okay?"

"Sure," he said, cutting off any more discussion by turning to look out the side window.

"Okeydokey," she muttered to herself and drove back toward the highway. When she spotted the auto parts store, she pulled into the parking lot and found an empty spot right by the entry doors. "You want to come in?" she asked Jake.

"No, I'll stay here."

She left the truck idling and hurried into the store. A clerk found the right battery for her, then she spotted a section of the store dedicated to artificial Christmas trees and decorations. As quickly as she could, she picked up everything she was going to need to decorate her and Roger's future real Christmas tree. Maybe there would even be enough to decorate a bit in the great room. She picked up several boxes of her favorite decoration—

candy canes—and had a full cart by the time she went back outside.

Jake got out of the truck and came around to her. He frowned at the full shopping cart, and she thought he might say something, but he didn't. He didn't meet her eyes, either. He just opened the large security storage box in the back of the truck bed, emptied the cart into it, then closed it.

"It looks as if we're in for snow soon. Let's get back to the ranch." He opened the passenger door and climbed into the truck, and she followed.

"Did you really go tail-over-head off of Moon Dance?"

He exhaled heavily. "Yes. I flew right over the saddle and did a face-plant on the ground. Now can we go?"

She wanted to take the tightness out of his expression. "I bet you got back on, didn't you?"

"I had to get back on or risk looking like a coward."

"My parents had a friend who had horses, and I rode a twenty-year-old horse named Old Dan."

He seemed impatient. "I bet you were really good at it."

"I didn't go tail-over-head when I tried to get up in the saddle for the first time."

Jake actually chuckled skeptically. "Sure, because girls are much more cautious and proper."

"Should I add that to your list?" she asked, wishing he could hear her sarcasm.

"Add what to what list?"

"The list with only *stupid jerk* on it right now, but I can add *sexist*."

He laughed this time and she loved the sound. "Sure, why not. So, you were a natural rider from the get-go?"

She crinkled her nose in a grimace. "No. I didn't get back on that horse or any other horse ever again."

He smiled at that. "Okay, the score for following through is Jake, one, Liberty, zero."

She shrugged. "Gloat if you must, but being up on that horse was terrifying. He was huge."

There was still a smile shadowing his lips, and it made him look younger and less tense. "You'll never know what you missed."

She shook her head. "If I'll never know, then it doesn't matter, does it?"

"Touché," he murmured, and she started the truck and pulled out onto the road heading south.

The trip back was silent until they were just past the blind curve on the county road. That's when it started to snow. "I'll get the battery changed before we go inside."

With a quick glance, she said, "It can wait until tomorrow." Then she focused on the road ahead and finally saw the boulders. They were already topped by clinging snow that was being driven by the wind. She took it easy driving between them and up to the house. When she stopped the truck by her Jeep, she laid her hand on his arm to keep Jake from getting out.

"I'll just say this, and I won't say it again. I really appreciate you staying another day or two. Without a phone, especially my cell, I'm kind of at a loss, and I'd feel better not to be here totally alone."

He only nodded, then said, "I'll get the battery in." He got out of the truck into snow and looked back into the cab at Liberty. "I'll get the battery and tools. You get in the Jeep to pop the hood for me." He swung his door shut.

Fifteen minutes later, Libby met Jake on the front porch after he'd changed the battery, and they hurried into the house together. It was warm and quiet being out of the coming storm. Jake stripped off his jacket and tossed it onto the cowhide bench, then he kicked his boots under the seat. He turned toward her as she nudged her boots under the bench by his. "That should do it, but have the Jeep checked by Henry in Eclipse."

"I will. I owe you big-time for the furnace and the battery." She hesitated, but had to ask, "You really are staying longer, aren't you?"

He shrugged. "I'm going to stay until the landline works and the storm's over." Libby was so relieved, she had to stop herself from reaching out to hug him again. He hadn't responded that first time, and she didn't want a repeat. So she clasped her hands together and said with feeling, "Thank you."

Jake just nodded again and turned away to head into the great room.

The wind suddenly ran over the house like a train gone wild, and Libby felt herself tense. Wind brought bad memories from a part of her past that she didn't want to revisit. She glanced out the window by the door. Large snowflakes swirled in the wind while the world outside turned white. She crossed to the great room and saw Jake standing by the couch unzipping his duffel bag. When he glanced toward her as she walked in, he was holding a rusted metal box about the size of a rectangular wallet in his hand. "You need something?" he asked.

She shrugged. "No, just...you know."

He pushed the box into the duffel, then zipped it up. She watched his shoulders moving under his black thermal shirt before he looked back at her. "No, I don't know."

She didn't want to be alone with the wind. She'd been alone one too many times as a child when the wind had come up and there was no one there for her. She didn't imagine that Seth had told Jake about that part of her life in foster care, and she found she didn't want to share it with him, so she shifted away from it. "I'm just wondering about something Seth told me to convince me to come here over Christmas."

He tossed the duffel over the arm of the couch and onto the floor with a thud, then turned to her. "He told you Santa lived here?" There was a hint of smile on his face that she welcomed very much.

"Not quite, but he did say Roger and I could have our own Christmas tree."

He took his time sitting down on the couch. "Sure you can," he finally said.

She went over to him, then sat down on the braided rug on the floor facing up at him. Crossing her legs, she said to him, "Do you know where there might be an ax around here?"

That brought a chuckle. "You want to play lumber jack, or is it for a nefarious reason?"

"Nothing bad. I need to chop down a Christmas tree. What's Christmas without a tree with candy canes, lights, tinsel and gifts under it?"

"Uncluttered," he said.

"Translation? Bah humbug."

He sat forward to rest his forearms on his thighs. "Your fiancé isn't big on it, I'd guess."

That took her aback. "Why would you think that?"

"You said he gave up the chance of coming here with you for Christmas."

"No, I said he had to stay longer on the work site, but he'll be here before Christmas."

"Really?" Jake asked.

"Unless something unexpected comes up on the site."

He frowned slightly. "So he wouldn't come then?"

His question was fair, but he sounded annoyed. "Does it offend you that Roger is dedicated to his work?"

"That's a strong word. Why would it offend me? He's your fiancé, and I sure don't know him."

"Yes, he is, and it's between us," she said, but that wasn't really accurate. Roger hadn't asked for her input about him staying on at the new site. She liked to think she would have probably agreed, if he'd asked her. She had to admit, he seldom asked for her input on his work or schedule. But it always worked out eventually.

Jake gave a wry smile. "He's going to be at the wedding, isn't he?"

She brushed that away, saying, "So glad you've agreed to stay."

"Do you always get your way?" he asked with a touch of teasing in his voice.

"No, but I am glad you're staying," she said genuinely. "It's better not to take chances like that."

"You're pretty cautious, aren't you?"

She couldn't deny being too cautious, too planned and too protective sometimes. She'd never admit to anyone that it scared her to think of just letting things happen. "I'm not usually very freewheeling. I'm a realist, and I like order. I might be a bit uptight."

"A bit?" he asked with a lifted eyebrow.

So, he saw her as an uptight, overly concerned person who probably never let go. Her early years of having no control over anything had left scars. She knew that. Roger had been a godsend. He was dependable and safe, and she loved him for being so dedicated to his work. His parents had been pushing about wedding arrangements ever since the engagement, but she'd find a way to control that, too.

"What's the craziest thing you've ever done?" Jake asked. "Don't say you've never had a crazy moment. Everyone's done something unexpected, even people who don't think they ever will. So, what was your moment?"

She wished she could tell him something

that would knock him off his feet, but her life hadn't been filled with crazy moments after she'd been adopted. She certainly wasn't going to bring up how she'd tried to run away from her first foster home. That was over and done. "What do you classify as crazy?" she asked.

"I'll give you an example. I'd only been here at the ranch a while when I got up on the garage roof to knock snow off. While I was up there, I tried to fly."

"Seriously? You thought you could fly?"

"No, I thought I could jump and glide long enough to make the guys watching me think I flew."

"Were you compensating for the horse incident?"

That brought a hint of a smile to his lips, and she liked it. "Maybe. But it sounded like a cool idea."

She studied him. "So was it cool?"

"I dropped like a lead balloon and broke my ankle in two places. The only cool thing about it was the freezing snow I was almost buried in when I hit the ground."

"Ouch," she said with a grimace. "I bet you never thought about doing that again."

"Of course I thought about doing it again."

"You would have jumped off the roof again?"

"Probably not, but I spent a long time trying to figure out how I could have done it right."

"You can't fly," she said, pointing out the obvious.

He shrugged. "No, but at the time, I thought I should have been able to glide. Now I'm still like that, either get it right the first time or figure out how to get it right the next time. I'm not done with anything until I've beaten it, or it's beaten me."

She'd never met someone like Jake, and his ideas kind of scared her. "What if being beaten means you break your neck the next time?"

JAKE STARED AT HER. He'd taken chances and had it backfired, but at least he'd tried. Giving up wasn't acceptable to him. "If I start thinking I can fail, I will," he said.

Most people like Liberty weren't equipped to understand a life lived in the moment. No matter how much he liked her smile or had thoughts about how lucky Roger was, he'd never put himself in a place where he had to worry about altering his life because of another person. It was why he kept clear of relationships and, to some degree, why he didn't involve his family in his life very much.

Jake knew about being alone, and he'd craved it since the accident. He also knew he wouldn't leave Liberty here on her own with no way to contact anyone when a storm was coming. It was why he'd agreed to stay at the ranch with her. He owed that to Seth, and now he felt he owed it to Liberty. He owed her for going with him to see Sarge. It surprised him how easily he'd accepted her help and how easily she'd given it.

"What about discretion being the better part of valor?" she asked. "William Shakespeare's *Henry IV*. 'Caution is preferable to rash bravery.'"

He sat back, getting a bit of distance from a woman who seemed to have the ability to challenge just about anything he said or did. "Shakespeare? Seriously? You're pulling out the big guns? No offense to old Will, but I think it's better to regret something you tried and failed than to regret something you didn't even try to do."

"Maybe not doing something and surviving is better than doing it just to say you did what you wanted to do."

"Wow, now that sounds boring," he murmured, not adding that it sounded suffocating. That was pretty much the main reason he'd never settle down and answer to someone else. He didn't think he could survive that.

Liberty looked down at the ring she had been rotating on her finger and stopped. He could see her exhale as she sat up a bit straighter before she looked back at him. "That wind sounds horrible outside," she said, totally going off subject.

"And we're inside," he said.

She took a deep breath. "I'm sorry, I don't… It gives me the creeps. I've never liked wind."

"But you don't mind thunder. Go figure that," he said.

"This is different."

He'd seen her uneasiness about it last night, but he didn't brush it off this time. He could see the tension in her body, the way she took another deep breath and exhaled. He wanted to know why it bothered her so much. "What happened with you and the wind?"

"Nothing, really." She bit her lip. "I'm sorry."

"Sorry? Why? Was it something you did wrong?"

"I'd rather not talk about it." She looked serious about that.

"Okay, but I'm sorry for whatever it was," he said, and meant it.

Color touched her cheeks. "It's nothing big at all. Just stupid stuff when I was little."

"Was it crazy stuff?" he asked lightly.

"No. Well, maybe. I was so young, just five, I think. So it was foolish, not wrong."

"Now you have to tell me what happened."

He could tell she wished she hadn't mentioned it at all. "I don't think I have to," she said.

"I told you about flying," he said. "That's still embarrassing to me since I never figured out how to do it right."

"Oh, okay." She started speaking so quickly he had to really concentrate to see what she was saying. "It was nothing. I was little and I got lost in some woods and it got really windy. I didn't know where I was, and the wind was so bad that the trees just groaned and made cracking sounds, and I thought they were all going to crash down on me. I was there all night before they found me."

He hadn't expected that at all. "You weren't hurt, were you?"

She blinked. "I was fine, just fine." She shook her head, and her brilliant hair drifted softly around her shoulders. Resting her hands on her knees, she looked right at him as she sat straighter. "I just remembered something that I did that was crazy," she said.

He was quite sure she wanted to forget about what she'd just told him. So he'd play along. "What was it?"

"I was almost eighteen when I did this, and it was dangerous." She gave him a "you asked for it" look then went on, "I was warned not to take the tags off my pillows, but I cut them off the first day I was in my dorm at college." She grinned at him. "Rebellious, huh?"

"Absolutely. You broke a federal law, lady." They both laughed, and it felt good, really good. He didn't want it to stop.

"I'll swear you're lying if you turn me in," she said.

"What's said here, stays here."

He liked the way that smile of hers showed up. "Deal." She paused. "Now that's settled, I've been thinking about some things I could use your help with. First, the space for Sarge.

I would love to get your input on plans I put together before I got here and ideas I have since checking the space in the west wing." She was really into her work. It showed on her face that she was suddenly in her element. "Secondly, I'd like you to think of something you wanted when you were living here but didn't get. I mean, really wanted and wished for."

He wasn't one to analyze things too much, especially the past, and he wasn't sure he wanted to go down that road. "Seth would be a better source for Sarge's space," he said. "After all, it's all his idea. Honestly, back then, I never asked for much, and I never believed in wishes, either."

"How about now?" she asked.

"I get what I want for myself and wishing is pretty much worthless."

"Wow," she said. "I'm sorry."

He didn't want that. "No, don't be sorry," he said quickly. "I'm just being honest with you."

"Okay, I understand." She stood and turned to pad barefoot over to the glass doors to the right of the fireplace. Jake looked over and saw beyond her that the falling snow was changing to larger flakes, and the wind was dying down. He watched Liberty watching the outside world and knew he'd said too much. Finally, he stood carefully and crossed over to her.

"Liberty?" She looked startled when she turned to him.

He tucked the tips of his fingers in the pockets of his jeans. "I've reconsidered."

"What?"

"I'll look at the plans and give you my honest opinion, and I'll try to remember what I wanted, beyond getting out of the system."

"Seriously?"

"Yes, seriously. If it helps you help Sarge and Seth, I'm all for it."

"Thank you." She smiled at him and clasped her hands together. The diamond sparkled. "Thank you so, so much."

Jake felt a tinge of jealousy that a man he didn't know would get to see that smile for the rest of his life. That didn't seem fair, and it made his throat tighten. "Sure, no problem."

"One more thing. I need to get the Christmas tree before you leave, because I might need your help getting it back here after I cut it down."

He hated to mess up her plans as a lumberjack, but he did. "I should have told you something right at the first. Sarge has a law around here that no tree is ever cut down just to be brought inside and decorated."

"I thought Seth meant that Roger and I could do it."

"Sarge always had a living tree in a wooden root box around here somewhere. He brought it in for Christmas and used it for a couple of years, until it got too big or too scraggly. Then he'd plant it outside and dig up another one."

"Do you think he still has one out there?" she asked.

"I don't know," he said, and had barely finished when she moved around him to head for the door.

CHAPTER SEVEN

JAKE KNEW WHAT Liberty was going to do, and he didn't argue with her. So five minutes later he found himself outside on the back deck, wearing the beanie Liberty had handed to him, along with his jacket and boots. The snow was still coming down, but it was barely two inches deep, and the wind had faded to little more than a breeze. Even so, the cold made his face tingle. He wanted to get this over with quickly.

Liberty looked along the deck in both directions, then said something he didn't catch before she started hurrying down past the great room to the back of the west wing. He saw her target by the railing at the far end of the deck. A cone-shaped pine tree sat in a wooden container that brought it up to about six feet in height. It was partially covered in snow.

As Jake got closer, Liberty turned to him.

"It's perfect, but now we need a broom to get the snow off before we can take it inside."

"How are we going to get it inside? It took two or three bigger kids along with Sarge to move these before."

She studied the tree, then crouched down and pulled the red gloves out of her jacket pocket to put them on. She brushed away the snow around the bottom of the wooden container. He was surprised when she uncovered a swivel wheel at one corner of the box, then a second one at the next corner. She stood and announced with a grin, "It rolls!"

Sarge must have had it done so he could move it on his own. "Let's do this tomorrow," he said. "I'm starving."

"We need to get the tree inside so it can dry off before we decorate it."

"Who's this 'we' decorating it?" he asked, but not unkindly.

"Well, I mean, I'm going to wait for Roger to get here to decorate it, but until then, it can be drying out, you know."

"How long does it have to dry out?"

"A day, or two, or maybe longer. Who knows?"

He didn't bother to fight her vague statement. "Okay." He eyed the snowy deck. "It's not very deep. You just need a cleared path to the door."

"That won't take long. Is there a shovel or a broom?" she asked.

He knew it was easier to just go with the flow, and he told her where the brooms were kept. She took off to get one. Even when the tree was finally inside, sitting in the great room just by the glass door nearest to the kitchen, Liberty didn't slow down. She actually wiped at the tree with towels to get clinging snow off its boughs, then laid more towels on the slate floor to catch the rest of the snow as it melted. Finally, she stood back and smiled at him. "Thank you. It's beautiful."

"You're welcome. Now, can we eat?"

"Of course. I can make us something," she said, and went around him to go into the kitchen, then the pantry. Jake turned to go after Liberty, but she was already coming back out. "Your choice," she said as she put a large can of pork and beans and one of chili on the kitchen island. "I might not cook, but I have the skills to heat up anything."

"I'm impressed," he said.

"You know what? I actually can do a mean frozen dinner, too. How about chili?"

WHEN THEY SAT opposite each other at the table to eat, Jake watched Liberty test her chili and smile. "It's not bad."

No smile should make his breath catch the way hers kept doing. There was something about her he couldn't pin down, and it went beyond her looks. Maybe it was her persistence or the kindness she'd shown while they visited Sarge. He didn't know, and he really didn't want to think about it. Before he could taste the food for himself, Liberty got up. "I'll be right back." She took off toward the entry and disappeared from his sight.

Jake felt cold air invade the house a minute later, and he realized she'd just gone outside. He was ready to go and see what she was doing, when she came back carrying two six-packs of bottled soda. She set them on the table. "I forgot about these. Sorry there isn't a variety, but they are icy cold."

Her face was flushed, and that smile was back in place. Both six-packs were cream soda with twist-off tops. She handed him a bottle, then she sat back down and reached for her own. Jake put his by his place and looked over at her. He didn't think he was frowning, but he saw her say, "Oh, you don't like it, do you? I know a lot of people don't." She leaned forward and stretched to pull his bottle over by hers. "Sorry, the milk was spoiled, and the orange juice is dicey. There might be a can of tomato juice in there. Or I can make coffee."

"I like cream soda," he said before she could get up and take off to the kitchen.

She looked at him skeptically. "Truthfully, you really like it?"

"I almost forgot about it, but I do like it." He reached to take his bottle back.

"You've got good taste," she said with a nod, then started eating her chili.

The meal was quiet with neither one speaking very much, but there were four empty soda bottles when Jake pushed his bowl back. He tapped the closest one with his finger. "I haven't had cream soda since my last birthday here."

She sat back. "When is your birthday?"

He found himself answering her honestly, something he seldom did when faced with that question. "I don't know."

"How can you not know when your own birthday is?"

That did sound strange. "When they found me outside the police station as a child, I knew my name was Jake, and that's all I could tell them. There was no note with me, so they guessed at my age, five, and they finally gave me the last name Bishop. I'm not sure why. My first caseworker asked me to pick my birth date. All I knew was Christmas and the Fourth of July."

"What date did you pick? No, let me guess. Christmas?"

"I picked the Fourth of July, and I got fireworks for every birthday after that, like clockwork."

That made her smile, but it was a soft smile, one that could have been sympathetic. "You could have said Christmas and had Santa and presents and a Christmas tree."

"At that age, I couldn't really remember Christmas very much. The first Christmas I actually remember was in the foster home, and I got underwear and socks. But I sure remembered fireworks, being scared at first, then being enthralled with them. I don't know where I was, or who I was with, but I remember it being exciting." He sat back in his chair as he murmured, "The things you don't forget."

Libby pushed her bowl out of the way, then leaned forward. "Did you remember a wish from when you were here?"

"To be honest, it would be what I said before. The only thing I wished for back before I got here was that I'd never gone into the system or that I could get out of it. That wish wasn't answered—well, not completely. But Sarge and Maggie were terrific."

"So it sort of came true."

"I guess."

"Is it good for you, being back here? I mean, despite the problems?"

He exhaled. "Being back here without Maggie or Sarge, it's not the same, but it's my home."

"What happened to Maggie?" she asked.

"She got sick about six years ago. It was her heart, and she passed a year later. We all came here near the end and stayed for the funeral, then we all had to leave again. I hated that, but I had a contract in Alaska that I couldn't get out of."

"That must have been horrible for all of you, especially Sarge."

"It was," he said, then pushed away the past, done with thinking back on things that only hurt to remember. He stood, collected the dishes and took them into the kitchen while Liberty put the rest of the sodas in the refrigerator. Jake glanced over at her after he closed the dishwasher. "Dinner was good."

"Thank you. I open a mean can."

He smiled at that. "I'd agree with you."

"Can I ask you a favor?"

"Sure, if I can do it."

"I need to get started working, and my drafting table is still in the Jeep. It's kind of heavy and awkward. But I need to set it up."

"Where do you want it put?"

She looked around the great room. "Do you think it would be okay if I set it up in the of-fice? The desk would be an awesome work area. If I set up the drafting table by the desk, I could swivel between both."

"Okay, I'll bring it in, but before I set it up, we need to put the Jeep and truck in the garage and out of the snow before it gets too deep."

"Okay. I'll get the office ready for it. I'm dying to really get down to work."

By the time Jake got the table into the

house and across to the office, he was surprised that Liberty had actually managed to push the large desk up against the wall under the back window. She looked at him as he propped the folded table against the office doorjamb. "Oh, good, you got it in."

"How did you get the desk moved? It has to weigh a ton."

"It has coasters under each leg," she said. "Also, I do some design work, and I move a lot of furniture when I'm staging finished properties. I'm no weakling."

He nodded. "The phone, did you check it?"

"Dead as a doornail," he saw her say. "Not that I know how a doornail can die." She sat down in the computer chair. "I blew it while we were in Cody."

"What are you talking about?"

She shrugged. "I really needed to call Roger and my parents, but I didn't even think about it while we had phone service. Roger doesn't know if I made it here safely or not. And his mother must be going nuts not being able to contact me."

"His mother?"

She shrugged. "She's very interested in our

wedding, and she needs to check in with me all the time. She emails and texts constantly."

"Wow, that could be trouble," he said with a mock frown.

"Oh, no," she said quickly. "No, not at all. I'm just busy, you know, and I have my own ideas of how I want my wedding to be."

"Well, the phone might be working soon," he said.

That was met with her saying, "Or maybe we'll be snowed in before they get it working again. We won't be able to reach anyone then." She stood abruptly. "The snow's not very deep yet. I'll drive down to the end of the county road to find a signal and call them."

He almost thought he'd read that wrong. "You'll what?"

"That's where I lost the signal before, and that's not far. I won't be long," she said, and walked out of the office. He followed her to the entry where she was putting on her boots. As she reached for her jacket, she looked up at him. "Just give me your keys for the truck, please."

"That can't happen," he said bluntly, astounded that the person who'd argued *he* was reckless was thinking of doing something herself that might not end well. "I thought you were all cautious and careful. Now you want to go out in the snow and just hope you make it back?"

She stood and put on her jacket, grinning up at him. "I'm not jumping off a garage roof. I'm going a short distance down the road. I promised my parents and Roger I'd call or text. I don't want them worried."

"So you'd rather break an ankle, figuratively speaking, than a promise?"

"I've never broken one bone, and I keep my word." She passed that off. "But never mind, I'll take my Jeep. It works now."

He could admit he was rash and daring at times, but she was just plain stubborn and frustrating. He couldn't let her leave alone, and he wouldn't. "No, if you're determined to go, you can drive my truck. It's been prepped for this kind of weather."

"That's why I asked to use it," she said, and held out her hand to him. "The keys, please?"

He was tired, but he was going for a ride. He put on his jacket and boots, then headed for the door, and he knew she'd be right behind him. She was. He went out and got into the passenger side of the truck, and she slipped in behind the wheel. When she was set with the pillows behind her and her seat belt on, he turned and held out the key fob.

"Couldn't you have given this to me in the house?" she asked as she started the engine.

"Could have, but I have a bad character flaw," he said.

"What's that?"

"I don't suffer fools easily."

"Fools?" she asked, making sure he could read her lips. "I'm not the one who tried to fly."

He actually laughed at that. "We're even," he said, then he held out his hand. "Give me your phone so you can drive. I'll watch for the signal."

"Oh, sure." She pulled her phone out of her jacket pocket and handed it to Jake.

Liberty drove slowly as she neared the boulders, which were starting to look like giant snowballs. Jake spoke again. "You've never driven in the snow like this, have you?"

She stopped before going onto the county road. "No," she admitted.

Jake looked down at the phone. "If you

have any trouble driving, I'll take over. I'm feeling fine."

She tapped his arm, and he glanced at her. "You promised you wouldn't drive."

"No, I never promised that."

As surely as the sun set in the west, Liberty didn't let up. "It was unstated, but I assumed that you agreed because you admitted you shouldn't be driving." She kept those green eyes on him and made no attempt to drive farther.

"I don't plan on driving before I leave here on my own, and I'll let you know when that's going to happen. Now, enough of that." He wanted to get something straight with Liberty, because he knew it could end up being a battle if he didn't settle it now. "We have to agree that we're only going as far as the highway. The snow's coming down harder, and driving will only get worse. So if there's still no signal at the highway, we head back. Agreed?" She bit her bottom lip, and he knew she was going to argue. He had to set a hard and fast quitting spot. "Or do we turn around and go back now?"

She hesitated, then she nodded. "Okay, okay."

He had to be sure. "Okay, what?"

"If there's no signal by the time we reach the highway, I'll turn the truck around and come back."

He wanted to laugh at the touch of frustration in those green eyes. He'd been right to get it settled. Liberty had told him she kept her word, and now she'd given it to him, however reluctantly. "Let's get this over with," he said, and turned to look down at her phone.

"No signal," Jake said when they finally got close to the entrance of the highway. He looked at Liberty as she stopped the truck and reached to take her phone from him.

She looked at the screen for herself. For a moment, he thought she was going to throw the phone out the window. Then she looked up at him. "Shoot, what a failure," she said. "I'm sorry."

"I guess you had to try."

"I just don't want everyone worried about me, you know. Roger and my mom and dad. I hate them being concerned when they don't have to be."

"Stop beating yourself up, and let's turn around and head back," he said, wanting to stop this conversation right here.

She handed him her phone. "I'll go closer to the highway where it gets wider and do a U-turn."

He felt her warmth still trapped in the phone's plastic cover. As she approached the entrance and started to make the U-turn, Jake saw the signal icon flash. One bar. "Go very slowly as you turn," he said and kept his eyes on the icon as she inched forward. Another bar appeared. "Stop," he said as calmly as he could and reached to put on the emergency flashers. "We have two bars. Stay right here and try your calls. I'll keep my eyes open for any cars coming this way."

Liberty reached for her phone, then quickly dialed a number. Jake saw the screen flash, then she sat back in the seat and held the phone up about a foot from her face, obviously making a video call. He could almost make out the head and shoulders of the person on the call with her, but the angle distorted it. All he knew was, Liberty was smiling as he turned away to watch the empty highway.

After a few minutes, he was getting uneasy just sitting in the middle of the highway entrance and turned back to Liberty, hoping she was almost finished. But she'd shifted to have her back against the door, and he could see what she was saying. "I really miss you and can't wait for you to get here." She paused. "I already have our Christmas tree ready to decorate."

Jake looked toward the highway again and couldn't see any cars through the snow in either direction. When Liberty tapped his arm, he thought she was done. She wasn't. She was holding her phone out with the screen toward him a foot from his face. He looked past it to see her say, "Roger wants to talk to you."

Jake focused on the screen. Roger was a man with dark eyes, dark hair and a short beard. The expression on his tanned face was serious. "Hi, there," Jake said.

Roger sat with his back to a long window that showed thin light spreading over a barren landscape "I don't know you, and you don't know me, but I need you to do me a big favor." Roger didn't wait for a response. "It sounds remote and rough out there. I need you to watch out for Libby for me. I'll make it worth your while. Just name your price."

Jake couldn't believe the man was actually offering to pay him to babysit Liberty. "I don't want your money."

"Good man. Put Libby back on."

That was that. Jake looked at Liberty, who wasn't smiling now. She reached for her phone and looked at the screen. "Roger, I told you I'm fine here." There was a pause, then she nodded. "I know you love me. I love you, and I'll be okay."

The man had said something else, and Liberty almost rolled her eyes. "No, I won't." A pause, then she said, "Miss you, too. See you soon."

She finally looked at Jake as she lowered her phone. "I apologize for Roger. He feels bad that I'm here on my own, but his work is so important. My work, laying out a floor plan, isn't even in the same universe as getting clean water to people to keep them from sickness or death. He'll get here as soon as he can."

She was explaining way too much about the man. "Let's get back to the house," Jake said. He was nervous just sitting there as the truck collected more and more snow on its surface.

"Okay," she said. "I'll just text my parents."

LIBBY WISHED SHE'D never insisted on driving in the snow to call Roger. If she hadn't been so distracted by Jake and Sarge when they were making the trip to and from Cody, she would have made the call and maybe it would've gone better. Now she felt disappointed and embarrassed that Roger would actually offer money to Jake to look after her.

Roger was still trying to figure out when he could leave to come here, and he wasn't certain about it at all. On top of that, his mother was anxious to speak to her. He'd asked Libby to make sure she called her soon since she'd been ignoring her emails and texts. Libby had hedged by saying they had to get back to the house. But he'd expect that call to his mother soon. She felt unsettled and not relieved at all to have contacted Roger, and the longer they'd talked, the more uneasy she felt. Things didn't feel right, and she didn't have a clue what to do to change that until Roger was with her in person.

Thankfully, Jake was silent all the way back to the house and didn't mention Roger's offer while Libby drove and tried to settle her nerves. Wedding jitters. That was it, she decided, but she couldn't shy away from the fact that the call she'd thought would excite her hadn't. She didn't feel reassured after speaking with him and only felt more pressure to please his mother. The call had been rushed and shorter than she'd needed, with nothing she'd hoped for.

The snow was still falling, the wind was growing and daylight was being blotted out. Libby breathed a sigh of relief when she saw the boulders caught in the harsh glare of the headlights. She turned onto the barely visible drive up to the house, then stopped by her snow-topped Jeep. Leaving the truck idling, she turned in her seat toward Jake. "You said we need to put the Jeep and truck into the garage, but what about the packages in the lockbox back there?"

"I'll get them inside before we go down to the garage." But he didn't make a move to get out. "Where did you say your fiancé is now?"

"Western Africa, a village in Mali, below the southern edge of the Sahara Desert. Roger's doing preliminary layouts and plans for a linked water purification system."

"How long has he been over there?"

"He'd been there three months when he got word of another project in that area that had finally been accepted, so he had to stay longer. Once, he was gone for seven months on-site."

"Were you two together then?"

"No, I met him two years ago when he came back to Seattle for a major fundraiser. They were moving the foundation offices into a building in the downtown area. I was doing the plans for redesigning and repurposing the existing available spaces to accommodate their needs."

"So he comes back for business and fundraisers?"

"Yes, of course." She felt defensive and found herself almost lying when she added, "He'll be back here for Christmas, then we'll head to Seattle after the New Year and finalize the plans for our wedding in March."

"Will he be around for the honeymoon or is he going off to Timbuktu while you worry about calling him?" Jake asked. Even a bit of a smile from him didn't soften his sarcasm.

She didn't like what he was saying at all. "I'm sorry Roger was rude to you, but he's really a very good man, and he's doing a very good thing for the world. He's never been to Timbuktu, but if he thought they needed him, he'd be there."

He studied her intently for an uncomfortable moment, then seemed to shrug it off. "Sorry, I'm no expert on relationships at all. I keep my distance, but I just get the feeling that you think what you do is less important than what Roger does."

She answered that quickly. "Roger saves lives."

She watched him take a deep breath, then he spoke. "I think that what you're doing with this land, with this ranch, for all the boys who will come here, might just be saving some lives, too," he said. "Think about the value of your own work."

With that, he turned away and got out into the wind and snow. She hesitated, his words touching her. She knew the ranch would be important to the kids, but she'd never thought of it as life or death, just a break from their lives for a week in the summer. Then Jake had said that to her. It stunned her that he saw that so clearly and she just now faced it. For some reason her eyes burned with tears. She swiped at her face and got out into the bitter cold. Jake already had the storage box open and was pulling out plastic bags. He handed her several, then picked up the rest and followed her inside.

After the security box was emptied and the bags left in the great room by the Christmas tree, Jake and Libby went back out and drove the vehicles down to the garage and secured them. As they headed back to the house, a fierce gust of wind hit Libby and literally knocked her into Jake. He caught her, making sure she was steady, then shifted his grip on her to put his arm around her shoulders. "Hold on," he said, and they headed up to the house. He never let go of her as he kept himself between her and the storm, and she felt almost safe in the wind for the first time she could remember.

Finally, they were in the house, out of their jackets and boots, and despite the heat from the furnace, Jake made a new fire in the hearth. Libby curled up in one of the chairs and watched him, his words coming back to her. Roger praised her work, saying how good she was at it, but he'd never suggested he thought the work itself was truly important. In fact, his mother had some idea she'd be working at their foundation after they married. She'd been ignoring that, but now it made her more unsettled.

She had to clear things up with his mother soon, but not over the phone. When she and Roger were back in Seattle, she was going to sit down with Gwyneth and explain what she wanted her wedding to be and what she'd be doing after the marriage. She could compromise on some things, but she wasn't quitting her job or having half of Seattle at the wedding. She was nervous about that talk, but she had to do it. She would. When Jake stood and turned from the hearth, he looked at her and asked, "What now? It's been a full day."

"I think I'll just sit here and enjoy the fire for a bit. What's the altitude here?"

"Five thousand feet, give or take," he said.

"I usually never think about going to bed this early, but I'll be ready tonight."

He moved the chair by her, then he sat down and leaned back. He took his time pushing the sleeves of his black thermal shirt up over his forearms and stretched his feet out in front of him. He finally looked at her again. "About what I said in the car. I just wanted to make sure you know how grateful we all are that you're doing what you're doing here.

Sometimes life-and-death actions can come in all forms. You're making a difference you might never know about, but you are."

Libby was touched by his words. "Thank you," she said. "That means a lot to me. I can only imagine how Roger feels helping so many people with what he does."

"You're right. What he does is a good thing that helps many people. But what if one of the boys who comes here for camp finds what he needs to keep going? What if he actually makes a life in this world instead of being written off? How important is that?"

She couldn't take her eyes off Jake as he spoke, and his words touched her again. She knew from Seth that Jake had been one of those boys who'd made an exceptional life for himself after leaving here. "It would mean everything to me. I hope that happens on some level for every boy who comes out here."

"That's what you're making possible, touching one life at a time with this project. Because of you, kids could be changed forever."

She knew how things could change the path of a foster child. She knew what it meant to have one gesture from another human being make all the difference. It certainly had for her, and she was where she was now only because of that gesture by her adoptive parents, the Connors. "What happened here that changed you?" she asked, really wanting to know.

He narrowed his eyes as he shifted and rested his hands on his stomach. "Nothing and everything, but it all came down to Sarge and Maggie. They did it one kid at time." He exhaled. "I was one of those kids, a boy so damaged I was written off by everyone... except Maggie and Sarge. They never gave up. Not once, and they guided me toward a life I'd never dreamed of. That's what you can do with the camp."

"You're right. I know that one person can change everything for a child," she said, so thankful for the Connors, who never saw her as a girl who wouldn't talk and wouldn't laugh and who cut herself off. They'd seen her as a child to love.

She had to say one more thing. "I don't want you to think the Roger you met on the phone is the Roger I know."

"Honestly, my thoughts back there about Roger were pretty simple. I wondered what kind of man leaves you here alone yet says he's worried about you being here alone?"

"Roger has commitments," she said, finding herself defending her fiancé again. She hated it.

"Being with you and making sure you're safe, isn't that a reasonable part of being committed?"

CHAPTER EIGHT

LIBBY LOWERED HER eyes to look somewhere around the buttons that were undone at the throat of his thermal. There was no heart in her to defend Roger anymore, so she wouldn't answer his final question. She got to her feet and said, "I think I'll finish getting the office ready."

Jake got up. "I'll set up your drafting table."

She nodded, then turned and headed into the office. As she sorted through the boxes she'd brought in, Jake put the table up and placed it right where she wanted it. He left enough space between the desk and the table for her to sit in the computer chair and swivel from one work area to the other. He attached a work light to the drafting table, and when he turned it on, it cast a clear light over the whole work space.

When Jake headed off into the great room, for some reason, she called after his retreating figure. "Roger and I are committed to each other, and he'll get here for Christmas, too." He kept going with no clue what she'd said, but in some way, she felt better when she sank back into the chair. Truth be told, she had no idea when Roger would show up at the ranch so they could decorate the tree for their first holiday together. He'd been so vague on the phone, not sure when he could leave the site. But he'd promised to try. That was the only part of the conversation with him that held any hope for her.

She didn't realize Jake had come back until he spoke. "Do you need more light in here?"

He was in the doorway holding a tall floor lamp with what looked like a cowhide shade on it. "First of all, tell me that shade isn't really cow skin before I commit to it."

He shrugged. "All I know is it's some sort of parchment that's been stained. Now, if we're talking about the bench in the entry—"

She grimaced. "No, I don't want to know, or I'll never sit on it ever again."

He held the lamp up toward her with a smile. "Binary choice. Yes or no? Take it or leave it."

"Yes," she said. "Maybe over there by the window."

He crossed to where she'd motioned to her right and crouched to plug it in. When he finally eased to his full height, she noticed fine lines at the corners of his eyes as he narrowed his gaze on her. "I need to say something. Whatever you and your fiancé do or don't do is none of my business. It obviously works for the two of you, so all that matters is you're happy with it."

She hadn't expected that at all. "I do miss Roger when he's gone, especially now," she admitted. "This is our first Christmas we can be together. He was gone last year."

He sat down on the wooden chair by the desk to face her. "In Africa?"

"Southeast Asia, near Cambodia. While he was gone, I blew up some pictures that his crew had taken at some of the sites. They were wonderful photos of children with huge smiles as they played in water and ran under water sprays that reflected rainbows. Their joy was breathtaking."

She had known only after he'd hung them in his office that those photos had made her realize she loved him. He'd rescued those kids by what he'd done for them, and maybe being there with those kids had done a lot for him, too. That resonated with her. She'd been rescued by the Connors and her parents had told her she'd rescued them, too.

"You obviously love him," Jake said softly.

"I do." She felt befuddled, a word her mom used when she couldn't think straight. Her last conversation with Roger had left her unfocused. She still wished she'd never made it, that she'd waited until they could've had an unrushed conversation. "I'm tired. I think I'll go up to bed now and get to work early tomorrow." She stood and without looking back, headed out of the room and didn't stop until she was upstairs in the master bedroom. By the time she changed into a T-shirt and pink pajama bottoms, she all but fell into the large bed.

With no fire in the hearth when she turned off the bedside light, the room was cast into deep shadows. As she tugged the blankets up over herself, that moment when Jake had said, *You obviously love him*, ran through her mind. She loved Roger, and everything would work out. "That's all that matters," she whispered into the darkness.

IT WASN'T ANY of his business, but Jake didn't regret correcting Liberty about the importance of what she was a part of at the ranch. He didn't know anything about relationships. He didn't need anyone complicating the life he was living. But he understood one thing: Liberty was going to be helping one boy at a time. Sarge believed that was the way to rescue damaged boys, and he had lived that with Maggie as his partner.

Sleep for Jake came well after midnight, and when he opened his eyes again, he blinked at pale gray light behind glass doors that were frosted over. As he pushed himself slowly up, pain came out of nowhere, a stabbing fire in his right ear. Then it faded and was gone. It was almost as if it had never happened, but he knew it had. He waited, but it didn't come back. As he sat there, he felt something else, something he couldn't figure out. Maybe a shift in the pressure in his ears. If it was better or worse, he couldn't tell. Although the sounds were the same, existing only under the muffling pressure, he thought something had changed.

He slowly got to his feet and waited. No nausea, no dizziness, no pain. He took a couple of even breaths and released them unhurriedly. Liberty wasn't in the kitchen, so he turned and slowly walked over to the office door in the jeans and thermal he'd slept in.

It was empty, totally unchanged from the night before. "Liberty?" he called as he turned to the great room. He waited, but she didn't show up. His chest tightened at the thought that she might have left to find a phone signal again. He padded in his socks across to the entry and over to the door to pull it open. The scene outside was still and pure white. No vehicle had left or arrived through the deep, pristine snow.

He turned, looked at the bench and groaned. Liberty's jacket and boots weren't there. She'd gone out on her own, but she hadn't left by the front door. He quickly put on his boots and grabbed his jacket before he headed back through the great room, through the kitchen and mudroom, to the back door. There was puddled water on the floor, melted snow, and when he opened the door, more snow fell in where it had drifted against the back of the house.

He stepped over it as he pulled his denim jacket on and did it up. When he looked down, he was standing where Liberty had stood when she'd walked out of the house. He looked at her tracks going to the edge of the deck, down the stairs, then north toward a large grazing area dotted with thick stands of trees blanketed with snow.

Flipping up the collar of his jacket, he went down the stairs and called, "Liberty!" With no wind, nothing stirred, and the tracks in the snow seemed to go on forever to the north.

"Liberty?" he called again as he started following her path. His breath curled up into the air as he plodded on. Halfway to the trees, he felt the wind starting up again, coming down from the west, and he felt the knit hat in his pocket where he'd stuffed it after the last time he wore it. He pulled it on and hunched into the wind.

He knew how much the wind had bothered Liberty and why. He tried to go faster. He called again, "Liberty!" Nothing. But as he got closer to the snow shrouded expanse of trees, he spotted something moving among the thick trunks and low branches. Then it was gone.

Just seconds later, Liberty burst out of the trees coming right for him. Her hood was down, her hair was loose and tangled, and snow clung to her jeans and jacket in clumps. He pushed to get to her as quickly as he could but felt as if he was running in mud.

"I heard you and—" Jake saw Liberty start to say when she got closer to him, but her words were cut short by a flash of movement as something struck her from behind. There was enough force to push her right at him, and the momentum sent them both tumbling back into the snow.

Liberty was on top of Jake, her face inches from his, and he was stunned to see she was grinning as if she was having a great time. Then she pushed against him and rolled off to his left into the undisturbed snow. That's when he saw her attacker. A huge, mangy-looking black dog stood motionless just inches away from his feet in snow up to the animal's chest. Each breath the beast exhaled rose up into the freezing air. His teeth weren't bared, but his amber eyes were fiercely glaring at Jake and his upper lip was quivering.

The dog flashed a look toward Liberty, who was struggling to get to her feet, then quickly back to Jake. "Don't move," Jake hissed without taking his eyes off the dog.

The animal turned to him when he spoke. Liberty kept moving and was on her feet, saying something to the animal that he couldn't make out. "Liberty be quiet," he whispered.

She turned, started to say, "He's just—" and was cut off when the dog rushed at her and brought her to her knees. The next thing Jake knew the animal was trying to lick her to death.

He saw her say, "Get back, you doofus. Get off me!" The dog actually moved back enough for her to push herself up to get her footing again. He rolled his eyes up at her, then slowly turned to look back at Jake.

"Can I move?" Jake asked Liberty.

"Sure," she said, and held out her red-gloved hand to him.

The woman seriously still thought she could pull him to his feet. He did it himself, getting up cautiously, then he faced her and the dog as he swiped at the clinging snow on his clothes. "What is that?" he asked, motioning toward the animal who seemed glued to Liberty's side now.

"It's a he, and he's a big baby," she said, her smile coming back. "He won't hurt you."

Jake wasn't so certain about her last sentence. He pushed his hands deep into his jacket pockets. "I thought he was attacking you," he said, unable to smile about anything right then.

"Oh, I was attacked, but not in a blood-thirsty way. When I stepped into the trees, he was there and dived at me. I thought he was a wolf at first, and I was going to be his lunch. But the only way he tried to kill me was by licking me."

"You're okay?" he asked a bit stupidly since the death-by-licking obviously hadn't worked.

"Just a mess," Liberty said. "I heard you and was trying to get out of the trees so you'd see me, then he headed off the other way. I thought he'd left until he hit me in the back." She was stroking the matted fur on his head as she kept speaking. "He's just hyper, and I think pretty lonely and hungry."

Jake exhaled, thankful his heart had re-turned to a near normal pace. The fear he'd felt in that moment, when he thought Lib-erty was in real trouble, seemed way off the charts. It was still raising his heartbeat, and he tried to breathe to push it back. "Why did you leave without telling me?"

"You were sleeping. It wasn't snowing, and I wanted to walk a bit before starting work. Then I got the idea to go and see the original cabin past these trees. Seth told me about it, that Sarge built it when he first came on the land." She paused. "You didn't need to come looking for me."

"I wish you'd told me before you took off," he said, not about to explain how worried he'd been during that long hike to find her. He looked up at the heavy clouds overhead, then back at Liberty. "Let's get back before it starts to snow again."

"I'm taking him with us." Her hand stilled on the animal's head. "He obviously has no place to go, and he'll freeze out here."

"Okay, but we need to get back."

"Thank you." She bent over the dog, saying something near his ear before she stood to look at Jake again. "He wants to come with me."

"So, you're a dog whisperer?"

"No, but I can tell he's alone and needs me."

A caseworker had come to the ranch when Jake had jumped off the garage roof and broken his ankle, intent on taking Jake back to a special facility for troubled youths. Sarge had challenged her immediately. *He stays here with us. He's alone and he needs us.* The worker had left without taking him.

Jake looked at the ugly dog, one ear up, one down, and his tangled, dirty fur. "He's all yours."

NOW THAT WAS SETTLED, Libby was hungry. Jake turned to retrace his steps, and she followed, staring at his back all the way to the house. The dog never left her side. She remembered what Jake had said about no ties, no relationships, and it was obvious that could even mean a relationship with a dog. That made her feel sad for him. A man who did amazing things routinely with powerful jets couldn't trust himself to even have a dog in his life.

When they arrived at the deck, Jake hurried up the stairs and into the mudroom. "Come on, buddy, we both need to warm up," Libby told the dog. "Just don't listen to anything he says."

Jake glanced at them as they stepped into the mudroom. "I guess he really is yours," he said with what might have been a "What

were you thinking?" look on his face before
he took off his jacket.

She liked that idea. He was hers. "Yes, he
is. And I'll clean him up, but before I do, I
want to say I was wrong not letting you know
I was going out. But the good thing is, I found
him." She patted the dog's head, knowing she
couldn't have just left him behind. He was
totally alone and had no one. She knew what
that was like, and she didn't want even a dog
to experience it. She was so glad he'd come
along willingly.

Jake barely acknowledged what she'd said.
"Yeah. Now, close the door before you freeze."
With that, he walked out of the room and took
his jacket and boots with him.

She sat on a wooden wall bench in the
mudroom with the dog beside her as she took
off her boots, her jacket and the wet gloves.
She spotted a towel under the bench across
from them and grabbed it to start drying the
dog's fur. He was as controlled while she did
that as he'd been out of control outside. Her
jeans were wet up to her thighs and her hair
was damply clinging to her face and neck. All
she wanted was to get into a hot bath.

Jake was by the fireplace when she cut

across the great room to go upstairs with the dog. If he hadn't spoken, she wouldn't have stopped. "Just let me know when you're leaving next time," she heard him say just before she stepped up into the entry. "It's too dangerous for you to be out on your own in this weather."

She stopped on the step up into the entry, waiting for him to glance over his shoulder at her before she responded. "I already apologized."

His gaze dropped to the dog. "He's not pretty."

"He will be. You just wait." She turned and went up to the master bedroom with the dog at her heels.

Almost an hour later, Libby sat on her bed in fresh jeans and a pale blue thermal top. She'd blown her hair dry and contained her ringlets in a high ponytail. The dog was lying by her bare feet. It had shocked her that he'd calmly stepped into the bathtub when she'd brought him close to the warm water, and he'd been patient with her fussing over him.

Now clean and towel-dried, he smelled good from the rose-and-vanilla shampoo she'd used to wash him. Jake was right—the dog wasn't pretty. Maybe that would come when he fattened up. He looked at her and whined softly in his throat.

"You poor thing. You're hungry." She got up. "Come on."

He was right with her as she went back downstairs. Jake wasn't in the great room, so Libby went into the pantry to find something to feed the dog. She actually found an unopened bag of dog kibble, and she sat in the mudroom with the animal while he wolfed it down. As he drank some water out of a large bowl, Libby heard footsteps overhead. When she went into the kitchen with the dog, Jake was stepping down into the great room.

"See if this fits him," he said as he walked over to her and held something out to her.

"Where did you get it?" she asked as she took a well-worn dog collar from him.

"It was made years ago for a dog named Pax," Jake said. "It's the beast's if he'll wear it."

"He's not a beast," she said, then turned to try it on him. He didn't object at all. "Thank you very much," she said to Jake. "Now he's fed, I need food."

AFTER EATING SOUP and sandwiches in silence with Jake, Libby watched him load the dishwasher. When he turned to her by the island, she said, "Do you think the snow's going to stick around for Christmas?"

"Pretty sure it will" was all he said as he went around her and down into the great room. He walked past the tree and over to the fireplace. She watched him crouch to freshen the fire, then she went over to the hearth so he could see her speak. She really wanted him to help her decorate the tree, because it was starting to really depress her to have it sitting there naked. She wanted to enjoy the tree and have it all spruced up for when Roger showed. So, she'd do it and surprise him when he finally got here.

But when Jake looked over at her, she couldn't ask him to help. He just looked tired. She shifted gears. "I'm going to do some work."

"Okay," he said, then turned back to the fire.

Once in the office, Libby finished getting the printer working and laid out the blueprints Seth had given her on the drafting board. She secured them in place, then moved back and opened her laptop. She couldn't go online with no internet at the ranch, but she could pull up what she'd worked out for the suite off the blueprints before she came to the ranch and add her new ideas to that.

She didn't know how long she'd been in the office, but when she looked up and out the window, daylight was waning. Snow was being swirled crazily by the wind. The dog had left without her noticing, and she got up to find Jake. He was on the couch and the dog was lying on the floor at his feet. She smiled as she went over to the pair, who both turned toward her at the same time.

Taking a seat on the couch by them, she reached to scratch the dog's head. "He's fickle, huh?" she asked.

"He's practical," Jake said. "And he's house-broken. He whined to get out and came back okay. I got away before he could start licking me when he came inside. He had some more food, too."

The dog had been at the house for mere hours, but it already felt like he belonged. "Thanks. I got lost in working on the plans. I'm glad you let him out. He's so skinny, but he smells good. All I had was my vanilla-and-roses shampoo for his bath, and I used it sparingly."

"What are you going to call him?" Jake asked as he turned to rest his left arm on the sofa back.

"I have a few ideas. Maybe Beau. I think he's got a good heart. Or Buddy, but that's kind of blah. Lucky, for obvious reasons." She hesitated, then told him the name she actually thought she liked the most. "What do you think of Pax?"

His reaction was to frown as he looked down at the dog. She killed the impulse to get his attention and tell him she'd go with one of the other names. But when he finally looked up at her, he surprised her.

"I think it fits."

JAKE KNEW THE name was right. "The Pax who wore that collar was at the ranch when I was. Sarge found him on the side of the road, almost dead. But he made it. He turned out to be big and smart and loyal. He looked like a Doberman/shepherd mix, but both of his ears stood up."

"Another survivor," he read on her lips.

"Sarge had a gift for knowing one when he saw one."

He saw her eyes become overly bright before she leaned down to get closer to the dog and frame his muzzle with her hands. Jake knew she spoke to him, but he couldn't see what she said before the dog licked her face. She turned back to Jake as she wiped at her cheek. He thought she looked sadly happy, if that was possible.

"You know, sometimes life just gets so good I can hardly stand it."

His life was surprisingly good for this brief bit of time. A warm house, a dog and this woman smiling at him—a scene right out of a Norman Rockwell painting. "The dog has it good," he conceded.

"So, he's Pax?" Liberty asked.

"Yes, he is."

"Thank you. I can tell he's been through a lot and now he's clean and fed and..." She shrugged, a shaky motion of her slender shoulders under her pale blue thermal. "He's got a new name and a forever home. When I leave here, he's coming with me."

He studied her and didn't miss the unsteadiness in her hand as she stroked Pax's head again. He would have given Liberty anything she asked for right then, if he could have. Agreeing the dog was hers was easy. "If he's here when you leave, he's all yours."

"Why wouldn't he be here?" she asked, a slight frown touching her face. "He knows he's wanted. No one ever ran away from being wanted."

Her words were tangling him up inside, and he didn't like the memories that came with them, of times when he hadn't been wanted. Before he'd come to the ranch, he'd run away four times and thought of doing it many more times. "Pax would be a fool to run away from you," he said before a bolt of pain shot through his right ear. It was gone before he could even raise his hand to touch it.

When he felt Liberty's hand on his shoulder, he didn't acknowledge it for a few seconds. When he finally looked toward her, any hope that she hadn't noticed what happened was gone. He could see it in her eyes.

She drew her hand back. "Are you dizzy or—"

"No. Just an earache. They come and go." Pax stirred, then eased away from Liberty and went closer to him. Before Jake knew what the dog was going to do, his front paws were on the couch, and his face was right in Jake's as he proceeded to lick him frantically.

"Get down!" Jake said sternly and was astonished when the dog moved back immediately and sat down on the worn carpet.

Liberty bent forward to stroke Pax's neck, then glanced up at Jake. "Are you okay?"

Jake wanted to get past whatever had happened. "Fine, good," he said. "So, what's on your agenda?"

"Work, but I sure wish I had cell signal out here. I hate being cut off like this."

"You know they have a word for your phobia?"

She frowned. "What phobia?"

"The fear of being without a cell signal. Nomophobia."

Her expression shouted skepticism. "You made that up."

"No, a guy named Cal Harris, who helps me with my hearing problem, brought it to my attention."

"So he made it up?"

"No, he's the one who read about it."

"If that's true, then you can understand why I want some relief from it?"

He knew she was working up to asking

about maybe going to find the signal she craved. Without saying anything, he slowly got up and went toward the entry. He was totally stable as he took the single step up, and he knew Liberty would follow him. She couldn't help herself. When he got to the front door, he swung it open wide and sure enough, Liberty was right there. When he felt her touch on his back, he smiled to himself. She was so predictable.

Pax shot past them and bounded out into the snow, leaping high in the air as he ran. When Liberty came around to his side, Jake glanced at her and saw the uneasiness in her expression as the dog headed out of sight. "He'll be back," he said.

"Did you open the door to let him out?"

The heat of the house was at his back, the cutting cold of the outside world at his front, and Liberty was right by his side. "No, that was his idea. I just wanted to see how deep the snow is so far. It's pretty deep, so going anywhere is out of the question for now." He hoped she got the point he was trying to show her.

Just then Pax was back, running full tilt for the door. Stepping aside, Jake missed the impact that would have surely buckled his knees. Once inside, Jake shut the door, and Pax shook so violently that a clump of snow from his fur flew through the air and caught in Liberty's hair by her right ear.

Without planning to, Jake reached to swipe it off, then found himself cautiously brushing the tips of his fingers down the satiny warmth of her cheek. For a moment he was mesmerized by the connection. Green eyes met his, and there was a flash, a moment when they both recognized that something more than casual contact was happening.

Jake drew back, but he wouldn't apologize. He wouldn't have meant it right then if he had. But he wouldn't touch her like that again. He saw Liberty start to say something, but she ended up turning away. When she met his gaze again, it was as if what had happened between them never had. "I've decided I'm going to decorate the tree now, before I go back to work."

"I thought you were going to wait for Roger to do it with you."

"I was, but I think I'd like to have it done when he gets here to surprise him. Would you sit on the couch and let me know if I put too much stuff in one area, or if the tree looks crooked?"

He could do that for her. "Sure."

She turned and headed into the great room with Pax all but glued to her. Jake went to the couch to grab a fresh thermal. Some snow had hit him too on the shoulder and melted going down his arm. But he stopped himself. Any other time he would have stripped off the damp shirt and put on another one, but he couldn't do that with Liberty around. For one, he didn't want to horrify her if she saw the scars on his back.

So he crossed to the chair Liberty had sat in earlier. He pulled the closest chair to it closer and sat down, putting his feet up on the second chair.

Liberty was taking packages of lights out of a plastic sack. As she opened the first box and started unwinding them, he spoke up. "You'd better test those before you put them on the tree."

"Yes, of course," she said, coming over to hand him the string she held. "Why don't you test these, and I'll test the next ones." His simple suggestion pulled him into what he didn't want to do—decorate the tree. He'd never liked the fuss around Christmas. He hated socks and underwear for presents and he hated getting an apple in the small stockings that hung on a shelf by whatever tree was in the house he'd been assigned to. But he'd swallow all of that to make sure the lights on Liberty's tree worked.

That led to opening boxes of ornaments and ropes of sparkling silver and gold tinsel. When the tree was draped in everything Christmas, he easily set a glittering gold star tree-topper in place. Then he stood back to assess it.

Liberty was right beside him, her arm brushing his. When he looked at her, she said, "I'll plug the lights in."

"No, I'll do it. You stand right there and get the full effect."

"Wait," she said, then ran to turn off the overhead lights in the great room and then the office. Finally, the kitchen went dark, and she came back to Jake. He could only make out what she was saying because of the glow from the fire in the hearth. "Okay, I'm ready."

He went to the side of the tree to plug in the lights, and he positioned himself so he could see her face before he put the plug in the outlet. As the lights flashed on, he was rewarded when she smiled, an expression of wonder and happiness. He could have looked at Liberty like that forever and never gotten tired of it. And oddly, he'd kind of enjoyed decorating the tree with Liberty. That surprised him.

CHAPTER NINE

JAKE WAS SO close to falling into a place where he knew he didn't belong that he had to get distance. His life was a mess, and even if he got back to that life, he wouldn't drag her with him. He had a feeling that if she was in his life, she'd complicate it on levels he'd never see coming. That couldn't happen. He'd seen it in other test pilots. They gradually walked away from their careers, usually saying they couldn't put their family through the worry that came on every test flight. Or they had problems because they hesitated or didn't go that extra step needed in a test. He never wanted to have to choose between what he felt born to do and caring about someone.

His life was only his to live.

And Liberty had Roger. He had no business even thinking what he was right then. "All the lights work," he said as he moved back to his chair to sit down and get farther from her.

"Wow control your enthusiasm," she said as the Christmas lights twinkled and danced off the shiny glass ornaments. "Not much for Christmas, are you?"

He shrugged. "I told you I'd take fireworks over Christmas any day."

"But this tree lasts for as long as you want to keep it in the house. You could keep it in until your birthday. Fireworks are gone as soon they explode."

Liberty hurried over to a bag that still had something in it. She took out several red-and-white boxes and brought them over to where he was sitting. "Candy canes, the final touch on a perfect tree."

She dropped the boxes on the other chair, then opened one and handed it to him. "You take the high part, and I'll take the low part." She grinned. "Maybe I have a bit of Scot in me."

He figured she had more than a bit of child in her, and he did what she wanted. When the tree was dripping with the red-and-white candy, he turned to her. "Anything else?"

"No, it's perfect, well, except for presents, but they'll come. It's the most beautiful Christmas tree I've ever seen," he watched her say. "The snow's outside, and all we need now is some Christmas music playing as we sip mulled cider."

"I can supply some music, but you're on your own with the mulled cider," Jake said. "But first, I'm going to find something for dinner."

When he went into the kitchen, he flipped on the overhead lights and opened the refrigerator. He was startled by Liberty's hand on his arm. When he turned, she said, "I found some meat in the freezer before I left this morning, and I took out two steaks. I'm not sure about how to cook them. Maybe fry them, or roast them in the oven?"

One way or another, she'd ruin the meat and he knew how to barbecue steaks but didn't want to right then. "That's too much to do," he said. "How about some packaged mac and cheese? There's always boxes of that here."

"I think I can do that," she said right away.

"No, I'll do it. You sit and enjoy your tree."

He turned away and headed for the pantry. This time she didn't follow him, and before long, he had the boxed pasta done and in a bowl on the table where he'd set two places for them. "Comfort food," he announced.

Liberty came toward him but went past the table and up into the kitchen. The overhead lights went off again before she turned on the light in the fan hood over the stove. When she came to sit down across from him, she asked, "Can you see what I'm saying without the overhead lights on?"

"Not a problem," he said, then thought of something and stood. He motioned to the bowl of pasta. "Help yourself. I'll be right back."

He headed past the pool table to a cupboard set flush in the wall to the left of the office door. He pushed a panel and it snapped open, showing old electronics from the seventies and eighties stacked on two shelves at eye level. The lower shelves were filled with LPs in their original sleeves, cassette tapes and CDs in jewel cases.

He switched on the CD player, which was the size of a small suitcase, then crouched to scan the lower shelves and saw what he wanted. He pulled out a CD of Christmas music and put the disc on the tray that automatically slid in. He turned and called to

Liberty. "Give me the thumbs-up when this is loud enough." She'd been watching him and nodded. He pressed Play, then slowly adjusted the volume until he got the signal from Liberty. He went back to the table and sat down again. "It's older Christmas music."

She smiled at him. "'Silver Bells,' one of my favorites." She glanced at Pax, who was settling by her feet. Looking up at Jake, she said, "Thank you, this music is perfect."

"I'll take your word for it," he said. Then he remembered something he wanted to say to her. "With more snow coming, will you promise not to push to get out of here to go to town for shopping or whatever until it's safe?"

She put another spoonful of macaroni on her plate, then looked up at him before taking more. "I knew that's why you opened the front door earlier. Sneaky," she said with a smile.

"What?"

"You let me see how much snow was out there so I wouldn't suggest doing something risky, didn't you?"

She got him good. "Well, did it work?"

"Actually, it did. It was hard enough driving last night, so, yes, I agree not to push to get out of here until the roads are cleared. Besides, they'll be ready tomorrow, won't they?"

This would test her agreement. "No, they start with the town first, next the major roads in and out, and then they make their way out here."

She rolled her eyes. "Great." Then she shrugged. "Okay, but the minute we can get back into town, I need milk, fresh fruit and some treats for Pax."

She seemed to be in a mood not to challenge him, so he kept going. "Okay, how about we take my truck into Cody, do some food shopping for you, find a cell signal to treat your addiction and see Sarge again when it's safe?"

"When did you start being logical and cautious?" she asked, and he knew that she was teasing him.

He knew exactly when he'd started—when he'd met Liberty. He wasn't usually protective, but he owed Seth that much, and he owed her, too. He didn't want anything to happen to her because he let it happen. When he finally left, he'd leave her here safe. "Enjoy it while it lasts," he said, and motioned to the macaroni and cheese. "Can I have some?"

"Yes, of course," she said, and pushed it over to Jake.

The food was passable, but the company was better. They talked about anything that came up without arguing. "I'll feed Pax after we finish here," she said.

The dog sat up to look from one of them to the other, as if he understood what Liberty had just said. When Jake said, "He's spoiled already," the dog's ear that could stand up did.

"He deserves to be spoiled. Everyone does, just a bit."

"Are you spoiled?" he asked as he pushed his empty plate back.

"No, I guess not. Well, maybe some." She smiled at that. "My mother always makes my birthday cake the way I like it."

"How's that?"

"I love carrot cake with sour cream frosting, and she makes it every year. It's wonderful."

He'd never tasted it but she certainly looked happy thinking about it. "When's your birthday?"

"New Year's Eve."

"So how old are you this year?"

"Guess," she said, smiling.

He shook his head. "Oh, no, I'm smarter than that. If I say too young, you'll think I'm lying. If I say too old, things won't go well."

"How old are you?" she asked.

"Thirty-two."

"Well, I'll be twenty-nine."

"What should I say? I would have never guessed that, then leave it up to you figure out why I said that?"

She broke into a laugh and shook her head. "If I were you, I'd stop while I'm ahead."

He wished he could hear her laugh. He realized he'd laughed more since he'd met her than in any recent time he could think of. She stood up. "I'll get the dishes tonight."

"Do you want me to restart the music?"

She stopped and turned to him. "How did you know the music had stopped?"

"I can't feel it anymore," he said with a shrug. "More Christmas songs?"

"Yes, please."

LIBBY SAT ON the couch by Jake with Pax lying in between them on the cushions. The Christmas tree lights and the flicker of flames from the fire in the hearth were the only lights in the space. It was beautiful. Jake had put the

music on repeat, and it was soft and sentimen-
tal. "White Christmas," one of her favorites,
started and she stroked Pax as he settled his
muzzle on her thigh.

Jake turned on the lamp on the end table by
him, then turned to her. "What song's playing?"

"'White Christmas.' Why?"

"You were smiling."

"I just love being warm and snug out of the
cold and hearing Christmas music."

"I think you're making me reconsider my
choice," he said.

"What choice?"

"Picking the Fourth of July. Maybe Christmas has its good points."

"If I could have named my birthday, I
would have picked Christmas," she admitted. "They are both spectacular days in the
year. Speaking of which, the man at the general store in Eclipse—Farley—said something when I asked about eclipses that would
be happening around here over the holidays.
There aren't any, but he mentioned that we'd
miss a Christmas Moon, by one day. Do you
know what that is?"

"I think Maggie and Sarge talked about it some, but I didn't pay any attention to what it actually was," he said.

"Not having internet is frustrating. I'd like to know about it."

"How about doing it the old-fashioned way? I remember Sarge had a book all about the moon, the mythology and what the phases mean. It should be in the office somewhere."

She got up, hurried into the office and flipped the light on. She scanned the shelves then spotted it. *The Fascinating Moon*. Jake was sitting with his head resting on the back of the seat, his eyes closed, and Pax was right up against him when she came back. She went over to the tree, took two candy canes and crossed back to the couch. She sat down and settled with the dog between the two of them, then opened the book. Looking at the index, she found the answer to her question was on page 115. She flipped to it and read the title of that section. "The Secrets of the Christmas Moon."

"Okay, tell me the secrets," Jake murmured and declined the candy cane she offered to him.

She read out loud about any full moon

in December being called a cold moon or snow moon. "That's okay, but not romantic at all," she said. "But, get this, if a December full moon rises on Christmas Day—so I guess you'd only see it Christmas night—it's a Christmas Moon." She scanned more. "It's very rare, only once every twenty or thirty years. Apparently, from this chart, this year the full moon rises on the day before Christmas, so I guess it could be called a Christmas Eve Moon."

"A full moon's a full moon," he said.

She read further. "There's some legends about it. You know, things passed down, and it got mixed up in magic and fables."

"What's supposed to be the magic of it?"

She scanned further. "Two things—first, you can make a wish and it will come true. Secondly, and the best, it's said that if a couple kisses under a Christmas Moon, they'll be together forever." She smiled. "Kind of sweet, don't you think?"

Jake shrugged that off. "Sweet is in the eye of the beholder," he murmured.

"Come on. You can't be that jaded about Christmas and romance, can you?"

He was silent, then said, "I've never been a romantic."

She shrugged. "Of course, men hate to admit to being romantic."

He exhaled. "Believe it."

"You don't date or anything?" she asked, realizing he was probably being truthful.

"I do, when it works for me, but I've got my career and with it being a questionable one, I don't drag anyone into it."

"I guess if you think you're dragging someone into your life, it wouldn't be very romantic, would it?"

Jake studied her. "You have enough romance in you to make up for the lack in me."

She closed the book. "Well, I still want to see a Christmas Moon. I bet Roger will feel more romantic about it than you do."

He laughed at that, but it was a rough sound without real humor in it. "Anyone would."

She stood with the book in her hand. "I think I'll go up to bed and read a bit."

"Let me know if you come up with more magic or myths," he said.

"Okay," she said as took the book, the

candy canes and looked down at Jake. "I'll give you every romantic detail."

Jake gave her a wry smile. "Oh, I know you will."

LIBBY WOKE TO thin sunlight coming in the windows and dressed quickly in a white sweater and jeans. She reached for the book about moons before heading downstairs with Pax at her heels. Jake was in the kitchen, and she could smell coffee in the air. "Good morning," he called over to her. "How about some breakfast?"

She tossed the book onto the couch, then nodded as she crossed to him. "I'm hungry."

He turned to take bacon strips out of the frying pan and laid them on a plate covered with a paper towel. "I am, too."

"What are we having?"

"There's no eggs left, so we're going to have bacon and peanut butter sandwiches for breakfast." When she wrinkled her nose at that combination, he said, "Oh, come on, they're good. I ate a lot of them as a kid. You'll love them."

She wasn't so sure about that, but she always liked the aroma of bacon cooking. By the time she had actually tasted the sandwich he'd made for her, she was a believer. "That was pretty good. I can't believe I've never had it before."

He gave her a "told you so" look. "Trust me. I won't steer you wrong on food."

"Good to know," she said. She finished the last of her coffee and put the mug down. "When you look at the plans for Sarge's suite, will you be totally honest with me about what you think of them?"

"I'll be honest."

"That's all I ask," she said. "Could we do it now so I can get down to work?"

"Lead the way," he said, and followed her into the office.

Libby turned on her laptop, pulled up her files on the ranch, then opened the one for Sarge's suite. She angled the computer toward Jake as he sat down on the extra chair. "Just scroll down and ask me if you don't understand something."

He quietly went through the documents, never asking any questions, then he finally sat back, hesitating before he looked at her.

"Well, what do you think?" she asked, bracing herself.

"Let me see if I get what you're doing. You want the two rooms at the end west hallway joined by taking out the closets where they butt up against each other. You're taking the small bath and the room between the back south-facing room and the office, too. Right?"

She was impressed that he got what she was trying to do. "Yes, half of the room next to here will be incorporated into the main area, and the other half will be for an enlarged bath specially designed for Sarge and an adjoining walk-in closet."

"I saw that."

"Well?" she asked.

"The bath will have a walk-in tub for safety?"

"Yes, also slip-proof tiling. The shower is low entry and with double benches and safety rails in it. What do you think?"

He took his time before he said, "I think you're spot-on, and it's good planning to take advantage of the existing plumbing and keep it on the south wall with the window."

"I take it you've done construction in your past?"

As he sat back, Pax came in to plop down on the floor by them. "I did some construction work after I ended my stint in the army and was trying to figure out how I could do what I knew I wanted to do with my life and still pay my bills."

"What did you want to do?"

"I knew a guy who flew commuter planes and I helped with some of the mechanical problems he had, and one thing led to another and he gave me flying lessons in payment for my work for him. From the first time I flew solo, I knew I wanted to fly and that lead to wanting to be a test pilot."

"Can I ask why you wanted to do that?"

"It's brains and skill, the combination that makes you think and push past boundaries. It's a challenge every day at work." He narrowed his eyes on her. "And don't give me a label, like an adrenaline junkie."

"I wasn't going to say that," she answered, although she had thought that when Seth told her what Jake did for a living. He'd even mentioned Jake was fearless and loved the rush of what he did. "But it does seem dangerous. Actually, I think I understand why you've kept your distance from Seth, Ben and Sarge, and why you haven't told them about your hearing problem. You really think you're protecting them, don't you?"

"It's for my protection, too. I can't concentrate on what I'm doing if I'm worried about them worrying about me. When I'm in the cockpit, I can't be distracted and play it too safe."

"But they know what you do. Seth's told me all about it, and you think they don't worry?"

"Knowing is one thing, being involved in it is something I wouldn't ask of anyone, especially someone I cared about."

"The places Roger goes to for the foundation projects can be pretty unstable politically. But I understand that it's part of who he is. That doesn't mean I don't worry or that I'm unaware that he could be in danger. Do you think Seth and the others don't understand how dangerous what you do is?"

"Of course they understand," he said flatly. "They know that I just do what I do, then I do it again. Simple as that." He stood, apparently ready to retreat. "I think your plan's great."

"Thank you, I really appreciate your input."

She hesitated, then stood to face him. "And your honesty about your life. I just don't—"

"You don't know the life I've lived. But my past is what made me who I am today. Yours did the same. But you've had a normal life, with good parents, a great job. I didn't come close when I was younger. I had someone drop me at a police station without even a tag that had my name and birthday on it." He exhaled harshly, then kept talking. "Then I went from house to house, never fitting in, never wanting to, until the ranch. But even then, I had to form my own destiny." He stared at her hard. "And I did. It centered on my job, and that is the only way I know how to make my life work. I've always been a risk taker, I admit that, and I'm doing what I love being a test pilot. Right now, I'm doing what I need to do to heal so I can go back to that life."

"I understand," she said, feeling vaguely unsteady as he spoke.

"That's my point, Liberty, you can't understand." He rocked forward on the balls of his feet. "No one who hasn't been in foster care could understand. How could you?"

His words echoed in her, and they hurt. She

understood him, why he was like he was, why he isolated himself, because she'd done the same thing before she'd been offered a real life, not just an existence. "My life wasn't always like it is now. I've been where you've been. I can tell you that a life where people depend on you and care about you and love you is a huge improvement over just trying to survive in foster home after foster home. Or getting lost in a windstorm and thinking pretty much that no one would even miss you." When her voice broke, she stopped talking, afraid she'd start to cry, and she didn't want to do that in front of Jake. She tried to take a breath before she managed to add, "That's why Seth and I became friends. We knew what the other had gone through, and where we'd ended up. I do understand."

His eyes narrowed on her as if he couldn't quite look at her. "You, too?" he finally asked just above a whisper.

"Yes, me, too." She swallowed hard. "Until I was adopted, which was something of a miracle for an eight-year-old who hated being touched and just wanted to be invisible." She swiped at her eyes and couldn't stop now that she was talking. She wanted Jake to know who she "really" was and why. "My fourth foster home was my last. The Connors asked to adopt me, and I couldn't believe they would want me. I knew that they couldn't love me. There wasn't anything to love. But they did and do, and I love them. They're my mom and dad. I'd give up just about anything in this world for them."

JAKE READ THE words on her lips, unable to move. Pax went closer to Liberty, pushing against her leg. She ignored him as she stopped talking and worried her bottom lip. Jake didn't want to see anymore. He really didn't want to follow his impulse right then and hold her and tell her that anyone could love her. "I am so sorry," he finally said before she could speak again. "I didn't know you were one of us."

"I just wanted you to know that I…" She shook her head sharply, then brushed at the tendrils of hair that had escaped from the ponytail. He saw how unsteady her hand was. "I don't tell people about it. Even my parents and I don't talk about it much. I hate to even think about it, actually."

He saw her release a heavy sigh, then look him right in the eye. "I promised you, before I left this house again, I'd let you know. I think I'd like to go out for a walk now and..." She shrugged. "I need to..." She didn't finish, but he was pretty sure she needed to be alone.

The change in her was startling. The pain he'd seen in her face when she'd told him about her past was gone. But now she seemed almost withdrawn. "Okay."

Unexpectedly, she took off her engagement ring and opened the desk drawer to drop it inside.

As she closed it, she said, "I should've taken it off sooner," then went around him and out of the office. He followed her to the mudroom and stood watching her get her outer clothes on, then put up her hood.

"Where are you going to go for your walk?"

"I want to see the original cabin. Seth said it hasn't been used for years, but Sarge kept it up and it's really livable."

"Sarge built that on his own when he bought the land. Then he married Maggie, and they needed a lot more space, probably thinking they'd have kids to bring up."

She met his eyes. "They did have a whole lot of kids they helped bring up."

"Yes, they did," he said, then found himself offering, "I could go with you, if you want, so you don't get lost?"

"No," she said, and he knew he'd been right. He'd let her go alone. "I won't get lost." Pax had been watching them patiently, but now he moved closer to Liberty and his tail started to wag. "I don't know how long we'll be, but I'm just going there to look around, then we'll head back."

She zipped up her jacket, then Jake said, "If the snow starts up again, just come back."

"I will," she said.

"Okay, then, I'm going to go down to see if the tractor's working."

She frowned at that. "Why?"

"There used to be a snow blade that fit it. I want to clear the drive as much as I can, and also the way to the garages so we can get the truck and Jeep out when we need to."

"You can drive the tractor?"

"Yes, I can drive the tractor. I've done it

before to clear snow and haul hay out to the fenced pastures."

"Oh, of course," she said but didn't look convinced. Then he understood. "I'm fine to drive it. I'm feeling good, and no more face-plants or dizziness. Besides, if things go side-ways, all I'm going to hit is snow and more snow."

"Okay," she said.

He wondered, as he watched her leave the house with Pax, how much self-control it took for her not to try to talk him out of driving the tractor. Her body language almost shouted that she thought it was a terrible idea, but she let it go. Maybe Liberty Connor was loosen-ing up.

Jake managed to fit the tractor with the blade and worked steadily clearing the snow. When he was finished, he drove the tractor back up to the house and left it there. He stepped inside the entry, but the place was quiet. "Liberty, I'm back!" he called.

He waited, but there was no dog and no Liberty. He went through to the mudroom, and her outerwear wasn't there, either. He'd figured maybe an hour to get through the snow to the small cabin, half an hour to look around inside, maybe forty-five minutes coming back because of her original tracks and the trip was mostly downhill. He checked his watch. She'd been gone for three and a half hours.

He opened the back door and looked outside. It was like a rerun of yesterday. Tracks on the deck in the snow, then more down below. Liberty's and Pax's paths ran parallel, making a straight line toward the trees in the distance. The thing was, there were no tracks to show they'd come back.

He went across the deck and stared intently into the distance. It was peaceful, and nothing moved in his line of sight. White on white. He stayed very still, then made up his mind. He wasn't going to wait for her to come back. He'd go and meet her somewhere between here and there.

Tired as he was, he set off. When he finally reached the trees, he saw she'd gone through them, and he did the same. When he broke out on the other side, the tracks continued north toward the cabin that was barely visible in the distance. With snow on its roof and drifts climbing halfway up the sides of the log walls, it almost blended into the land around it.

He saw her trail. Thankfully it looked as if she'd made it to the cabin safely. He thought of heading back and letting her come at her own pace, but he couldn't. Not until he knew she was safe. He couldn't fight a protectiveness that nudged at him. Maybe knowing what she'd gone through as a child had affected him more than he'd realized. But he didn't want her to be out there alone if anything happened. The image of that tiny girl huddled in the storm without any real hope that someone would miss her ate at him. He kept going. He was within a hundred feet of the cabin when his leg muscles started to burn, and he stopped. The porch was completely buried in snow, and only the tops of the two front windows were visible. Then he saw smoke rising into the still air. It came from a vented outlet that he knew was for the potbelly stove in the living area off the kitchen.

He yelled as loudly as he could, "Liberty! Pax!"

The next moment, the dog was there, storming around from the back of the house. Jake barely missed being laid out in the snow again by yelling, "Stop! No, Pax, no!" Just a few feet before impact, the dog stopped, spun around and headed back the way he'd come. Jake followed him up and along the side of the house. As he rounded the corner at the back, he saw Liberty standing on the small stoop by the back door.

Her jacket was gone, but her boots were on and her hair was free from the ponytail to fall around her shoulders. "Jake, what are you doing here?"

CHAPTER TEN

THE BACK OF the house was protected from the wind, and the snow was half as deep as it was elsewhere. Jake went closer to the stoop. "You've been gone for over four hours."

"Oh, gosh, I'm sorry," she said, then backed up toward the open door. "Come on in. It's freezing out there."

He was on the stoop in one stride and in the small mudroom with one more step. It was empty. Two more steps and he was in the tiny square kitchen with its small refrigerator, stove and cupboards lining the walls. After all the years since he'd walked into the cabin for the first time, he was struck by how it looked as if time had forgotten it. Nothing was changed.

He turned and stepped into the living area that took up the rest of the front of the cabin. The potbelly stove was radiating heat, and

Liberty was already sitting on a small sofa that still had the dustcover over it.

"Look," she said, obviously pleased with herself. "I got the stove to work, and you won't believe it, but the electricity is still on."

He crossed a worn rug on plank flooring and sat down on the sofa as he undid his jacket and turned to look at Liberty. "What have you been doing?"

She shrugged. "Enjoying this place. This is just a wonderful house. It's tiny, but it's lovely. I mean, the furniture is all here, and there are no mice or rats running around. The bed in the bedroom is beautiful, wrought iron with scrolling at the head and feet, and it almost takes up the whole room. I wouldn't change a thing. It's got everything you need. It's compact and comfortable and sweet."

He would have never called a house "sweet" but if he had to, he guessed this cabin might be a contender. "For eclipse watching, we all staked out our viewing sites on the ranch, but Sarge and Maggie always came up here to watch the skies together."

Liberty seemed pleased by that information. "Oh, that's romantic. Maybe they saw a Christmas Moon from the porch."

He couldn't help smiling at that. "As I remember it, they did. Maggie was thrilled." Funny he hadn't remembered that until right then.

"I wonder if Sarge had the idea of bringing a wife here sooner or later when he built it?"

"I don't know. He met Maggie just before he was deployed, and she was out of reach for him. She was the only daughter of a wealthy rancher near Jackson Hole. She was younger than him, too, so it was hands-off. But when he came back after his time in Vietnam, he bought this land. I think things changed for both of them around then."

"A soldier coming home to find the woman he'd probably fallen in love with at first sight before he was deployed." Liberty sighed and hugged her arms around herself. "Boy, are you trying to make me cry?"

"No," he said, and hoped she was kidding. "So, you lit the stove?"

She was distracted immediately. "I found wood in a covered box at the back of the house." She looked over at Pax lying out in front of the stove, then back at him. "I know why Pax was at the trees when I found him. He was living here, well, not inside, but near the wood storage out back, which, by the way, is full." She shrugged. "Anyway, there's an opening in the stone foundation where he was staying. Can you imagine how cold that had to be?"

Jake certainly could. "He's a survivor for sure," he said.

"Yes, he is. Has anyone actually lived here in recent years?"

"Yes, off and on. Friends, people who needed a place to stay. Sarge and Maggie had their breaks up here when they needed time away from the boys."

"How did they get up here? I mean, that walk is beautiful, but it's uphill and not short or easy if you had to do it more than once a day."

"Sarge cut a road that goes east from here, then dips down to the county road near the blind curve. That was the original entrance for the ranch."

"Would it work for my Jeep?"

"If you bladed it."

"Seth said that he'd like me here as much as possible during all the phases of the work when it really starts in the summer. I think staying up here would be close enough to the work without being buried in it. Plus, I'm even closer to the campsite locations and the original mess hall and bunkhouse that we're going to repurpose. Do you think it would be okay if I stayed up here instead of at the house?"

"Well, I don't see why not, but what about Roger? How would he react to living in a four-hundred-square-foot house out here with no Wi-Fi or cell signal?"

"Come on, Roger's used to roughing it when he's on-site. I think I could make it work," she said but she didn't sound totally convinced she could. "When he's gone, I could stay here, and when he's back, I could be in Seattle when I had to be."

"Don't you have other clients besides Seth?"

"I finished my last job just before I came here, and my boss agreed I'd be on this job exclusively until it's complete, so that's not a problem. Anyway, I'll talk this over with Seth when I can. He understands about…things."

"You're right," Jake agreed instantly. It was her business to sort out. "Seth will understand. He knows you and Roger."

She turned and reached for her jacket. She looked back at Jake when she spoke again.

"I'm going back to the house. Are you coming?"

"I'll shut down the stove, then I'll come back," he said.

Pax was with Liberty as she went through the kitchen and walked out the back door. Jake stayed where he was to give her a head start so he wouldn't say anything else about Roger on the way back that he'd regret. He had no right to question her relationship.

He crossed the room to tamp down the stove, then he started back, taking his time and keeping his distance. When he arrived at the house, he took his time putting the tractor, which he'd left by the front door, away in the hay barn. Then headed up to the house. He hoped Liberty was working. He could lie down and try to shut off his thoughts for a while.

He'd barely stepped into the entry when Pax ran out of the great room. The dog was going so fast, he almost skidded to a stop when he saw Jake. He had a candy cane in his mouth and Liberty was right behind him. She made a grab for Pax, but he gave her the slip and was a blur as he ran through the still-open front door and disappeared.

Liberty frowned at Jake. "Why didn't you stop him?"

"I didn't know I was supposed to." He'd fallen into the middle of whatever had been happening and didn't have a clue what the dog had done.

She motioned to the door. "You need to go and get him."

"Me? Why? He'll be back."

"Yeah, to steal more candy canes," she said, and dropped down on the cowhide bench.

"Stealing candy canes?"

"He cleared more than a dozen candy canes off the bottom level of the tree while I was working in the office." She took a deep breath then exhaled. "I was busy and he was with me, then he wasn't with me for what turned out to be a long enough time for him to strip the lowest branches of the tree of candy canes. He was in the middle of stealing the next one when I spotted him." She shook her head. "I never should have yelled at him or run toward him. I probably terrified him, and now he's out there running scared. Candy canes have to at least make him sick. I don't even know exactly how many he's eaten."

He crouched down in front of her. "Liberty, I've never heard of a dog overdosing on candy canes."

He could have kept his words to himself, because she didn't acknowledge he'd even said them. "You have to find him, then we'll go and look for a signal and call a vet."

"Liberty, we can't. I cleared all the way to the boulders earlier, but the road is impassable."

"But what if he gets really sick?" She looked around Jake, then stood suddenly, almost bumping into him, but he took a step back. She pushed around him and opened the door. Pax was there. He usually dived into the house, but he just stood in the opening looking up at Liberty. The candy cane was gone. He had no idea what she was saying to the dog, but she ended up crouching to hug him.

He went over to the door. "Let me close this."

Liberty stood and tugged Pax by his collar to get him out of the way. Then Jake turned, and Pax was all but glued to Liberty's leg again. "Told you he'd be back, and he doesn't look much worse for wear."

"Do you think he'll be okay?"

"Yes, I think he'll be fine. He's always

with one of us, so we can keep an eye on him. Now, if you're working in the office, I'll watch him."

She stroked Pax's head. "I guess that will have to do."

LIBBY WAS GOING to redo the candy canes and make the bottom half of the tree a no-candy-cane zone. "I think I'll keep his targets higher, then I'll get to work." She could tell Jake was tired, but he followed her into the great room and they started putting the candy canes higher up on the tree. When they finished, he settled in the chair positioned to half face the tree and half face the chair Libby sat down on. "I wish we had some milk. I'd make hot chocolate. That always feels so Christ-massy."

"What's with you and Christmas that it's so important to you?"

She hesitated. The story of her Christmas addiction was something she'd planned to share with Roger on their first Christmas together, a way to get closer so he understood her better. They hadn't had last Christmas together, so she'd waited. The thing was, she thought she knew Roger well but lately was starting to wonder if that was true. She felt off, as if her thinking wasn't right. When she'd put her engagement ring away in the desk earlier, she thought it was to keep it safe, but now she could admit to herself she'd been relieved not wearing it. As beautiful as it was, she never felt comfortable with its weight on her finger reminding her that she was going to change her life a lot in the next few months.

Jake, on the other hand, knew her background now. He'd lived part of it, and she found herself thinking she might just tell him of her connection to Christmas. She loved the story herself. Perhaps later she'd tell him but not right then. "Maybe when we have some good hot chocolate, I'll tell you my story about Christmas. But no milk and no marshmallows mean no hot chocolate."

"I didn't even know people made hot chocolate with milk until I got here. The stuff I had was made with water, and I got used to it."

"Whoa, that's sounds bad. But there's cocoa powder and water, and if you like I can make you some while you keep an eye on Pax."

"Sure, if you want to."

She got up and headed to the kitchen. As she made the hot cocoa, she watched Jake in his chair, his eyes closed. Once she poured the thin-looking drink into two mugs, she went over to him. She nudged his foot with hers and his eyes flew open; then he exhaled. She held out a cup to him. "I hope this is what you remember."

He sat up straighter and took the offered drink, and she sat opposite him, cradling her own in her hands. She never took her eyes off Jake as he took a sip then rested his mug on his thigh. "It tastes just like I remember."

"Really?"

He smiled. "Yes, really. Thank you."

She lifted her mug in a salute. "Here's to hot chocolate made with water," she said, and took her own sip.

She froze for a second, spit what she had in her mouth back into the mug, then got up and headed into the kitchen. It was horrible, all thin and powdery tasting. She didn't think even marshmallows could make it drinkable. She poured it out in the sink, rinsed her mouth with water, then went to the tree, got a candy cane and sat down facing Jake again.

He was lucky he wasn't laughing at her, but

she could almost see him trying to control it. "That was horrible," she said, making sure he saw her lips. "Just disgusting."

He shrugged, and the smile was close to showing up. "I had no idea you were going to make some for yourself. I thought you had coffee in your mug."

"If that's what you remember and you like it, you're very mistaken." She made an exaggerated grimace. "It tastes like dishwater."

"Have you been drinking dishwater again?" he asked, and his smile finally showed up.

She couldn't help grinning herself. "It might be better than that stuff." She held up the candy cane. "I need this to get the taste out of my mouth." She bit a small piece off the end, then sighed. "Much better. A candy cane can cure a lot of things. By the way, Pax seems okay, doesn't he?"

"He looks pretty good," he said, then shifted to stretch his feet out in front of him. She saw Jake hesitate, as if something had stopped his motions for second, then he set his mug on the floor by his chair before he settled. She wondered if it was his ears, but she wouldn't ask. "What music's playing?"

"'The Christmas Song.' You know, chestnuts roasting and all that. It's really nice. Oh, there's still those two steaks for dinner, if you'd like?"

"Thanks, but I'm not hungry. Make yourself something," he said, and closed his eyes without asking her about Christmas again.

Libby got up and as she passed Jake to go to the office, she looked down at him. She couldn't imagine being in the system as long he had. It seemed certain that he'd never had a lot of what she'd received from the Connors. She just wished she could turn back time and give him that present. He deserved it.

JAKE WAS IN the old cabin. Music was playing from somewhere, a song he recognized. "Have Yourself a Merry Little Christmas." He heard it as if he could really hear, and Liberty was there, in his arms, her head resting on his chest as they moved together to the music. He could hear her singing along, her voice soft and honey smooth, and all he wanted to do was hold her like that forever.

He woke with a start, still in the chair in the great room, no lights on except for those on the Christmas tree. No music, no Liberty singing, just noise and pressure in his ears, and Pax pawing at his leg. Jake groaned, hating the punch of his reality as it hit him again. "Okay, okay," he muttered as he pushed himself upright in the chair. "Give me a minute."

The dream was gone. He got to his feet carefully but felt steady, and set the mug down on the hearth. When he turned to go to the entry, he saw light spilling out of the office and Liberty working on her computer at the desk. He watched as she tucked her hair behind her ear.

He turned away and went to let Pax out. The night was still and bitterly cold, but he could see the glow of moonlight here and there where the clouds were thinning. Pax ran off, and Jake waited, his mind on the dream and the sense of loss he felt when it was over. He hated it. He had to leave the ranch soon and start forgetting about Liberty. That wasn't going to be easy. He wouldn't really forget, but he wouldn't be close enough to catch the hint of roses and vanilla or be on the receiving end of her smile. Pax was back quickly, running past Jake, as anxious to get out of the cold as Jake was right then.

He was startled when he turned and Liberty was stepping into the foyer wearing pink pajama pants and an oversize T-shirt. "He woke you up?" she asked.

"Yes, he did." He wouldn't tell her how the dog waking him had snatched him out of what had felt like happiness and back to being alone. It killed him that the dream would always be a dream. His choices, his life—and this pseudo version of home and hearth wasn't a choice. But that didn't mean he'd forget that dream anytime soon.

"I'm sorry."

"I was just his closest mark," he said. "Are you heading to bed?"

"I don't know. I've almost got the revised layout done for Sarge's space, and I want to go over it again."

"Did you get something to eat?"

"Yes, some soup and fishes."

"Fishes?"

"Oh, sorry," she said. "My mom always made toast with soup and cut it into dunking strips she called fishes."

He watched her expression, part happy about the memory and part wistful. He'd remember this someday and smile. And he'd remember sitting by the Christmas tree with her as if he actually belonged in her life. "I'll have to try that sometime," he said.

"I can make you some right now, if you'd like?"

"Thanks, but I'm okay."

"You know, I just realized, I can make the music as loud as I want, can't I?"

"As long as the house doesn't start shaking." She headed over to the music cupboard and adjusted the volume knob. Just when he started to feel discomfort from the vibrations in the air, she stepped back. "Is that too loud?"

He went over and leaned around her to turn the volume down. "There, that's good."

"What songs are on the CD?"

"Just older holiday songs mixed in with some Christmas carols."

He took a breath then asked, "Is 'Have Yourself a Merry Little Christmas' on it?"

She smiled. "Yes. It played maybe five minutes ago. I love that song."

He followed her lips, but he heard her in his head as she spoke. It was her voice from his dream. "Oh" was all he could say.

Liberty studied him for a moment, then said, "Thanks for taking care of Pax," and headed into the office. Jake cleaned Pax off, then lay down on the couch. As he closed his eyes, the dream ran through his mind of Liberty singing that song as he held her. *Crazy coincidence.* But he'd "heard" her sing it, and now that voice was fixed in his mind.

Morning came the next day with no snow falling and the wind barely there, but the cold was just as intense. Jake left Liberty a note on the back of the front door, *Going to check county road. Back soon.* Then he walked down the drive toward the boulders. When he got to the rise, he saw a snowplow going past the entrance, piling snow up on either side of a single cleared lane.

He turned and went back to the house. When he took the steps to the porch, the door opened, and Pax darted out past Liberty. "Good morning," she said with a smile as he stamped his feet to get the clinging snow off before he stepped inside.

She closed the door, then turned to him as he unbuttoned his jacket. "So?" she asked, still in her pajamas with her hair loose.

He saw the hope in her green eyes, and he gave her the news. "The plows have cleared the road to the highway. It's only one lane wide, but it's drivable."

He barely saw her smile before she was hugging him, her face buried in his chest. He felt as if he was living that dream when she'd been in his arms, and he closed his eyes and let himself hug her this one time. When she moved back, he met the full impact of her smile. "This is great! Let's go," she said. "I just need to change and get my phone, then I'm ready."

With that, she took off up the stairs, and he went to sit down on the bench. He was playing with fire. His determination to keep his distance had bitten the dust. He couldn't even avoid her hug. Worse yet, he wasn't at all certain he would try to avoid it. Right then, he made himself a promise, one he wouldn't break. As soon as the landline was connected, he was leaving. If Liberty had been someone passing through his life whom he was attracted to, he might have played it out. But she wasn't looking for anything from him. She'd be married soon, and she was Seth's dear friend.

He saw her at the top of the stairs, still smiling as she hurried down and over to him.

Wearing a dark green sweater and jeans, with her hair back in a ponytail, she sat down by him on the bench. She put her boots and jacket on quickly, then stood. "I'm ready," she said, but hesitated. "What about Pax?"

"What do you think? He could stay here if you put out food and water. We shouldn't be more than a couple hours."

She crouched in front of the dog and spoke to him, and Jake wished he could see what she was saying. The dog sat down, and she stood. "Ready?" she asked Jake.

"Is he ready?"

"Yes, I explained why we're going away, and I think it's okay."

He wouldn't challenge that statement. "So now that we can get to town, the plan for today is getting something to eat and do grocery shopping, then head to Wicker Pines to visit Sarge, right?"

"That's the plan." He saw her hesitate before she asked, "How are you doing?"

He felt the dream haunting him as he read her lips. He still imagined her voice. "I'm okay," he said, and reached into the pocket of his blue plaid flannel shirt, which he wore under his jacket. He took out an old photo he'd found and held it out to her. "This was taken on the first day Sarge and Maggie moved into this house."

When Liberty took it, Jake watched her study the photo of a young, strong Sarge with his arm around Maggie, a delicate-looking woman with red hair and happiness radiating from her. A soft smile touched Liberty's lips as she asked, "Do you think I can make a copy so I can put it up in Sarge's suite for when he comes home?"

"Sure."

"You know, I think I do look a bit like Maggie."

"Yes, you do." He didn't want to add anything about their other similarities, such as their smiles, their kindness or how both could walk into a room and life got better. That would only make things harder on himself. "Sarge's life revolved around her."

She fingered the edge of the old photo. "No wonder he's so lost without her."

To have one person so important to you that your life would cease to be worth living without them seemed unthinkable to Jake. He got to his feet and wanted to leave, but Liberty was still staring at the photo. When she finally looked up at him, he saw her say, "I need to put this away."

"Okay. I'll bring the truck up from the garage and meet you out in front."

She went back toward the office while he slowly got to his feet and crossed to the door. Pax just sat there. "Protect this place," he said to the dog, then Jake stepped out and closed the door behind himself. He paused to take stock of how he felt physically. Something was different besides that delusion that he could almost hear Liberty speaking. He wasn't dizzy or nauseated, and pain didn't come despite the horrible cold. He figured he'd find out sooner or later and headed off to the garage.

By the time Liberty came out the front door, the truck was idling by the porch steps and the interior was warming up. Jake sat on the passenger side watching her as she got in behind the wheel and closed the door. She readied herself with the pillows, adjusted the seat and secured her seat belt. Then she finally looked at him. "I hope Pax is okay."

"He'll be fine," he said, hoping he was right. "We won't be that long."

"Okay, let's go," she said, and backed the

truck up to turn it and head down the drive. She stopped before she turned onto the cleared lane of road and looked at Jake. "We're probably safer with Pax at the house instead of in the truck. If he'd come, he probably would have been so excited he would've tried to give kisses and licked one of us to death," she said.

He actually chuckled at that. "I guess dogs don't learn to kiss by practicing on the backs of their own hands, or paws, as the case may be."

"Is that how you learned to kiss?" Libby asked.

He liked that gleam of humor lingering in her eyes. "Why would you think that?"

"Just a guess that comes from seeing my share of preteen boys kissing the backs of their hands."

He laughed again. "Busted, huh?"

"You bet. Although my Dad told me I couldn't tease them about it."

"Kind man." Jake motioned toward the road. "Should we go?"

"Sure," she said. Jake knew she couldn't face him to talk while driving, so they drove in silence on the cleared lane to the highway. She stopped just before the turn to get on the northbound side and took her phone out of her jacket pocket. She looked at Jake. "I've got a signal, and I want to call the veterinarian for Pax. Do you know his name?"

"Lucas Patton."

While she got the number, she made her call, then explained to Jake. "Dr. Patton said there was nothing in candy canes that would hurt Pax. He wants me to bring him in for a checkup soon."

"So no death by candy cane?" he asked, not bothering to hide a grin.

She looked a bit embarrassed. "No, but it can harm his teeth."

"A toothless dog," he said, the grin still there.

CHAPTER ELEVEN

WHEN THEY FINALLY arrived in Cody, the main street was almost cleared, but their progress was stop-and-go, dictated by a street plow plodding along ahead of them. Libby tapped Jake's arm when she had to stop because of another plow coming out of a side street. "I saw a sign for a market ahead, so we can pull in there."

"Maybe they'll have a deli or something and we can get some food."

The cars in front of them started moving, and a few minutes later, Libby pulled into the cleared parking lot for the market and found an empty spot close to the entrance. As she brought the truck to a stop, Jake said, "I'll stay out here. If you come across a roast-beef sandwich with everything but mayo, could you get me one?"

"Okay," she said.

Libby came back out shortly after with a

shopping cart full of bags. As soon as Jake saw her, he got out and came around to open the security box. While he took care of putting the groceries away, she carried one of the bags around to get behind the wheel. When he got in, she held out a wrapped sandwich to him. "Roast beef with no mayo," she said as he took it from her. Then she handed him one of two bottles of cream soda. "I found these in the cooler."

He smiled at her. "Great," he said.

She laid her sandwich out on the console and unwrapped it. When she picked up her soda, Jake lifted his bottle to hers in a salute. "Here's to people with kind hearts," he said, his eyes holding hers as he took a drink.

"Is it a good or bad thing to have a kind heart?" she asked him.

He hesitated, then lowered his bottle. "In this world, sometimes it's a very rare thing."

Libby nodded at Jake. "I think you're right."

She stayed parked while she ate part of her sandwich, then rewrapped the remainder and put it back in the bag. Jake was finished with his when she pulled out of the parking lot and headed north to go to Wicker Pines.

When Libby drove the truck into the cob-blestoned parking lot at the rehab, they were the only vehicle in the visitor's area. Libby heard a beep from her jacket pocket and pulled out her cell. It was a warning that it was almost dead. "Shoot, I should have charged my phone," she said as she stopped the car and turned to Jake.

He tapped a slot in the console between them. "Grab the cable and charge it while we're inside."

"How's your phone for a charge?" she asked as she did what he'd said.

He took his out and turned it on. "Good."

"Okay." She turned off the truck and got out, but Jake wasn't making any move to do the same. She went around and opened his door. He was looking intently down at his phone. She tapped his arm.

Very slowly, he turned toward her frowning. "Sarge isn't doing well. Seth's calling Max Donovan, the sheriff, to ask him to go to the ranch and get me to come here."

Her heart sank. "Let me call and see what's going on, unless you want to do a video call?"

"No," he said right away, and handed his phone over to her.

She could feel his eyes on her as she stood by the open door in the cold and called Seth. He answered right away. "Jake! Finally."

"Seth, it's me, Libby. Jake just got your message, and we're at Wicker Pines ready to go in. What's going on?"

"Sarge is running a high fever, and they're trying to figure it out. I'm stuck in New York. There's no flight out because of a freaking snowstorm. Ben's caught, too. I've been trying to contact Jake since Dr. Miller called me."

"There's no cell signal at the ranch, and the landline's down."

She heard his rough exhale from the other end of the line. "Max is almost to the ranch."

"Do you know the sheriff very well?" she asked.

"He's an old friend."

"Well, there's a dog in the house named Pax, and he's all alone, and if we have to stay here longer, he might not do well. Do you think your friend could check on him to make sure he's okay?"

"I'm sure he will. Let me talk to Jake."

She looked at Jake and motioned him to get out of the truck. "Jake's heading inside right now. We'll call as soon as we know anything."

She ended the call and handed Jake his phone. She told him what Seth had said. "We need to find out what's going on with Sarge."

Jake turned and headed toward the entry, and Libby had to half run to keep up with his long strides. When they were buzzed in, Julia was there to greet them. "You made it. I'll get you in to see Sarge as soon as Dr. Miller finishes some tests. Right now, Sarge has a fever that's far too high, but he's resting comfortably. They're working on adjusting his medication." She motioned to a pair of wingback chairs near the desk. "Have a seat and try to relax. He's in good hands. I'll come back to get you as soon as possible."

"Are you sure we can't go in now?" Jake asked.

"I'm sorry, no." She seemed sincerely apologetic. "In the meantime, I promise I'll keep you up to date."

Libby turned to look at Jake, who was staring as Julia went through the double doors. He spoke without looking at Libby. "I should just go back there. What are they going to do to me if I do?"

She could see his jaw working, and she stepped closer to him to touch his arm. He glanced at her. "They could have you removed physically, and you could see the sheriff when he comes to take you to jail."

He took off his jacket and laid it over the back of the chair, which had a view of the double doors as well as a side door. He sat down, his eyes on the exits to the room. Libby did the same with her jacket, then sat facing Jake and leaned forward to touch his knee. She didn't pull back until he looked at her. "If this was a really dangerous situation, they would've had him taken to a hospital, airlifting him if they had to. Money is no object with Seth. You know that. So this isn't good, but it's obviously something they feel they can handle."

She expected him to close his eyes and shut her out, but he never looked away. "It is what it is," he finally said on a heavy sigh.

"Is that your motto?"

"It has been for quite a while."

"My dad's kind of like that. He takes what comes and makes it work and never complains. I wish I were more like him. I mean, I've learned so much from him, even if I wasn't there with him from the start of my life."

Jake narrowed his eyes on her. "How long were you in the system before the adoption?"

She knew that answer pretty quickly. "Four years, two months and eleven days. How about you?"

His expression tightened as he looked down at his hands resting on his thighs. "Almost ten years from the time I was dumped at a police station until I went to the ranch. I don't count my time with Sarge and Maggie as the system." He shifted his hands to the arms of the chair and gripped them. "How did you get into the system?"

"My mother was a single parent, and my father's name on my birth certificate was 'unknown.' My mother got sick when I was three, almost four. She didn't make it." She had to swallow. "The only real memory I have of her is the scent of the vanilla-and-roses shampoo she used."

"So, you were adopted by your foster parents?"

"Yes, Susan and David Connor. I was eight years old when they asked to adopt me." She exhaled. "They're wonderful. They took me in and gave me a home and a great life."

Jake held her eyes. "A real calm in the storm," he said in a low voice.

"Yes, peace and safety and real love. Although, for a while, I thought they could send me back, even though I was adopted. The concept of being with them forever was hard to get my mind around. But when I did, wow, it was great. My new parents gave me a choice of what I wanted to be called. I decided I wanted to be a Connor like them, and they said I could choose any name or names I wanted. So, I went from being Grace Good to Liberty Grace Connor. The judge in the adoption court gave me a stuffed bear named Liberty. I really liked the name."

"And you never looked back," he said.

"Well, I always remember the storm's out there. And the foster camp, if it turns out right, could be the calm in the storm for so many boys."

Jake looked more tense, but when he spoke, his words were measured. "I'm just glad that you're out of the storm."

That simple statement made her so aware of the man across from her she could barely breathe. Then Jake darted a look behind her at the same time she heard footsteps. She turned, and Julia was there. "You can go in now." Jake got to his feet and was heading for the doors before Julia finished her sentence.

"Thank you," Libby said to the woman, then hurried after Jake. She was surprised to find him standing just inside the double doors in the hallway, his hand pressed to his right ear. When he saw her, he lowered his hand and turned to keep going.

Libby didn't say anything, but she knew something had happened again. If he wouldn't mention it, she wouldn't ask. She stayed by his side until they were outside the door to Sarge's room.

Julia hurried up from behind them. "The doctor said he'll be in to speak to you as soon as possible." She was carrying their jackets, which they'd forgotten. "I'll put these here," she said, and laid them on one of the padded benches by the doors.

When Julia was gone, Libby looked up at Jake. "I'll stand where I did the last visit, directly across from you. So if you have a problem, just give me the high sign."

He turned toward the door but didn't move

to open it. Libby realized the man who took massive chances every time he went up to test a jet was worried about pushing through the door in front of him. He was afraid of what he'd face on the other side. She didn't even think about it before she reached for his hand and laced her fingers with his. There was no reaction at first, then he was holding on to her. He closed his eyes momentarily, then reached to push back the door with his free hand.

When they stepped inside, Sarge was awake, his face flushed. The man was looking over at them. Libby couldn't tell if he recognized Jake or not. She was praying he did. Jake went toward the right side of the bed, still holding tightly to her. Sarge looked up at Jake then spoke, his voice barely above a whisper. "Oh, my boy, Jake."

Libby felt a tremor run through Jake before he let go of her to reach over the safety rail for the older man's hand. He held on to Sarge. She went around to stand where she'd promised.

"Heard you were sick," Jake finally said.

The older man started to say something, but a coughing fit cut off any words. When the doctor entered, Libby waved slightly to get Jake's attention. He looked up, then over at Dr. Miller. Libby moved back to let the man get closer to the side of the bed where she stood. "Glad you made it," the doctor said to Jake.

"What's going on?" he asked bluntly.

The doctor patted Sarge on the shoulder and said to the man, "We'll be right back, Sarge." He glanced at Jake. "Maybe Ms. Connor can stay with him while we talk outside."

Jake looked over at her. "I'd like her to hear what you have to say, too."

"Okay." The doctor nodded and headed back to the door.

Libby followed them out and angled herself so Jake could see her, and so she could see the doctor.

"I never like to go over things with the patient there. They can get confused and take things the wrong way."

"What's going on?" Jake asked.

"There's an infection that we didn't expect, and he was put on an antibiotic regimen, but the fever's tough. We're adjusting the meds to hopefully boost their effectiveness, but we have to do it slowly."

"He'll be okay, won't he?" Jake asked.

The doctor exhaled. "Right now, it's pretty much about getting the right dosages. Once that happens, our hope is he'll start to improve."

"How long is this going to take?"

"I honestly have no idea, but I'm hopeful we'll see something in the next four to five hours."

"I'll be here."

The doctor nodded as if he'd expected what Jake said. "Of course. We can accommodate that."

Jake turned and reentered Sarge's room without waiting for any more discussion. Libby lingered to speak to the doctor. "Please, just keep us in the loop so we know what's going on. If something goes sideways, please tell Jake when I'm with him. He's very close to Sarge."

The doctor didn't hesitate. "I understand. I'll be back after I check on lab results."

"Can I use a cell phone in here?"

"Yes," he said, then left.

She quickly left a message for Seth, telling him what was going on, then she went back in the room to be with Jake.

He was sitting in a straight-backed chair he'd positioned near the safety rail on the right side of the bed. Sarge was motionless, his eyes shut, and he looked more flushed. Libby crossed to Jake and laid her hand on his shoulder. When he glanced up at her, the pain she saw in his eyes hurt her. "You know how strong he is, and they'll get the right medication."

Jake spoke as he looked back at Sarge. "He's burning up." She reached down to touch the man's hand. His skin was paper dry and abnormally hot. She went around the bed and pulled a chair up so she could see Sarge and Jake at all times. She knew that Jake's world had to be tipping precariously close to the storm.

As the time ticked past, Libby slipped out to make calls to Seth and keep him up to date. Max had checked on Pax, and the dog was okay. Libby tried to call Roger twice but hadn't been able to connect. Her parents weren't answering, either. By late afternoon, the fever gave no signs of breaking. A look out the window showed clouds darkening and dropping lower. Still, nothing changed for Sarge.

Finally, she got up and went around to Jake, crouching by his chair to lay her hand on his arm. He didn't take his eyes off Sarge as he said, "If nothing changes in the next hour, I'm going to insist that they get him to a hospital, or they get someone here who knows what's going on."

She waited until he finally looked at her. "It's your call," she said. "I'll go and talk to Julia. She seems to be on top of what's happening. I'm worried about Pax, too. I know we're going to be gone a lot longer than we thought. I don't want to leave here to go all the way back to the ranch, but maybe I should later on, if I have to."

"No," he said quickly. "Call Seth and tell him to contact Max and see if he wants a place to sleep over for the night. He can stay at the ranch with Pax and be closer to town."

"Would he do that?"

"If he can, he will. It can't hurt to ask."

"I will," she said, then left the room. She almost walked into Julia, who was coming toward her with a tray and two covered dishes along with a pot of coffee.

"I know you two haven't eaten, so I brought you dinner," she said.

"Thank you so much." Libby took the tray from her. "I'll take it in."

"Okay, is there anything else I can do?"

"Jake's pretty stressed. While I make some phone calls, could you be with him? He doesn't want to talk, but I'd feel better if he isn't in there alone."

"Of course. I'd be glad to do that. I can take care of a few things for Sarge while I'm at it."

Libby went back into the room with Julia and set the tray on the small cabinet by Sarge's bed. She turned to Jake and laid her hand on his shoulder. "Julia brought dinner for us. She needs to do a few things in here, so I'll go and make a call, then be right back."

Unexpectedly, Jake laid his hand over hers and said, "Thank you." The contact was gone as he turned back to Sarge.

Libby found the reception area empty, so she sat down and dialed Seth. She told him Sarge's condition still hadn't changed and talked to him for a while, then asked if he could call the sheriff to see if he'd stay at the ranch for the night. After that, she put in a video call to Roger with little hope of connecting after all the failed attempts. She was surprised when he picked up.

"Roger, hey, I've been trying to get a hold of you for hours."

He looked tired, his khaki shirt rumpled, and for a man who was very precise about his appearance, he looked rumpled, too. His dark hair was askew, and he seemed stressed. "Sorry, I've been busy. Everything's happening at once around here."

She needed this connection so much right then—to see him and hear his voice. "I miss you. Do you know yet when you'll be here?"

He shook his head. "I don't. I can't cut this job short, but if I can try to hurry it along, I will. You never called Mother, did you?"

She bit her lip, and told him the truth. "I'd rather wait until we go back to Seattle together to talk things over with your mother and father. I think you need to be there with me."

He frowned. "Come on, Libby, she's not going to wait that long. She's excited about everything. Just call her. She's found a veil for you that's, according to her, beyond perfection."

"I have a veil," she said, and knew her voice sounded a bit tight. Right then she didn't care. "There's a lot going on here, too. We're at the hospital with Jake's foster father. He's pretty sick."

"Oh, sorry. I hope he improves," he said, quickly, then kept talking. "I need to get going, but call Mother, please."

"Roger, I don't think—"

"I don't have time to worry about veils and the music and the food. Right now, she's looking at a string quartet. I'm too busy here to do that kind of thing."

Libby hated what he was saying. Even more, she hated herself for how badly she needed to hear that Roger understood what she was going through. "We're at the hospital, and I don't know what's going to happen."

"Sorry, sure," he said, brushing that aside. "I have to get off of here."

"You will be able to be back for Christmas, right?"

She heard him sigh heavily. "I'll try, and if I don't, it's just a day on the calendar. We can pick any day we want when I get back." He glanced away from the screen, then at her. "Gotta go. Love you," he said, and the screen went blank.

Libby would've cried if she hadn't felt so shocked at his throwaway words about Sarge's condition and Christmas just being any day they chose. She almost didn't recognize the man she'd just spoken to, the man who cared so much about the people he was helping. Instead, he'd seemed self-absorbed and disinterested. She knew that much of their relationship had been long distance, with him traveling, but she truly believed she knew him. Now she wasn't sure what to believe.

She did know one thing. She didn't think she'd worry about calling Roger again for a while. That thought took her aback, but it didn't change the way she felt. They needed a break; at least, she needed a break that had little to do with the physical distance between them. She had to refocus on what was truly important right then—Sarge and Jake.

When she got back to the room, Julia left. Libby crouched down beside Jake again.

"Did you talk to Seth?" he asked right away.

"Yes, and he said he's got the corporate jet ready, but the airport's still not letting anything take off or land. He said not to worry about the sheriff. He'll get in touch and work it out. I also told him about you thinking you needed to get Sarge moved, and he said since you're here, you do what you think is best. He trusts you."

Jake surprised her by asking, "If he were your father, what would you do?"

For that moment, she could see the fear Jake had of doing the wrong thing. She stood and looked down at him, then motioned him away from the bed and over to the door. She slipped out in the hallway and turned to him as the door shut behind them. "The doctor's right. Sarge shouldn't hear us talking."

"I agree. Now, what would you do?"

She let herself reach for his hands and held on to them. He stared at her, but his hold on her hands tightened slightly. "If he were my father, I don't think I'd have him moved just yet. It exhausted him coming here and now that he's sick, it seems too chancy. Especially with the bad weather. But whatever you think is best. You know him. I barely do. Whatever you decide, I'll help you any way I can."

He closed his eyes, then said on a heavy sigh, "Thank you." She could tell he was exhausted, probably more emotionally than physically.

"You need to eat and take a break."

He let go of her hands and sort of agreed. "I guess so."

Neither one ate much once they were back

inside, and then Jake went back to sitting beside the bed watching Sarge. Libby wanted to try to distract him, and said, "Sarge and Maggie were really good together, weren't they?"

"Very good together," he murmured.

"What did Maggie call Sarge?"

"Jimmy, always Jimmy," he said, and stood, grabbing his jacket off the chair's back. "I'm going to stretch my legs. I won't be long. Come and get me if anything happens."

JAKE LINGERED IN the failing light and cold, leaning against the truck as he breathed in and out. He stayed still, letting the light wind brush across his face. He'd barely kept himself together watching Sarge today. Then he'd seen some of his own concern in Liberty's eyes when she looked at the sick man. She had no dog in this fight, but she was here, worried and doing anything she could to help. She'd held his hands when he needed an anchor, and he'd held on to her. She had a good heart.

When he finally stepped back into the room, Liberty was in the chair he'd been using, but she'd moved it closer to the bed. She was leaning forward, her hands holding on to the top of the safety rail and her forehead pressed to them. She slowly turned as he approached her, and he could see it in her face—nothing had changed.

"He's sleeping," she said.

He slipped off his jacket and tossed it onto a nearby chair then went closer to look at Sarge. He seemed less flushed, but that only made him appear weaker somehow. Closing his eyes to block what he was facing, Jake was startled when he felt Liberty's touch on his cheek. She didn't pull away when he looked at her. For a moment she was that anchor again—the only thing keeping him from slipping into a nightmare.

He saw her say, "You need to sit down." She drew back and he felt a sense of aloneness that started to smother him. He took his seat again but didn't look back up at Liberty. He wasn't sure he wanted to see the soft smile that shadowed her lips. A sad smile.

He didn't know how much time had passed when he glanced over at Liberty again. She was sitting in a chair she'd pulled up to the safety rail facing him. He watched her reach under the lower metal rung to lay her hand over Sarge's. She held it for a moment, then stood and brushed the tip of her finger across the sleeping man's forehead. Before Jake knew what she was doing, she had the call button in her hand and was pressing it.

"I think that he's—"

Jake was on his feet now, his heart hammering. "You think he's what?" he demanded.

He saw her clearly say, "It's changing, Jake." Julia hurried toward them, and he couldn't see what Liberty was saying to the nurse. Julia checked the monitor, then did a digital reading with a forehead thermometer scan. She studied the screen that kept track of his vitals.

Liberty's full attention was on Sarge, and Jake was about to scream when Julia looked over at him and smiled. "His temperature's coming down. It's one hundred even, and his vitals are stronger."

Liberty was beaming at him. "I thought he felt cooler, and he is. The fever, it broke, didn't it?" she asked Julia.

"It looks like it has," she said. "I'm going to get Dr. Miller."

Liberty went over to Jake. Her hand covered his where he gripped the side rail, and he saw her say, "The medication's working, Jake."

He felt unsteady and turned his hand to

hold on to hers. Then he looked past her at the door as Dr. Miller came in. The man nodded to them, then repeated what Julia had done moments ago. Sarge began to stir.

Finally, the doctor looked over at them. "He's coming out of it," he said, then took Sarge's temperature again and smiled at them. "It's good. I'll be back soon."

Jake looked at Liberty. "It's over." He eased his hand away from hers, making himself finally remember his second promise. It was too easy to accept her support, to hold on to her, and he couldn't keep doing that.

"Do you want to call Seth?" she asked him.

"After the doctor comes back," he said, and turned to Sarge. He saw the man's eyes flutter, then they were open and gradually focused on him.

"Jake," he saw the man say, then he looked at Liberty. "Who…are you?"

Liberty took her position across the bed from Jake. Sarge turned to his right. "I'm Liberty Connor," she said to him.

Sarge glanced back at Jake. "What's going on?"

"You've been sick," Jake said gently.

"Oh," he said, as if that explained every-

thing, then he turned toward Liberty. "You...
you're Liberty?"

Jake watched her smile at the man. "Yes,
and I'm from Seattle. Lots of rain there, but
no snow like you get here."

Jake maneuvered to get a better look at
Sarge speaking. "My Maggie was supposed
to move to Florida." He coughed, then said,
"But she stayed here for me. She said she
never missed going to Florida, but I know
she did."

Liberty shrugged. "When you're really in
love, you're more concerned about being with
that person than about rain or snow or heat or
cold or anything else going on around you."

Sarge worried the hem of the blue blanket
with his hands. "I loved Maggie, but she had
to go. She couldn't stay." He raised his hand
and laid it over Libby's. "You didn't want to
go, did you, Maggie?" he asked as he looked
up at her pleadingly.

Jake knew it could happen, but seeing
Sarge confused like this still hurt horribly.
Liberty covered his hand with her other palm
and said, "No, I didn't want to go. I never
wanted to leave you, Jimmy, not ever."

Tears welled in her eyes.

"I know, I know," Sarge rasped. "You and me… I love you so much."

"I love you, too." Her voice wavered, but she managed to finish, "I always will, Jimmy."

Sarge's eyes fluttered closed again. A moment later, Liberty was easing his hand back onto the blanket as he drifted back into sleep.

She took what looked like an unsteady breath, then reached for the chair and dropped down on it.

Jake couldn't take his eyes off Liberty. She swiped at her cheeks, then took another breath, and he knew she'd gone above and beyond anything he could have expected from her. When she finally looked at him, he said, "I'm staying, so why don't you drive back to the ranch and rest up and make Pax happy."

"We'll talk about this after Dr. Miller comes back," she said without hesitation.

CHAPTER TWELVE

IT TOOK TEN long minutes that seemed like forever to Jake before Dr. Miller came back. But the wait was worth it. The doctor quickly checked Sarge before he announced, "Ninety-nine even. The meds are working, and his vitals look very good. There are some tests still pending, but he's doing well."

Jake bowed his head and covered his face with his hand while he tried to breathe in and out, then a touch on his shoulder made him look to his left. Dr. Miller was there. "Why don't you two go home and rest?"

"I can't," he said.

"Mr. Bishop, you two need it. You go back to the ranch I've heard about. He'll be asleep for quite a while, probably well into tomorrow. We'll call you if we need to, and you can call us anytime."

"We have no cell service out there, and our landline's down from the storm." Jake sat back. "I can get a hotel or something close by."

"We have a guest cottage that you two are welcome to stay in until you feel you can leave. Think about it, and I'll be back in a bit." Dr. Miller left.

Jake looked at Liberty, who stood watching him. The small guest cottage wouldn't work for the two of them, at least, not for him, so he had to convince her to go back to the ranch. The line between doing the right thing and doing what he wanted to do was very thin right then. He took a breath and said, "Call Seth."

Liberty took out her phone. "Seth needs to see you and talk to you. Why don't you do a video call? You did fine with Roger."

"Okay," he said, and she put in the call, then handed him the phone as Seth showed on the screen. "Hey, Seth."

"Jake. What's happening?"

"It's all good, better than good," he said. "The fever's broken. The doctor said that this is a win."

"Thank goodness," he saw him say. "Boy, am I glad you and Libby are there with him.

Ben and I couldn't have gotten there. This storm is unbelievable."

"I'm here and staying, so you take care of what you need to there. When he's awake, maybe we can get him on a video call with you and Ben."

"Absolutely," Seth said. "Oh, Max said to tell you the dog is doing great, and thanks for giving him a place to crash between shifts."

Jake didn't think he read Seth right. "Max... he called you? How, if he's still at the ranch?"

"He said the landline's up and working again. He called in a favor and the phone company got it fixed."

"Terrific. I'll call you soon," he said, and hung up.

Before Jake could say anything to Liberty, the doctor was back, "So, are you staying here?"

Jake exhaled. "It seems the landline is fixed at the ranch."

He looked at Liberty and said, "If it's okay with you, we'll both head home."

She nodded and Jake spoke to the doctor. "As long as you call us when Sarge is awake or if something comes up, we'll go back to the ranch."

"I will certainly call either way."

Jake stood, holding to the rail for a second to make sure his legs could support him as the doctor left.

Liberty came closer and smiled at him. She'd done so much, been so caring, and just having her there had made all the difference for him. She'd grounded him when he'd felt as if he were going to scatter into nothingness. He owed her more than she'd ever know. "Are you ready to go?" she asked.

"Just a minute," he said, and turned to bend over Sarge. "I know you probably can't hear me, but I'll be back tomorrow, and we can call Seth and Ben." He rested his hand on the man's shoulder. "You're going to be okay," he said, then turned back to Liberty.

Without a word, she reached out to him and held to him tightly for a long moment. He let himself hold her, then knew he had to let go, even though he never wanted to. She looked up at him, concern in her green eyes. "Are you okay?"

He exhaled. "I'm doing a lot better."

"Me, too," she said, and slipped her arm in his. "Now, Pax is waiting."

JAKE WAS AT the foot of the staircase when Libby came downstairs with the dog after changing into black leggings and an emerald green oversize shirt. Her hair was free around her shoulders, and her feet were bare. She stopped on the last step. "Did Max leave?"

"Yes, he had a call. He said to say goodbye to you, and he thinks Pax is a lucky mutt," he said. "I finally put the groceries away."

"Oh, I'm sorry I didn't get a chance to thank him enough for helping with Pax and getting the phone fixed, but I wanted to get comfortable when we got back."

Jake let his eyes flick over her. "I'd say mission accomplished."

"Why don't you change and I'll make some real hot chocolate with whole milk. I'll add a candy cane to stir it with."

"Okay, you make the drinks, and I'll get the fire and music going."

Libby got busy in the kitchen while Jake restarted the music and laid the fire. By the time the flames were leaping in the hearth, she was back with two mugs in her hands. Jake took one and sat in what was becoming his chair, positioned to face the tree and her. As she settled across from him, she was watching him, probably to see his reaction when he tasted the hot chocolate.

He stirred with the candy cane, took a drink, then grimaced. "Talk about drinking dishwater," he said.

She looked stunned and he quickly said, "Kidding, just kidding. It's wonderful."

"That's mean," she said, but smiled with relief. "I'll forgive you because you restarted the music."

"You said you'd tell me why Christmas is such a huge thing for you, as soon as you had good hot chocolate to drink."

She hesitated. "Why are you so interested?"

"I can see how important it is for you to do Christmas up right with Roger. I'd like to know why."

She took a drink before she answered him. "We've never spent Christmas together. He was gone last year on-site, and I wanted this one to be special."

"But why are you so Christmas-crazy?" Jake said.

"This is good hot chocolate, so, okay. I'll tell you. The second year I was with the Connors, they asked me if I liked being with them, and I said I did. Then they said, if I wanted to stay with them, would it be okay if they adopted me. They actually said they loved me, which I didn't particularly believe, but I agreed. We went through so many court visits and interviews." She smiled slightly. "Then we went to court just before Thanksgiving, and the judge was nice and let me pick out that teddy bear from a bunch she had in the courtroom. I think I understood the adoption would come soon but was afraid to ask anything about it in case it didn't happen."

She sighed, and the smile lingered on her lips. "Then Christmas was getting close, and one by one the other kids were switched to a placement somewhere else, and on Christmas Eve I was the only one left. We were sitting around the Christmas tree, and I told Dad and Mom that I was sorry I didn't have a Christmas present for them."

She closed her eyes for a moment, then blinked and looked back at him. "Well, they both got up and came over to me on the couch and sat down with me between them. Then they hugged me, and Mom was crying, and Dad said that I was the best Christmas present they'd ever been given."

She bit her lip, but Jake could tell it was

more to fight the tears he saw become bright in her eyes. She took another breath. "They told me we were a brand-new family, a real family, and nothing could ever change that. And Christmas is the best time of the year for families to be together."

She wiped at tears that ran silently down her cheeks. "My family. All mine, really mine, and they loved me, and I believed it. I've loved Christmas ever since, and with Roger, I want the same thing. Real family and real love."

Jake released a breath he hadn't even realized he'd been holding. That had all happened years ago, but Jake felt such happiness at what Liberty had found on that Christmas Day. "I see why it's so special to you." And why she was wanting Roger there this year. She was planning a new family, and Roger was the main part of that plan. Another barrier fell in place, blocking him even more from ever believing he could be anything Liberty wanted.

She stood quickly, looked at him and said, "Pax wants in." Then she walked across the room to the entryway. Jake waited, then finally Pax came running toward the Christmas tree. The dog looked up at its candy-cane-free branches, then flopped down onto the floor, looking totally bummed out.

"He knows what he likes," Jake said.

Liberty sat down and looked over at him. "Can I ask you a favor, please?"

After what she'd told him moments ago, he'd do any favor she wanted from him. "What's that?"

"I had always planned to tell the man I married that story before I shared it with others. It was sort of like, 'here I am, and this is who I am.' I mean, he knows I was adopted when I was young, but I wanted him to understand why I'm the way I am now. Everything in life changes us, and that changed me forever. So, if you talk to Roger some time or other, could you not mention I told you about it, please?"

He hadn't expected that to be the favor. "I won't mention anything about it."

He saw her shoulders lower as she sighed, then she sank back into the chair. "Thank you so much."

Roger had a lot of wonderful things coming to him when he married Liberty. "No problem," he said, then shifted everything. "How many days until Christmas?"

She frowned as she was obviously trying to figure that out. "Soon we'll be at the twelve-day mark. You know, like the song, 'The Twelve Days of Christmas'?"

"I hate that song. Who in their right mind would give a lady a partridge in a pear tree?" When Liberty laughed at that, Jake could almost hear it, soft and sweet, like her voice was in the dream. His chest tightened. He was losing it. "Yes, and why would she want eight maids a-milking?"

"How about six geese a-laying?" she asked and was laughing again.

He thought he'd never seen anyone as beautiful as Liberty was at that moment.

"Thanks, but no thanks," he saw her say. "But the five golden rings, now, I'd take them in a heartbeat."

He thought about the ring she'd been wearing when he'd met her. She probably would have five golden rings from Roger sooner or later. He drank more hot chocolate, knowing he was leaving soon now that the phone was repaired.

"Why don't you go and check the phone and make sure it's working?"

"I can't believe I didn't when we got here," she said, then immediately got up and carried

her mug with her into the office. He expected
her to call Roger or her parents if the phone
was connected, but she was back in less than
a minute. "It has a dial tone," she said.

"So you can call Roger."

Instead of a smile, that brought a frown that
tugged a fine line between her green eyes.
"Yes, I can." Then she totally changed the
subject. "I need to sleep down here tonight."

That was not going to happen. "Why?"

"Because I won't hear the phone ring if
I'm sleeping upstairs. Just in case they call
from Wicker Pines. I'll be back in a bit," she
said, and went into the office again and closed
the door this time. She was right, and she
had to be downstairs to hear the phone. He
could sleep upstairs in his old room, and Liberty could come and get him if anything happened.

A sudden pain hit him in his right ear. It
was gone almost immediately. It didn't leave
dizziness or nausea in its wake, but he could
still feel a tight sensation in that ear, an odd
feeling.

He decided right then that when he left
here, he'd find a hotel in Cody near Wicker
Pines, then contact Cal. He wanted to find

out what was happening with his hearing, and Cal could arrange for the best of the best, courtesy of Madison, to come to Cody to check him out.

He drained the last of his drink and stood carefully. He'd come here alone; he'd leave alone. That sounded so empty to him, but he'd designed his life that way, and it was what it was.

LIBBY SAT AT the desk with the receiver in her hand but didn't put in the call to Roger. When a loud beeping sound came from the earpiece, she put it back on the cradle. She wasn't going to tell him about her first Christmas as a Connor over the phone. He wouldn't have the time to listen. She'd share it when he got here. She figured she'd told Jake about it because he was a fellow ex-foster child. That was probably it.

She knew who she really wanted to talk to and reached for the receiver again and called her parents. It was good to hear her mother's voice and the excitement in it when she told her more about the summer camp. That lifted her heart. To know they were with her uncle and his family for Christmas made her happy, too. She just wished that Roger had shown as much excitement about what she was doing as her parents did.

When she'd hung up, she went back into the great room. Jake was crouched by the hearth putting more wood on the fire. All the lights were off except for those on the Christmas tree, and "I'll Be Home for Christmas" was playing. She stood very still, taking in the scene in front of her.

She had an apartment in Seattle, but this place felt like home to her right then. She knew she'd speak to Seth about the cabin, to see if she could use it while she worked here. That made her smile. Jake stood and spotted her across the room.

He motioned to the couch. "It's all yours for the night."

"Thank you," she said, stepping closer. "Just for tonight."

"Did you get a call in to Roger?" he asked.

"I didn't call him. I talked to my mom."

"She's okay?"

"She's fine. She and Dad are in Georgia with my dad's only brother and his family. They're having a great time, and they're planning on coming out here in the spring to see what I'm doing."

"That's good, right?"

"Yes, great," she said, and bit her bottom lip.

"Why don't you seem thrilled?" he asked.

That took her aback. "Why would you ask that?"

"I've noticed when you're bothered and trying to figure things out, you have a tell."

"What?"

"A tell, like in a poker game. It's something that a person does that they don't realize they're doing, such as if they have a good hand, they might fidget with their chips or tap their fingers on the felt. If you know what to look for, you can almost read their minds."

"Okay, what am I doing?"

"You bite your bottom lip or sort of nibble on it when you don't know what to say or if you're bothered. It's never when you're happy or sure about what's going on."

She barely kept herself from putting her hand over her mouth. She was bothered, but she didn't like him seeing that so easily. "Seriously?"

"Yes. Now, what's going on? Is it me?"

"No, it's not you. I'm just thinking, period," she said and turned to go to the couch and sit down. Jake followed her and took time turning on the side light before he sat down, too.

"So, what are you thinking about?" he asked.

"I really don't want to talk about anything right now."

He didn't move for a long moment, then stood and said, "Okay, sleep well." With that, he walked away and out of the room. She heard him going up the stairs, then his footsteps overhead. When there were no more sounds from him, she sat there with the music still going and the fire crackling. Jake had caught her. She was bothered, but it wasn't about work or the weather. It was Roger, and that worried her more than she could say.

JAKE'S DREAMS USUALLY dissolved upon waking, and he just remembered if they were good or bad, until he'd dreamed about Liberty dancing with him. He remembered that one perfectly. Now he knew he was dreaming again, but he was in the old cabin, going to the door, stepping outside onto the porch. It was a clear night with snow everywhere.

He knew it was cold, but he didn't feel it as he scanned the landscape, sparkling in the glow of a full moon.

He was in that shifting reality where he could hear Christmas music, with no idea where it came from. Then he looked into the distance from the top step and saw Liberty making her way slowly toward him, a red beanie covering her hair, her green jacket on, and she was illuminated perfectly by moonlight.

"Liberty?" he called. She stopped and looked up, saw him, then she smiled and waved. He was down the steps quickly, sinking into knee-deep snow and starting to feel the cold. "Liberty!" he called. Then she was almost there, holding out her hands to him, laughing.

"I want to stay here with you." Her voice came to him soft and honey smooth, but her words became a lie as she started to recede before he could touch her hands. She was leaving, going back, fading until she dissolved into brilliant prisms of moonlight. He lunged to grab her, but all his hands held was the sparkle of moonbeams. Sorrow flooded through him, then everything became soft nothingness.

When Jake woke up, it was because Liberty was standing over him. Her hand was on his shoulder, gently shaking him. "Sorry to wake you up," he saw her saying. "But I wanted to call Julia and talk to her, if it's okay with you?"

He was having trouble shaking free of that dream, that sense of loss, but Liberty was right there. There were no moonbeams, just her dressed in jeans and a white cable-knit sweater. She'd pulled her hair back from her face in a knot at the nape of her neck and looked as if she'd slept well. He could barely focus, the dream overlapping with reality. "Sure, call her, and I'll get myself together."

He freshened up and dressed in jeans and a gray thermal shirt. When he went downstairs and stepped into the great room, Liberty was just coming out of the office. She was smiling and something in him eased. "Sarge is sleeping. He woke to eat breakfast, then fell right back to sleep, and they're encouraging that. So she suggested that we hold off until tomorrow to visit. He doesn't seem to remember much about being sick, but he's coherent when he's speaking. Pretty good, huh?"

"Yes," he said, happy for that. But he knew that it was time for him to leave.

"I can't wait to see him again," she said.

"Me, neither." He wanted her there when he walked back into Sarge's room tomorrow. He'd take a day to go with her to see Sarge, and when they got back, he'd explain he had to leave. He could be out of here before dark tomorrow night and contact Cal.

"I forgot some things yesterday because I only went into the food section at the store. I'd like to get some real dog shampoo for Pax. Also, I really want to get some marshmallows to make more hot chocolate. I was thinking I'd go to Eclipse since it's closer than Cody."

"It should be pretty clear on the highway for you."

"You aren't going to come?"

"I can stay here with Pax until you're back."

"Oh, I forgot. I want to go by the vet's with Pax, too. He said to drop in anytime. But I don't have a clue how to get there. I thought you could come along and show me, and you know him, too."

"Maybe he has a cure for candy-cane addiction."

She laughed at that, the way she'd laughed in the dream, and he put that sound into his reality. "Pax still hasn't forgiven me for taking the candy canes off the lower part of the tree."

Jake had no dizziness, no nausea, no pain. He could go into Eclipse with her today. "Okay, I'll go with you to Luke's."

"Thank you. Oh, one other thing. Seth called right when I hung up with Julia. He's really tied up with work, but since there isn't an emergency any longer, he's planning on coming closer to Christmas. He and Ben will fly in and stay at Wicker Pines in one of the guest cottages, so they can spend all their time with Sarge. Seth thinks he's going to be seeing you, too."

"I hope he can stay more than just a day or two," Jake said.

"Will you be there with them?"

He didn't have any idea yet where he'd be on Christmas, so he told her the truth. "I don't know."

JAKE AND LIBBY never got to Eclipse. They ended up heading to Cody after Julia called the house again to tell them Sarge was asking for Jake. So, they'd headed north to Wicker Pines. The visit had been wonderful, and Sarge had been thrilled with the two-foot-tall potted live Christmas tree they'd gifted him, which Libby had remembered seeing in the store on their first trip. It came with multicolored twinkling lights already on it and some red and green decorations attached to the boughs. The rehab room had brightened up, and so had the man in the hospital bed. He'd been lucid and participated in conversation, even correcting Jake a few times when he got a name or place wrong.

"He's doing well, isn't he?" Jake asked as Libby drove out of Cody and onto the highway heading south. Snow was cleared past the shoulders of the road now, and the traffic was light.

"You don't have to answer me on any of this, okay? I just want to say it."

She gave him a thumbs-up and he kept talking. "Getting the tree for Sarge was a great idea. That really made him happy. Calling Seth and Ben was an even better idea. All things considered, I'm glad we came here today." He chuckled softly. "Also, thank you for getting me a knit hat while you were in the store. Green was a nice choice. Christmassy, you know."

Libby couldn't resist glancing at him long

enough for him to read, "Thumbs-up is boring." Then she looked back at the road. She'd never been bored around Jake. She liked talking to him. She liked seeing him smile and she liked the way he cocked his head slightly to one side when she spoke.

"A conversation face-to-face is the best way to talk to anyone. So, for now, you drive, and I'll shut up."

She gave him a thumbs-up but flashed him a smile before focusing on the road.

When they got to the ranch and let Pax out to run, Jake shifted over behind the wheel so he could put the truck in the garage. Libby went into the house. It was warm, and the Christmas tree glowed by the hearth. Fresh pine smelled so wonderful in the space. She took off her boots and jacket, then sank down onto the couch.

When she checked her cell, she saw that while in town she'd missed four texts and two emails. She exhaled, then turned off her useless cell phone and pushed it into her jeans' pocket. She had the landline now, but she still wasn't sure about talking to Roger just yet. She didn't want to feel as if she was intruding on his work and keeping him from something more important than talking to her.

That thought almost took her breath away because she knew it was true. She closed her eyes tightly and that didn't change anything. Right then, what he was doing on-site in Mali was more important than she was, than their wedding was, probably more important than being here for Christmas with her.

She was startled when she heard Jake say, "Do you have time to talk?"

He was standing over her and she got to her feet. She couldn't talk to him. "You know, I need to get work done. I'm slacking off."

"Maybe later," he said, and she had a feeling she should have agreed. "Whenever you can spare some time today."

She sighed. "You know what, sit down and we can talk. Work can wait for a while."

Jake hesitated, then sat on the couch.

Instead of staying next to him, she sat on the old rug facing him, crossed her legs, and took a breath. "Okay, now we can talk."

He was frowning. "Is there something wrong, something you didn't tell me at Wicker Pines?"

She blinked. "What? No, nothing."

"I know you talk to Julia a lot and thought

maybe she'd told you something you didn't think I should know."

"Why would you think that?"

He shrugged. "You tend to want to protect people."

He was right, but wrong at the same time. "Nothing is wrong at Wicker Pines. I promise. I'm working through some things, but they aren't about you or Sarge. Julia is really thrilled with his improvement both physically and emotionally since you've been there for him."

He seemed to ease up at her explanation. "That's good."

"I'll tell you anything I find out. I promise, and I keep my promises."

"Yes, you do," he said. "So, what's bothering you?"

She didn't plan on it, but she found herself telling him about the decision she'd made about Roger's mother and the wedding. It just spilled out and Jake silently let her talk. When she finally stopped, he actually smiled at her. "So, the real Liberty Connor showed up after all?"

She didn't understand. "What are you talking about?"

"You finally drew a line in the sand. You're going to have a face-to-face with your future mother-in-law and negotiate. I think it's a great plan. And, knowing you, you'll end up getting a lot of what you want for your wedding."

He got all of that out of her rambling dissertation. "You know, you're right. I can't believe I just kept letting it go, all the calls and the texts and the ideas for the wedding, and her expecting me to work for the foundation…"

"Why did you?" he asked.

She knew why. But it was embarrassing. "I hate to admit this, but his parents, their position, their money, their station in life, it's all so far beyond mine. They know about my foster care years and the adoption, but I think they wish he'd asked someone better qualified to marry him, a socialite or whatever."

"What does Roger say about your plan for a meeting?" he asked.

She wished he hadn't brought it up. "He wants me to take care of things. But I think it should be both him and his father there, too, so there's no misunderstanding."

"You're right. It should be. It affects all of you."

"I know, but he's so busy and has so much going on. I can't ask him to just let everything go to be here."

"Liberty, you're going to marry the man, whether it's at the justice of the peace's office or in a palace. Maggie and Sarge had their problems with her parents, but the two of them stuck together, immovable, and her parents came around. They were in it together, all the way to the end. Just my opinion, but he'll be here at Christmas and things will probably calm down, then maybe he'll agree to go to the meeting. Him going to the meeting can be his birthday present to you. How's that?"

She wished it was that simple. But from the way Roger had spoken so cavalierly about their wedding, she was wondering now if he'd even be here at Christmas. "Yes, maybe. I don't know. I'll figure it out."

"Maybe you need to call Roger and have him come back earlier? Not for a showdown, but so you and he can be alone. I'll be gone, and the two of you can have your privacy to work out whatever's going on."

"I can't demand he drop everything to come here."

"Then you drop everything and go to him?"

She wished she wanted to do that, because she might have. But she knew if she intruded at the site, he might not even have any free time to be with her. Then it dawned on her that she didn't want to leave the ranch. It felt right being here, and even more, she didn't want to leave Jake and Sarge. They were becoming important to her. "No, I can't do that. He needs to concentrate on what he's doing."

"What about your mother? She must be excited about you getting married."

"Oh, she is, very excited about it." In that moment it hit her, and it hit her hard—she had been shutting her own mother out of the wedding plans worrying about Roger's mother. That made her feel slightly sick.

"All I wanted to do was plan my own wedding. Ever since I was small, I wanted my mom to make my wedding cake, not have some fancy seven-tiered wonder on stilts. I wanted to wear her wedding dress, and only invite close friends and family."

"That's what you should have."

"I don't think his mom and dad see their

only son getting married in anything less than a huge production for hundreds of guests. I'm not sure how I can get a compromise, but I'm going to try."

"Is eloping an option?" Jake asked with a smile.

She chuckled at that. "Only if Roger doesn't mind being disowned." She exhaled. "I'll do the meeting on my own, if I have to." Hesitating, she rocked a bit closer to him. "Between you and me, his parents kind of scare me."

CHAPTER THIRTEEN

JAKE THOUGHT THEY'D talk a few minutes, then he could broach him leaving in a few hours. But he could tell Liberty was dead serious. "How do they scare you?"

"With their expectations," she said simply. "And I sure don't want to embarrass them in any way in front of their friends."

"How could you possibly do that?"

With a seriously intent look in those green eyes, she said, "For an example, at the reception they want a six-course meal for three hundred guests. His mother wants pampered salmon. No joke. Add high-priced champagne, along wine from their own label *and* a string quartet for the music."

He shook his head. "Wow."

"If they have the string quartet, you know what means."

He didn't. "No, what?"

"Slow, romantic music, like waltzes or classical pieces, and dancing them in a dress with a twenty-foot train."

"No conga lines?" he asked, hoping against hope that he'd finally get a smile out of her. That didn't happen.

"I wish," she said, and her shoulders sank on a sigh.

Then he thought he understood one of her problems. He rested his forearms on his knees and leaned closer. "Let me guess. Liberty Grace Connor doesn't know how to dance, and Roger and his parents don't have a clue that you don't have a clue."

She looked embarrassed, then nodded. "I don't and they don't."

"Why not?"

"Roger and I never had an occasion to dance, so it never came up. I kind of thought I could take dance lessons while Roger was away, then I came up here, and that's not going to happen before he comes back."

It seemed surreal to him that he was discussing her wedding with her, and even more disconcerting, he wanted her to have the wedding she wanted, which really sounded pretty impossible after what she'd just told him. "You should be able to be honest with him."

That brought color to her cheeks. "I'm not sure how he'd react."

"You've never had an argument with him?"

She shook her head sharply. "No. Just about our plans I had for us before the wedding, and things are just sort of out of whack right now. He's there. I'm here. If I could just get the dancing thing to go away, I could deal with pampered salmon."

"You are a bit of a control freak, aren't you?" he asked.

"No, well, maybe. I don't like surprises, and I don't like not knowing how things will go. And I don't like feeling stupid." She shrugged. "Okay, I need control. I admit I feel safe with control. Is that what you mean?"

In all of his adult life, Jake had never felt such a need to make someone smile and relax as he did right then. That was ridiculous. She rubbed her bare ring finger as she lowered her head. Of all of her worries about the wedding, there was nothing he could do about any of them, except for one—dancing. He'd do one last thing to help her before he drove away.

"It's not hard to dance," he found himself saying to try to encourage her.

Liberty looked up at him as she tucked her hair behind her ears. "Easy for you to say."

"You never went to your prom or anything?"

She nodded her head. "I certainly did in my junior year. A kid named Kevin asked me to dance. I crushed his feet so badly that he tripped and went facedown on the floor. He never spoke to me again."

"That sounds pretty rough," he said, barely holding back a smile.

She cocked her head to one side and narrowed her eyes on him. "Don't tell me you can dance?"

"Sarge had us all go through his idea of a social manners course while we were here. It included dance lessons."

"You're joking, aren't you?"

"No, I'm as serious as Kevin's crushed feet."

She almost smiled. He'd come so close. "And you did it?"

"Sarge wanted us to at least have a semblance of manners. He was big on his boys having skills."

Color deepened in her face. "I have skills, no matter what anyone might think."

He'd worded that wrongly. "Dancing is a learnable skill. If I can learn to dance, you can."

"Thank you, but I wasn't thinking of the two-step."

He clicked his tongue at her. "Liberty Grace Connor, I do believe you might just be a bit of a snob yourself."

He liked it that she blushed so easily. "Sorry, what I meant was, they won't be doing the two-step at my wedding."

"Too bad. Your future mother-in-law might lighten up if they did. However, despite doing a mean two-step, my skills go beyond that."

"And you were good?"

"I was good. I am good."

"Okay, if you're good, could you show me the basic steps for the waltz?"

He could show her the steps... "I'll try."

"Shoot, I'm sorry. Of course, you can't hear the music."

He didn't know why her saying that shook him. He'd give anything to wipe that look of sympathy off her face. Then he thought of a way he might be able to do that. "Pick a song, any song that you think is slow and nice and memorable. If it's in Sarge's collection, I'll know it. He always said, 'If you feel the beat, you'll move your feet.'"

She shifted. "I love Christmas music, but I don't want to dance to 'Jingle Bells' at my wedding."

When Jake moved to stand, Liberty scrambled to her feet. He felt steady and headed past the pool table to the closet that held the CD player. When Liberty came up behind him, he asked, "What is your favorite slow Christmas song?"

"I guess, 'Have Yourself a Merry Little Christmas'?"

He hadn't thought about that song for years until it had invaded his dreams. "Is that what you want?"

"It is, as long as it's okay with you?"

"You've got it," Jake said. Five minutes later, the worn braided rug was rolled back, and the music was ready to play. Libby had thankfully thought of Sarge before they started. Knowing she wouldn't be able to hear the phone ring over the music, she'd called Wicker Pines and spoken to Dr. Miller himself, who'd told her Sarge was sleeping and his numbers were their best yet. Jake turned the volume higher on the CD player until he was satisfied.

Then he came across to where Liberty stood in the middle of the cleared area in front of the couch. As they faced each other she pointedly looked down at his feet protected only by his socks. "I told you about Kevin, so maybe your best bet is to put on boots."

"I'll take my chances," he said. "Face me with a bit of distance between us so you can see my feet clearly, and I can see you singing," he said. "I'm leading, so if I step back, you step forward, and if I step to my left, you step to your right. Got it?"

"I think so."

"I'll show you the basic steps, and you watch. Can you sing the words, so I know where I am in the song?"

"Sure, if that makes it easier." She waited until the song began again, then Liberty began to sing along to it. Jake moved easily in a simple pattern. They went through the full song twice as she watched him move, then she looked at him. "Can we try it now?"

Jake blinked at her. "What?"

"I want to dance. I thought this was what we were leading up to. I think I can do it now."

His heart sank. He'd been stupid, thinking

he could just show her the steps and have her mimic them. Now she wanted to dance with him, and he wasn't sure he could be that close to her and keep a mental distance. "I don't know if you need to."

"I do," Liberty said as she came closer.

Jake stared at her as she put her hand on his left arm then lifted her right hand, waiting for him to take it in his. He couldn't back out, and he took her hand and lightly placed his other hand on her waist. He kept space between them. "Whenever you're ready," he told her.

Jake watched her lips as the song started again. It was like the dream; he could almost hear her singing as they started the pattern. At first, she failed miserably, stepping on his feet twice, not that she had much weight behind the contact. He hoped she'd give up then, but she kept going, starting the song again, and this time she began to move with more assurance and matched his steps.

When the song finished, she was smiling. "I think I'm almost dancing."

"You are," Jake said. "Liberty Connor can do anything she sets her mind to, apparently."

His eyes held hers. "That's one thing I do know about you."

"I'm trying," she said, then added, "I think I might be able to dance at my wedding and impress everyone."

"That's the Liberty Connor I know and—"

Jake turned abruptly, leaving her standing in the middle of the floor. He felt stunned at what he'd almost said. Love? "I want more bass," he called over his shoulder as he headed to the CD player.

He adjusted the equalizer and tried to concentrate on what he was doing. It wasn't love that he'd been feeling. He reasoned he felt a need to protect her. He'd feel that way around anyone he cared about. He cared. That was that.

Maybe now she'd say she knew enough to get by at the wedding. But when he looked, she was still there waiting for him. He had no choice, so he went back, faced her and got ready to endure the torture of feeling her in his arms and the scent of roses and vanilla with each breath he took.

"Wait and we'll catch the beat," he said, not looking at her directly, but just past her.

He finally looked at her mouth and saw

her singing. "Okay, start." Surprisingly, they caught the right moment, but she looked down at the same time and stepped on his foot. He stopped, ready to call it a day, but she had other ideas.

She gave him a wry smile, and he read her lips. "Sorry, but I warned you. One more time, please."

"Okay," he said, and she started singing again. She was right with him, step for step, easily following his lead now. It was as if it clicked for her, and she moved, coming closer and closer against him. He shut his eyes when he inhaled her scent as she rested her head on his chest. He hated it that holding her felt so good, that her slender body seemed to fit perfectly against him. Then her left hand moved up his arm and he felt it at the side of his neck. He closed his eyes so tightly color exploded behind his lids and he was holding his breath when Liberty stopped dancing.

That was it. He opened his eyes. That was all he could take. Then Liberty looked up at him, her gaze vaguely unfocused as if she'd been lost in the moment. His world shifted on its axis when she smiled slowly up at him. "You are a terrific teacher."

He felt as if he'd heard those words, and he found himself leaning down. His lips touched hers, and they were soft and warm. For a treacherous moment, he let himself get lost in the contact, the way her mouth parted for his, the feel of her against him, his arms around her. It wasn't a dream, it was reality, and it was something he'd wanted since he'd first looked into those green eyes. He'd wanted it every time she'd touched him, and every time she'd smiled at him.

Liberty slowly moved back, the kiss over, lowering her left hand to his chest to press weakly against him. When he looked down at her, he thought he saw what he was feeling echoed in her eyes, then it was gone when she spoke. "I…I didn't mean to… I…"

He felt a cold distance growing between them even though she was still so close he could feel each breath she took. When he felt the steady beat of the music start again, he said, "Liberty, I'm…" He couldn't finish.

She wrapped her arms around herself. Her tongue nervously touched her lips for just a moment, and he was pretty sure her taste would still be lingering on his lips if he dared to check. "This can't happen, Jake. I'm marrying Roger."

He saw her shoulders tremble when she exhaled again. "This was…impulsive and not real. But Roger's real. My life with him is real."

"And this is just the calm in the storm," he said before he thought about it.

"No, it isn't." He saw real intensity in her eyes now. "I'm not going back into the storm. I'm going back to my life."

He had to stop any more of her words before they completely destroyed him, even if he couldn't hear them. "No. Please." He drew back and told a painful lie. "It was just a kiss, nothing to get upset about."

She looked as if she was going to cry. "I'm sorry," he watched her say. "I'm so sorry."

She turned away from him to cross to the CD player. He felt the music stop abruptly. Without looking back, Liberty went into the office and closed the door. The action was final.

Jake knew what a mess he'd made of everything. He should never have agreed to dance with her, ever. What difference would it make at her wedding if she still had to have everything she didn't want? Why had he believed that it would be okay, that he could help her? He should have taken a step back, been smart enough to think about it without acting on it. But whatever sanity he'd had left fled for one stunning moment.

After putting the braided rug back in place, he looked around. The office door was still firmly shut. Even Pax was smart enough to know trying to get into the office was a bad idea. Jake ran his hands roughly over his face, then went into the east wing to take a hot shower. He'd be out of here in an hour. He couldn't offer Liberty what she had with Roger, and he wouldn't get in the way of her engagement and her happiness. He would let her know what he was going to do, though, and not just walk out. He owed her that. But he had to get out of there as soon as he could.

After his shower, Jake dressed in jeans but had to go out to the great room to get a clean shirt out of his duffel. He flipped on the overhead lights and crossed to the couch to crouch over his bag and take out a white thermal. His old metal box fell out, and he looked down at it. It was rusty, and the pictures of a jet fighter that had once been on the top had faded to almost nothing, but it held a lot of him inside. It held his whole past. He pushed it back into the bag, then stood and shook his shirt out.

When he tugged it over his head, Pax came running at him from the entry.

He waited for the dog to get to him, but Pax went right past. Jake turned to see the dog's target. Liberty. She was standing on the far side of the pool table looking at him, her eyes wide and her hand clasped over her mouth. She looked horrified, and Jake realized the huge mistake he'd made because he'd been so distracted. Enough was enough.

He turned, reached for the duffel, and dropped it on the couch. It hit the cushions just about the time he felt Liberty's touch on his shoulder.

LIBBY TRIED TO catch her breath before she went toward Jake. The image of his back was seared into her mind. A long scar from the cap of his left shoulder angled downward toward his lower right spine. More scars, smaller but just as disturbing, showed a random record of something horrible that he'd survived. She got to him and felt him flinch when she touched him. But he didn't turn to her when he spoke.

"I'm leaving."

She drew her hand back and stayed put.

With a deep sigh, Jake finally looked at her. "What more do you want?" he asked weakly.

"What happened?"

"I'm not big on analyzing what I do," he said. "I told you a kiss was just—"

"Not the kiss. Your back."

"It's my business," he said, and turned to grab the duffel bag.

She couldn't pretend she hadn't seen the scars. She couldn't pretend it meant nothing to her that he'd obviously been hurt so badly. It scared her to think he might have died. There would have never been a Jake Bishop in her life. She couldn't image a world without Jake in it. She kept waiting. When he looked back at her, it chilled her that his face was devoid of any emotion, even anger, and he was holding the duffel at his side. She reacted without thinking, grabbing at the side strap of his duffel and jerking it out of his hand.

Keeping her eyes locked with his, she dropped the bag on the floor by her feet. "Please, after everything, tell me what happened."

She knew he could force his way out, but he didn't. He sank down on the couch. Even when she sat beside him, he didn't look at her. After a nerve-racking wait, Libby touched his forearm. He jerked away and turned to her.

"Just tell me," she said.

"I'll make this fast." He shifted toward her and took a deep breath. "The fact is, I'm legally bound to not talk about anything to do with my situation. Sorry."

"You can trust me," she said simply.

There was tension between them. "Trust has nothing to do with it. I'm legally constrained."

"Okay, then. I'll tell you what I think."

"Liberty, no."

She didn't stop. "You were in an accident of some sort, probably while you were under contract, and it could have killed you."

He just stared her.

"You're healing physically, but it's your hearing you want to get back, which seems a good bet with all the advances in medicine nowadays. But you're here, not somewhere getting an operation. You're here, waiting for something. I don't understand."

He didn't move.

All she wanted to know was that he'd be

all right. "How long until you'll get surgery?" she asked.

He looked as if he just wanted her to stop and accept what he'd revealed to her without digging. "Maybe never."

"Why?"

"I'm in a situation where if I do the wrong thing, I'll lose my life the way—"

"You could die?" she gasped.

"No, I'll lose my life the way it was before."

Libby just stared at him, unable to speak now.

"I'll give you one huge piece of information, then I'm done here. Test pilots can't be compromised physically. Hearing damage is a big eliminator. And I'm legally bound to disclose surgical intervention to any prospective employer. That means they wouldn't hire me, and they shouldn't. My career could be gone."

"So, a plane blew up with you in it. You won't tell anyone because you want to get back in a plane that could possibly blow up with you in it again, if you heal naturally? And no one will ever know what happened."

"No, it's not just that—legally I can't tell

anyone," he said. "Whatever I've told you is between us, right?"

She got up and stepped over his bag to get right in front of him. Then she crouched, waiting until he finally looked at her. "What are your chances of healing without surgery?"

"Twenty-five percent, and right now, I have to focus on Sarge, and on my own healing… I'm leaving."

The idea of him leaving and just disappearing from her life was more than she could deal with right then. He looked tired, too. "Get away from here, if you want to, but wait until morning and get some sleep. I promise I won't say anything about this to anyone. It's your story to tell."

Jake sank back on the couch. "I'll be out of here at dawn." She knew she was frowning, because he frowned right back at her. "What now?" he asked.

"Nothing at all. You said it's none of my business, and I get that."

"Then why are you so ticked off about it? It's my life, my problem. I should've left as soon as I found you here. You're not part of this and I don't want you to be. I don't want anyone to be part of this. It's mine. I'll do it on my own. Whatever happens, it's all on me."

"But I feel sad for you," she admitted honestly, figuring she had absolutely nothing left to lose with the man.

"Don't you dare," he said through clenched teeth. "That is exactly why I don't want to be tied to anyone, to rely on anyone. I don't want sympathy or pity. I just want to hear!"

A bit of anger was edging out some of her sympathy. "Good for you. Do it your way. Give up everything, maybe even your chance at ever hearing again, so you *might* be able to do what you want to do."

His voice dropped low. "Don't lecture me on what my life should be or what you think of it, and I won't lecture you on your life choices." Without warning, his face twisted in a grimace, then both hands went up to press against his ears, hard. She reached to try to help, but he pulled away from her, his hands still over his ears. She didn't move. Slowly he lowered his hands. When he opened his eyes, he sat straighter. "It's an earache," he said.

With that, he stood slowly, waiting a moment, then looked down at her. "Good night." He headed out of the room.

She heard his steps on the stairs to the second level, but she didn't move. She sat there for a long time just staring across the room at the lit Christmas tree, where Pax was sleeping. Standing, she crossed to a chair by the fire and sat down facing the flickering flames. She knew she wouldn't sleep, and she couldn't stop going over and over what Jake had admitted to her.

She knew he'd leave. He wanted it that way.

LIBBY STAYED IN the chair until she fell asleep, not wanting to use the couch again. When she finally woke, she twisted right away to see if Jake was on the couch. He wasn't. The duffel bag wasn't there, either. She got up and went to the master bedroom, then dressed in jeans and a bright red flannel shirt. With her hair loose, she went out onto the walkway and looked at the bedroom door to her right. It was slightly ajar, and she moved quietly toward it. But when she looked inside, the bed was made and there was no duffel bag in sight. He'd left.

Slowly she went down to the entry. There was no smell of coffee or cooking of any sort. She stopped on the last step and saw Jake's jacket and boots still at the cowhide bench. She'd missed them on the way up. He hadn't left. Then he was there, coming out of the west wing hallway, dressed in a green thermal shirt and jeans. He saw her, paused, then went past her into the great room. She waited, then followed him. But she'd barely taken the single step down onto the slate floor when she heard the shrill ring of the landline phone. She hurried past Jake to get to the office and grabbed for the receiver. "Hello?"

"Surprise, Libby," she heard in her ear.

She sank down in the chair as Jake looked into the room. "Roger?"

Jake walked away as Roger asked, "Libby, are you okay?"

She must have sounded as stunned as she felt. "I'm just surprised. How did you even get this number?"

"My assistant found it for me."

"Your assistant?"

"Well, he's my assistant while I'm in the New York office."

"New York? What are you doing there? The last time we talked, you were coming here when you left the site."

"No, I came here. In fact, I've just arrived

and have to hit the ground running to head off a situation with the foundation's board of directors."

"You flew back to New York to meet with the board?"

"More like to deal with the board. I have a lot of work to do here, but I called to tell you I'm here if you want to come for a quick visit?"

She was dumbfounded, trying to figure out what he wanted her to say. "Roger, I can't just leave here. I'm working, and I have things I have to deal with."

"Okay, sure, I understand. You're working, and I'm working. That's okay. Right now, it looks as if I'll be in Seattle the day before Christmas. I'll see you there. My parents are excited about you being there."

She didn't want to leave here to go to Seattle and have Christmas with Roger and his family. She didn't want that at all. "I don't know."

"Wow, don't get too excited."

"I am excited about having Christmas with you. But I thought it would be here. I honestly can't just up and leave like that."

"You can work when you go back after I'm

gone or ask the firm to send someone up to cover for you."

"Why can't you come here? This place is incredible, and I already decorated the Christmas tree. It's real and it's beautiful."

"Don't worry, my parents will have a great tree."

She tried one more time. "Roger, I really want to stay here for Christmas. I want to show you the original cabin on the property. It's so nice, all cozy with a potbelly stove and a breathtaking view. I was thinking we could stay in it when I come back later to continue with the project. I want you to see the plans for what I'm doing here."

"Libby, I'm trying to work this out. I only have so much time, and I really need to use it to straighten things out here. We can talk about this later."

She was wasting his time, and she felt it. This was all about Roger, and not about what she wanted or why she wanted it. She let go. "You go ahead and do what you need to do, and I'll stay here and get my work done."

He exhaled, and she knew she'd taken a burden off him. She wondered why she wasn't angry, just disappointed. That wasn't right. In fact, that was wrong on so many levels, for an engaged couple to be okay with not being together. "That works for me," he said. "We'll meet up in Seattle."

He wouldn't come to the ranch. He didn't want to. How sad that them being separated was fine with him. "I guess."

"You know," Roger said, "I wish I hadn't had to come back for the board's vote."

So he came back for a vote. She let that sink in. She wasn't a priority for Roger at all. He cared, but not enough. "You can handle it, I'm sure."

"Yes, I will handle it."

"About Christmas…" she said, then altered the rest of her words to suit what she was feeling and knew right then. "You know, Roger, I love what you do and why you're doing it. Your passion for it. That's awesome. You were born to do what you do."

"You understand me," he said simply.

"I love you," she said, and meant it. But she knew right then, she wasn't *in* love with him. Maybe she never had been. She didn't know. "You're a good man," she said honestly as she opened her eyes.

She was startled to see Jake in the doorway

watching her. Roger was saying something about Seattle, but all she could focus on was Jake with his jacket and boots on, holding his duffel bag at his side.

CHAPTER FOURTEEN

"ROGER, HOLD ON," Libby said as she put her hand over the mouthpiece. "Roger called to say he was back. He's in—"

Jake cut her off, "Just wanted to tell you that I'm leaving now." With that, he turned and strode back through the great room. Libby dropped the receiver down on the desk, then hurried after him. She almost tripped over her own feet trying to get to the step up into the entry before he did. She barely made it, and he stopped a few feet from her.

"Thank you for all you've done and for dealing with me," he said, choosing not to look directly at her, but just beyond her left shoulder. "It's time for me to head out."

Libby waved her hand in front of him to get his attention. "Where to?" she asked when he finally looked at her.

"I'm not sure."

There was no real emotion on his face. "Jake, we need to talk. Please."

"No. Go and talk to Roger, and be happy."

"Can't you just give me a few minutes?"

"Why?"

She fought for the words, then simply said, "I care about you."

He went very still, studying her for an uneasy moment, then said, "I didn't ask you to."

She blinked rapidly, her eyes burning now. "You don't want…"

"Honestly…" He closed his eyes briefly, then looked at her again. "My life isn't even close to what your life is. It's a mess and I have to focus on it." He lifted his free hand and touched her cheek. "I wish you well, you and Roger, and that your first Christmas together is all you want it to be, and that your wedding, big or little, will be good."

"Jake, I…" She felt tears threatening and had to swallow. "I need you to…"

"You need me to do what?"

She bit her lip and exhaled. "I need you to be safe and you can't drive."

"I haven't had any dizzy spells. I'm okay to drive."

"Okay, I…I really hope you can get back to the life you want so badly."

He stood very still. "Roger is a very lucky man."

"No, he's…" She hurt so much she didn't think she could breathe. "Can't you stay, just a bit longer?" She was thankful he couldn't hear her voice when it broke.

"No, I have to go," he said. He went to the door.

He only stopped because Pax ran up to him and blocked his way. Jake looked down at the dog, then stroked his head before reaching for the handle. Liberty moved to grab Pax by his collar as Jake opened the door. Without a backward glance, Jake was out and closing it behind him.

Libby let go of Pax to move to the side window by the staircase and watch until Jake was out of sight, heading down to the garage. Moments later the truck came into view and swung to go down the driveway. She couldn't look away until it was out of sight over the rise. Pax nudged Libby, and she crouched to hug him when he whined. "I know, I know," she whispered. "I tried to get him to stay."

He licked her face, but just once, then headed down into the great room.

She went back to the office and reached for the receiver. "Roger?"

The dial tone buzzed in her ear. Of course he'd been too busy with business to wait for her to come back. She dropped the phone in the cradle and whispered, "Goodbye, Roger," and no one heard her except Pax as he came in and pressed against her leg.

Libby looked out through the back window and saw snow starting to fall from leaden skies. Whatever she and Roger had was over and done. Maybe it had been over and done earlier, but she hadn't been smart enough to know it. She'd call Roger soon and let him know, then send the ring back, but right then, she knew it was the right thing to do.

She just wished Jake were still here. She felt empty with him gone, as if she didn't fit, and she'd never experienced that when Roger had been gone. If what she felt for Jake was love, it sure didn't feel good right then.

Sliding the top drawer of the desk open, she reached in to pick up the engagement ring but hesitated. The rusty box she'd seen Jake put in his duffel bag days ago—then again last night just before everything had fallen apart—was sitting in the drawer. He must have put it there earlier when she'd seen him coming out of the west wing. She ignored the ring and picked up the box to set it on the desk.

She hesitated, then opened it. On top of the contents was a paper folded in quarters with her name scrawled on it. Jake had left the box behind on purpose.

She picked up the folded paper, opened it and read. *Liberty, if you're reading this, I'm gone. If I were a different man, I might have stuck around to see what could have been. But I am who I am, and I accept that. I'm leaving my past here. I don't want it. Hope you'll finally see a Christmas Moon with Roger. J.*

The writing started to blur and when her hands became unsteady, she let go of the paper and it drifted down onto the desk by the box. Jake was who he was. She agreed with that, but it didn't make the hurt she felt any easier to bear right then.

She looked down at another folded paper, yellowed by age. When she picked it up and opened it, there were two thin sheets. The top sheet had a header that read, *Bishop,*

Jake, #ML8180. Under that was an official-looking government stamp, and below that, a morass of legalese. It outlined the "full and complete responsibilities and liabilities" of Child Protection Services "for the aforementioned child."

She slid it aside to read the paper under it. Its header was painfully brief, only *#ML8180* was at the top, not even a name. She read the single-spaced print that laid out everything about a little boy who had been abandoned at a sheriff's station. No background, no vitals, a guess at his age as five. His mother, father and birthday were all unknown.

She looked down into what remained in the tin—a pack of photos held together by a rubber band and, with it, a small gold coin, about the size of a silver dollar. Maybe it had been a medal or a charm, but whatever had been engraved on it had been worn off long ago. She laid it on the papers, then arranged the photos—all of the same boy—in what she thought was chronological order.

The first picture was of a small child dressed in jeans and a red striped T-shirt. He stared into the camera with large, bewildered blue eyes under a mop of pale hair. His lips were pressed together. At the bottom of the photo, someone had handwritten, *#ML8180/5 yrs/assigned to care*, followed by a date.

The other pictures showed that lost child morphing over the years into a teenager. In the last photo, he was rangy and lean, his features sharper, with a shock of dirty-blond hair, a clenched jaw and blue eyes narrowed with defiance. *#ML8180/15 yrs/reassigned.* Her heart simply broke.

She couldn't even imagine what Sarge and Maggie had faced with Jake and how hard they'd had to work to rescue him. But nothing the couple could have done would have taken away the scars from the boy's past.

She was crying now but paid no attention to the tears as she quietly admitted to herself what she should have realized before now. She loved him. She loved him for who he'd been, who he was now and who he'd become. But his decisions had robbed her of any chance to really love him. Even if she went after him, she knew without a doubt he'd send her away. He'd made it clear that whatever their destinies would be, they wouldn't be together.

JAKE DIDN'T GET more than halfway to Cody before he'd had to pull off the highway. The pain in his ears had come suddenly and so intensely that it was all-encompassing. He couldn't drive. He waited until the pain lessened before he got out his cell phone and put in a video call to Cal. He explained what was going on, and where he was.

"Stay right there. Do not drive any farther. I'll have someone there in ten." The man paused. "Hold on. Okay?"

"I'm trying," Jake said as the call ended. "I'm trying," he repeated in the empty truck.

CHAPTER FIFTEEN

LIBBY DROVE INTO Cody to visit Sarge around noon on Christmas Eve day. When she was buzzed into Wicker Pines, she found Julia in the reception area sitting in a wingback chair beside Sarge, who was in his wheelchair. "This man has been waiting for you to show up ever since you called," Julia said as she stood.

"Liberty," Sarge said with a smile, his eyes clear. His hair was combed back from his weathered face and he was wearing a plain T-shirt and jeans. He looked better every time she visited. She bent to kiss his cheek, then sat in the chair Julia had vacated for her. "You are looking spiffy," she said.

"Thank you, ma'am." Sarge smiled at her. "I told Jake that once when he was all dressed up, and he laughed at me. That boy has an attitude problem."

"He can have an attitude," Libby agreed.

Since Jake left, Libby had found her life going in a different direction than she'd ever thought possible when she'd left Seattle. She was going to complete the camp and everything that entailed, then she would look into opening her own firm in Eclipse or maybe in Cody. Roger was gone, and she was okay with that. Jake was gone, and she tried not to think about it. She was exhausted from crying and worrying about him.

Sarge was becoming important to her, and she came to visit him pretty much every other day. The other days she worked on the plans for his suite and had preliminary contractor meetings to start the remodel right after the new year. And she forgot about everything else. When Sarge and Maggie's dream became reality, she was going to be right there to see his face when he understood how loved he was. That kept her going.

Sarge looked at the present she'd almost forgotten she was holding in her lap. "What's that, chocolates?" he asked.

She held out the green-foil-wrapped gift. "No, it's not chocolates, but it is for you."

He took it and laid it on his lap. "I'll open this on Christmas," he said. "Thank you."

Julia got closer to Sarge, glancing at Libby. "You can open one present on Christmas Eve, you know."

He seemed hesitant, then Julia said, "I can't wait. Can I open it for you?" When Sarge nodded, she reached to slip the red ribbon off the foil and tear the paper at its seam. Libby watched the man's face as Julia took the lid off the box. A simple eight-by-ten-inch silver frame held an enlargement of the picture Jake had left with her. She would make a larger version to hang in Sarge's new space at the house.

Sarge didn't take it out of the box, but stared down at it, then a smile Libby had never seen before on his face was there when he looked up at her. "That's me and my Maggie," he said.

"You two made a beautiful couple," Julia said. "Why don't we go and take this to your room to see where you want to put it."

Sarge nodded and looked at Libby. "Come on, Liberty."

She was so relieved he'd called her by name. Dr. Miller had approved her giving him the picture, but she'd worried it might cause more confusion. It hadn't. Maybe it would later on, but for now he knew who she was and who Maggie had been. Julia pushed him in the wheelchair as they went back to his room.

Libby stripped off her jacket and tossed it on the bench by the door and thought she should have dressed up for Christmas Eve. Instead, she wore a pink thermal top, jeans and boots—her everyday wardrobe now.

She crossed to Julia and Sarge. "Libby, did you know that there's going to be an almost Christmas Moon tonight?" Julia asked as she positioned Sarge by the low table that held his Christmas tree.

"An *almost* Christmas Moon?" Libby asked.

"That's what I call a full moon when it's on Christmas Eve and not Christmas night," the woman said.

"A real Christmas Moon is pretty rare," Sarge chimed in as Julia made sure to set the picture down by the tree where he could see it. "Maggie used to wish to see one and finally did from the porch of the old cabin. It was beautiful, and it made the snow dance. That's what Maggie said."

Libby smiled at him. "She probably thought you made that happen for her."

"How do you know I didn't make it happen?" he asked her with a twinkle in his eye. She loved seeing him like this and couldn't help wishing Jake was there.

"I'm sure you did," Libby said as she took the chair Julia had brought over for her and sat down by him.

"His therapy is going great," Julia said. "He's starting to use the walker, and he can move pretty well with it."

The door suddenly swung back, and a man looked inside. He was sturdily built, maybe in his forties. He had a shaved head and wore casual clothing. He stayed in the doorway as he looked over at Sarge, then seemed a bit taken back when he noticed Libby. "Oh, uh. Sorry, didn't mean to interrupt anything."

"Hey, there," Julia said as she approached him.

"Can I speak to you?" the man asked her.

Sarge spoke up. "Have you met Liberty?"

"No, I can't say I have." The man came over to where they sat. "Pleased to meet you, Liberty." He held out his hand to her, and his grip was firm. "I've heard all about you."

"She's Sarge's favorite visitor," Julia said.

"I'm flattered," Libby said without pointing out that Sarge was limited on the number of visitors he could have just yet. Even Jake hadn't shown up here after he'd left. She looked at the sign-in book every time she wrote her name in it, just in case his name was there. It never had been.

Julia looked over at the man. "You said we need to talk?"

"We do," he said, then spoke to Libby. "Nice to meet you. Cool name, by the way."

When he and Julia left the room together, Libby spoke to Sarge. "Does he work here?"

He looked confused for a minute, then said, "I don't know, but he was a marine and hangs out around here."

"Oh," she said, then, "Seth and Ben will be here first thing tomorrow for Christmas. That's pretty great, isn't it?"

"Yes, my boys," he said. "That's the best present."

Julia came back in and seemed rushed as she spoke to Sarge. "Any requests for dinner?"

"Anything but that vegetable stuff," he said.

"Okay, got it." She glanced at Libby. "Are you going to hang around long enough to eat with Sarge?"

She hadn't planned on it this visit, but she found she didn't want to get back to the ranch too soon. "What time is dinner?"

"Around four. You're welcome to stay."

"Yes, thanks." She asked Sarge, "Do you want to stay in here for dinner or go to the fancy dining room?"

"I'll stay in here with you."

"Okay, I'll go and put in your orders," Julia said before glancing at Libby. "Are you coming for Christmas?"

"No, the boys are going to be here, and they need time together with Sarge. I'll see them later."

"Okay," Julia said, then left.

Sarge sighed as he looked at the picture. "My Maggie. So long ago."

Libby touched his hand. "Good memories, though."

He looked at her, some sadness in his eyes, but no confusion. "Good memories," he said softly.

Then his gaze shifted past her, and he suddenly smiled. She turned to see what he was looking at, and her world almost jolted to a stop. Jake was there, his eyes on Sarge, and he was smiling. She'd thought she might see him again, sooner or later, and she'd truly believed that she could handle it if that happened. But his sudden appearance in jeans, a loose white shirt open at the throat and tooled Western boots robbed her of any of the peace or the acceptance she thought she'd found.

Jake finally saw her and his smile vanished. He turned, and she knew he would've walked right back out if the other man she'd just met hadn't been standing in the doorway.

She heard Jake say tightly to the man, "Tell me you didn't know?"

"I can't do that," the man said.

Libby just wanted out of there. She looked away from the two men and said to Sarge, "I need to go and see about something. You visit with Jake, okay?"

"Yes, okay," he said, but looked confused.

She stood and kissed him on the cheek, then turned to head for the door. Jake made no eye contact as she went around him, and the other man cleared the doorway for her. As Libby slipped out into the hall and the door closed behind her, Julia came toward her.

"I'm so sorry. That was all Cal's doing."

Cal? That name sounded familiar. "What did he do?"

"He didn't tell Jake you were in with Sarge."

"I can't understand how Jake didn't know I was here. I'm parked outside, and he knows my Jeep. My name's in the guest book, too."

It didn't make any sense to her, but she didn't care. She was leaving. Sarge needed to see Jake without any emotional undertones from her, and she wasn't certain she could be close to Jake without doing something she'd regret, one way or the other. "Could you please explain to Sarge that I had to leave? I won't be here for dinner."

"Are you sure?"

"Very sure," she said, feeling off-balance from the shock of seeing Jake. "I'll…call before I come back."

"Okay…but Sarge is going to be disappointed. He's very attached to you."

Libby was attached to Sarge, too. "I'll come back after Christmas. Oh, shoot, I left my jacket on the bench in his room."

"No problem, wait here and I'll get it."

But Julia didn't bring it back. The man called Cal came through the door to hand it to her. "Julia said I owe you an apology, and I know I do. I thought Jake needed to see you and hopefully talk to you. I was wrong. I really do apologize."

She took her jacket and slipped it on. She barely knew what to say. "He doesn't want to see me."

Cal smiled slightly. "That's what he believes, I guess."

Before she could respond, Jake came out into the hall. "Cal, what are—"

As Jake stopped dead, Cal said to him, "You know what, you're on your own." Then he walked back through the door, and Libby was left facing Jake alone.

His blue eyes never left her face. "I thought you were gone."

"Don't worry. I'm leaving," she said, and would have if he hadn't spoken again.

He surprised her by saying, "That picture you gave Sarge, he's thrilled with it."

She didn't want small talk. "I thought you were gone, too. Then you just…just show up."

"So did you," he said with a shrug, his voice almost flat.

"I'll let you get back to visiting Sarge. I know he's happy you're here. I'm glad you came back for his sake." Nerves were beginning to make her feel light-headed, and she tried to leave again. "Goodbye," she said, but he stopped her with a question.

"How's your dancing?" he asked as if he was really interested in it.

"I don't dance anymore," she said. She still played the Christmas music, but never "Have Yourself a Merry Little Christmas."

"Oh, that's too bad." He seemed genuinely sorry. "What does Roger think about that?"

She exhaled to try to ease the tightness in her chest. "He doesn't care one way or the other."

"Is he at the ranch?"

"No." Roger had contacted her once since they'd broken up. He'd left a voice mail on her cell to let her know he received the ring, and he couldn't fathom what she'd done to the two of them. It hadn't angered her or hurt her. She was just relieved it was over. "He's back on-site," she admitted.

"You're okay with that?" he asked as he took a step closer to her.

Libby couldn't take any more polite questions and answers. "Goodbye, Jake," she said, then turned and walked away, making her escape. She hurried down the corridor, through the reception area and out to her Jeep, the only vehicle in the parking lot. There was no huge black truck anywhere in sight. She got into the Jeep and started the engine, but she wasn't going anywhere until she calmed down enough to drive.

She gripped the top of steering wheel, then leaned forward to rest her forehead on her hands. She tried to breathe evenly, then the passenger door opened suddenly. She turned, and Jake was slipping onto the passenger seat. He glanced into the back seat, then looked at her as he closed the door. "Pax didn't come with you?"

"No, he's getting fat and lazy," she muttered, and sat back in the seat.

"You never let me ask a question," he said, gazing at her.

"What question?"

"Are you spending Christmas alone at the ranch?"

His features seemed sharper, and she could see more fine lines at his eyes. She didn't want to be this close to him. "If I answer you, will you go away?"

"Depends," he said.

She sighed heavily. "No, I'm with Pax at the ranch."

"That's okay with you?"

She knew what he was trying to ask, so she told him. "Roger and I aren't together anymore."

Jake really looked legitimately surprised. "What?"

Libby held her left hand up and wiggled her bare fingers. "See, no embarrassingly huge diamond to throw at you."

He didn't smile at that. "Do you always tell a man that you love him and think he's terrific, then break up with him?" he asked.

"What are you talking about?"

"I saw you saying that to Roger on the phone."

She started to bite her bottom lip but stopped and took a breath. "I did love Roger, but I was never *in* love with him."

She heard Jake release a harsh breath before he asked, again in that flat tone, "You canceled everything?"

"Yes."

She could feel the tension growing in her and she just wanted him to get out, but he kept talking to her. "No dancing, no three hundred guests or a string quartet?"

"No engagement, no wedding, so no dancing," she said.

He frowned slightly but took his time to speak again. She couldn't read what he was thinking. His face was almost devoid of emotion, and she found she hated that. Then he asked, "Why did you break up?"

"It doesn't make any difference. I just didn't love him the way I should have to marry him." It sounded simple, but nothing had been simple for her ever since she'd met the man across from her. As much as she wanted to, she couldn't just say, "I love you, Jake, that's why I could never marry Roger," because she couldn't take him walking away again. She wasn't sure she could survive that one more time.

"I am sorry," he said in a low voice.

She swallowed hard. "I had planned so darn much that I didn't see the truth, only the plan."

"It's not too late, is it?"

She took a shuddering breath as she closed her eyes tightly. Then she made herself look at him again. She didn't know how to ask him what he meant by that.

"You deserve to be loved," he whispered.

She stayed very still, afraid if she moved right then, she'd start crying. She waited, but Jake didn't say what she wanted to hear. He didn't say one thing about loving her. She finally managed to say, "So do you. Now, please, I need to go."

Without speaking again, Jake turned away from her and stepped out of the car. She watched him walk away toward the entrance, never looking back, and she knew right then that loving Jake had never been optional for her. She simply loved him and didn't see any time in the future where she wouldn't love him. But that was for her to figure out. Jake was so closed down that she doubted he'd know love if it came to him. That was sadder than never loving at all. She put the Jeep in gear and drove away.

JAKE ALMOST KEPT walking back to the cottage he and Cal had been staying in since he'd been brought to Wicker Pines after having his attack while driving. While Jake healed, he'd been able to spend precious time with Sarge when he knew Liberty wouldn't be there. Now Sarge expected him back, and he wanted to see more of the man today. He headed to Sarge's room, and when he stepped inside, Cal was still there.

Cal got up, patted Sarge on the arm and said, "Semper fi." That made Sarge smile. Then Cal turned to Jake. "We've been talking marine to marine."

"We're staying to have dinner with Sarge," Jake said. "Could you let Julia know?"

"I'm on it."

As Cal left, Jake sat down in the chair next to Sarge. "You're looking great," he said. It was such a relief to be able to visit the man and have him there, both physically and mentally.

"Do I look spiffy?"

Jake laughed at that. "Yes, you look very spiffy."

Sarge looked at the picture Libby had gifted him. "Maggie isn't here," he said. "I wish…" His voice faded off, then he looked at Jake. "I miss her."

Jake reached to cover Sarge's hand with his. "I miss her, too," he said. "She did love Christmas, didn't she?"

"Yes, she sure did." He looked at Jake. "She would be happy you boys are here. I think she'd like Liberty, don't you?"

Jake glanced at the photo and for a moment, he was looking at Liberty, then that illusion was gone. "Yes, she would have liked Liberty."

CHAPTER SIXTEEN

JAKE SAT WITH Sarge after dinner until the man fell asleep, then he stood to go back to the cottage. When he stepped out into the hallway, Cal was sitting on one of the upholstered benches against the wall by the door. "He's asleep," he said. "It's going to be a big day tomorrow, and he needs his rest."

Cal motioned Jake over to the bench on the opposite wall to face him. "Sit for a minute," he said, and Jake knew something was coming.

But he sat down, anyway. "Okay."

"So, you let her leave?" Cal asked.

Jake exhaled. "I had to."

Cal shook his head. "You know she's not engaged anymore, don't you?"

"That doesn't change anything."

"I don't understand how you can love her and let her go."

Those words tore at Jake. "How can I love

her and not let her go? I'm not what she needs. I can't be."

"And you won't even try," Cal muttered.

Jake stood. He'd had enough. But Cal wasn't finished. "Yeah, go, run away."

Jake stood very still in front of the man. "I'm going to get some sleep."

"You do know that, after everything you've told me over and over again about your time together with Liberty, she's the best thing that's ever happened to you. Don't you?"

Jake had accepted that before he'd even left the ranch, but he was perfectly wrong for her. He'd admitted he loved Liberty slowly, but it was there. He more than loved her, if that was possible, and he wanted her happy with someone she deserved. "I can't change the way things are," he said tonelessly.

"You told her you loved her, and she walked away?"

"Of course not."

"You're the one who told me once that it's better to do something and regret it, then regret never doing it. I think you're right. You'll regret this for the rest of your life."

Cal reached into his pocket, then handed Jake the truck keys.

JAKE STOPPED THE truck beside Liberty's Jeep and looked at the glowing Christmas lights she'd strung along the railing of the porch. There was a huge wreath on the door, and smoke was rising out of the chimney into the night sky, which was dominated by a rising full moon. No lights showed in the windows. He turned off the truck and took the porch steps in a single stride before he knocked on the door. Nothing happened. He tested the doorknob and opened the door.

When he stepped inside, he saw Liberty's jacket on the cowhide bench and her boots under it. She was in the house. He took off his jacket and boots, leaving them by hers, then went to the archway. A dying fire in the great room flickered and sparked. The kitchen was dark, the office door was open to show more darkness, and the only light came from the Christmas tree lights and the flickering fire in the hearth. He clicked on the wagon wheel chandelier in the entry.

Pax came first. Jake heard the tapping of his nails on a hard surface above him, and he turned in time to see the dog running down the stairs toward him. When Pax got to him, Jake bent down and let him lick his face a few times before he stood to get out of range. "Okay, so, where is she?" he asked.

He got his answer when Pax turned and headed back to the stairs, where Liberty stood at the top of the staircase. "Hey," he said as he stood by the archway. "Your door wasn't locked." He couldn't tell if Liberty was stunned into silence, or if she wasn't going to talk to him at all. "I apologize for barging in like this."

She hadn't been in bed, at least not for the night. She was still wearing what she had on earlier, but her hair looked tangled around her shoulders. She came down, then stopped on the second step from the bottom. "Why did you?" she asked.

He exhaled, then moved closer to her. "I wanted to finally have that talk to explain something important."

She frowned. "Is Sarge okay?"

"Yes, he was asleep when I left."

She wasn't going to make this easy, not that he expected it would be. But he wasn't going to leave until she heard him out. "Can we sit somewhere? I'm not used to looking up at you," he said with a soft smile.

She didn't answer but came down and

passed him to go into the great room. He followed her as she went by the couch and chairs and headed to the office. She flicked on the lights and went directly to sit in the chair behind the desk before she turned toward him. Jake put the wooden chair in a position to face her, but not too close, then sat down. He looked at her, then glanced away, unsettled by the flat expression in her green eyes.

That's when he saw the old box he'd left for her sitting on the desktop. Liberty reached for it, then pushed it closer to him before she looked at him again. "This is yours," she said.

"I don't want it."

She turned to open it and took out the medal. "Do you want this?" she asked as she laid it by the box.

Actually, he had regretted leaving it with the rest of the things he never wanted to see again. He reached for it, felt its weight in his hand, then shifted in the chair to tuck it in his watch pocket. "Sarge gave it to me when I left for boot camp. It was one of his medals he'd been given when he was in the marines."

She clasped her slender hands in her lap. "Is Cal waiting in the truck for you?"

"No," he said, repeating, "You forgot to lock the door. Anybody could walk in here."

She pressed back in the chair and gripped the arms with her hands. "I didn't bother to. I've been changing, actually. You know, when I came here, I couldn't let things go. And, yes, you were right, I was uptight, cautious, worried and overreacted. I drove you nuts."

"I never said that."

"No, but I know that's true. Now I'm learning to be more in the moment. Goodness knows, I still backslide, but in general, I'm rearranging my life. I'm not pushing for what I think I want but trying to let life happen." She sighed. "Letting go has been working for me, so far."

"Letting go of what?" he asked.

"Roger, that's all over. I let go of the idea of making partner at my firm in Seattle. I'm starting my own firm around here when I finish this project. I'm not holding on to things just because it scares me to let go of them."

Her words struck him hard. Did that mean she'd let go of anything they might have had? He hoped not. "I always thought your persistence was unstoppable."

"It is, pretty much," she said with a touch

of what he thought might be pride. She tucked her hair behind her ears and said something that had nothing to do with what she'd been telling him. "I wanted Sarge to have that picture to remember what he had, not what he doesn't have now," she said wistfully. "When he looks at it, he smiles a wonderful smile." She took the original out of the desk drawer and laid it on the desk by him. "Thanks for letting me borrow it. I have a larger one to put in his room when he comes home."

He reached for the photo and put it in his shirt pocket. When he'd told Liberty she had a kind heart, it had been an understatement. "You're..." He couldn't catch the right words for what he saw in her right then.

"I'm what?" she asked and looked tired, as if she'd had enough and wanted this all over and done.

"I have never met a woman like you," he said. He leaned toward her and felt his own heart catch. "You're beautiful, intelligent and persistent and have the kindest heart."

She stared at him silently as color touched her cheeks. He kept talking, needing to say these things to her. "When I left here, it was one of the hardest things I've ever done, because I wanted to stay. The truth is, I left because I was sure I'd give you more pain than happiness if I stayed. I was sure you were better with Roger, or with anyone but me."

"But you never asked me what I wanted," she said.

Cal had been right about that. "I came to talk to you, because I want you to know that, if things were different, if I was different..." He let his words die out when she almost grimaced.

"You didn't have to come all the way out here to tell me that. Your note made that very clear. You are who you are." Pax pushed at her hand, but she ignored him. She looked right at Jake. "It is what it is, right?"

"What fool told you that?" he asked wryly.

"It doesn't matter," she said. "If you're waiting for me to tell you you're right, I'll do it. You're right. You're wrong for me, and I'm wrong for you. There," she said. She started to stand but ended up dropping back down on the chair as if her legs had suddenly given out. "You can leave now with a clear conscience."

He knew right then that if he walked away this time, he'd go headfirst into the storm.

Maybe that was his destiny, the one he'd fashioned on his own. He wouldn't leave here unless he had no hope left.

"You were right about me, about a lot of things," he said, "I need to stop shutting people out of my life. I never meant to hurt you, never."

She looked so sad right then. "Liberty, tell me what would make you happy?"

"Why do you want to know?"

"Just tell me."

So SHE TOLD him the only thing that would ever make her happy. "If I was loved and loved someone, the same way Sarge and Maggie loved each other, the way he still loves her, that would make me beyond happy." She shrugged.

"I always thought theirs was a one-in-a-million love," Jake said softly.

She closed her eyes as she murmured, "Maybe it is." She understood right then that a one-in-a-million love was something unbearably painful, unless both people felt the same way. Slowly, she opened her eyes and Jake was still watching her.

He rubbed both hands over his face, then

cleared his throat. "I have messed things up in my life, but I'm not going to do it again, even if it won't make any difference."

"What are you talking about?"

He crouched down in front of her, but he didn't touch her. "Listen to me, and if you want me to go when I'm finished, I will, and I'll never bother you again."

She bit her lip, then nodded.

"I did something pretty stupid, and I know now what it cost me. I've never thought I could be tangled up in anyone else's life, because I knew that I was in this alone for the duration. Then I met you, and you began to shape my world, to make me question everything I'd believed was true about myself. Then I walked out. I left you behind. I thought you were going to be married, that you'd have the life you wanted, and I wasn't what you wanted."

"Jake, no, I never… You're wrong."

"I've never wished that I was wrong before. But if you asked me what my wish was when I came into this house earlier, I'd tell you. I wished I was finding you in the great room, that you were glad I was here, and I knew as long as you were there, I wasn't alone.

Between you and Pax, I've been pulled into wishing this was my life, that you were the best part of that life." He exhaled in a rush. "I guess...my final wish would be that you loved me as much as I know I love you."

Libby stared at him, stunned. She could barely believe what he was saying. It was everything she'd hoped for. "You...you really wish that?"

"Yes, please, give me a chance to love you. I can't walk out of here alone." His voice was low and unsteady. "I've done that once, and without you, it was a whole new painful definition of alone for me."

She smiled at him, her heart so full she could barely breathe. "Jake Bishop, I love you."

She leaned toward him, then his arms were around her, pulling her up and tightly against him. She could feel his heart racing in his chest, and she inhaled the scent of him. She was home. Finally. In the home she wanted for the rest of her life. "You really love me?" she heard him say.

"I love you so much, I don't even have a word for it," she said against his chest, then realized she wanted him to be able to read what she'd just said.

She eased back enough to look up at him, but before she could repeat it, Jake was smiling at her. "We'll figure out a word for it. We can work on it for years and years and years and years, if we have to."

She suddenly realized what had just happened, and she could barely ask, "You…you heard me?"

He framed her face with his hands, and unsteadiness was in his touch. "Yes, and you sound just as I remember."

"But…but, we've never spoken to each other before."

"No, but you spoke to me in my dreams." He brushed at the dampness on her cheek she hadn't been aware of. "Please, don't cry."

"These are happy tears," she said.

"I never understood happy tears," he whispered to her.

"They're special, only for when life is just so good you can't believe it. Like now. It's a Christmas miracle. You're here, and you can hear me. You…were in the hospital?"

"Sort of. I've been at Wicker Pines with Sarge in a cottage at the rear of the property.

I had some sort of attack as I was driving to Cody, and Cal went into action. Next thing I knew, he had my old boss agreeing to have me treated there as long as it didn't become public knowledge. We underestimated the security and privacy there, believe me, and no one knew I was there, except a few staff members and Sarge. They flew in one of the specialists I'd seen before, and there was a correction of some sort, maybe from the altitude or just healing. They aren't sure."

"They didn't operate?"

"No, but I might have to have a procedure in the future. I only have 50 percent hearing in my right ear. So, I'm not sure, but…"

She touched his lips with her fingertips. "Later, tell me it all later. It's a miracle, no matter what happened." Then she stood on her tiptoes to whisper, "I love you. Now, can you just kiss me?"

Before the last word died out, Jake pulled her closer and he kissed her. Everything fell into place, into something that Libby had only dreamed of before. She felt complete, and she knew being here with Jake was where she'd been heading all of her life. In his arms, holding on to him, breathing him in and being loved by him.

She drew back and sighed. "What now?"

"That depends on you," he said in a rough whisper.

"Depends on what?"

"Whether you'll marry me." He shook his head. "I never planned on saying that to anyone. You know, we can wait and see how things go, and then you can decide if you want to. I'm going to be around here from now on. I know I'll need to find work. Even with the healing, I can't fly yet. So I'm thinking I might be able to contract as an instructor sooner or later, but for now, I'm staying right here."

"Good, because I'm staying where you're staying, and going where you're going. That's the way it's supposed to be when you get married, isn't it?"

"Are you sure?"

"Yes, as long as you'll accept my dowry."

"What are you talking about?"

"It's not much, just the little cabin beyond the trees. Seth wants to give it to me as a bonus for my work on the camp. Ben and Sarge agreed. I was expecting to be there with Pax." She touched his beard-roughened chin and smiled. "What do you think?"

"I think this is Christmas Eve and we have someplace to be."

THE PORCH OF the old cabin was the perfect place to watch the moon rise huge on the horizon, its light blotting out the shadows all around Jake and Liberty as they sat on the top step. They were wrapped together in blankets they'd found inside after they'd managed to drive Jake's truck on the original access road to the cabin.

"An almost Christmas Moon," Libby said, making sure Jake was looking at her. "I think the same magic applies to an almost Christmas Moon as a Christmas Moon. You get to make a wish, and they say the couple that kisses under that moon are together forever."

Jake smiled at her. "I don't need a wish. I'm luckier and happier than I have any right to be right now. But the kiss…well, that's different." When he kissed her, everything made sense, and *happy* didn't begin to describe how this man made her feel.

He drew back and was grinning. "That seals the deal. This is forever. We'll be here whenever the Christmas Moon shows again. But next, a small wedding, family, close friends, a carrot cake wedding cake with two tiers tops, and you wearing what your mother wore at her wedding as long as the dress train isn't longer than two feet. And no dancing."

She laughed softly. "Wow, you were really paying attention. But I want to dance with you at our wedding."

"Really?"

"Just wear good boots," she said, and they both laughed, holding on to each other as the almost Christmas Moon lit up the world for them.

EPILOGUE

Eclipse Ridge Ranch, Valentine's Day

THE WEDDING WAS a simple ceremony with family and a few close friends in the great room at the ranch. Farley and Libby's dad had cleared the deck of snow to do the barbecuing. The carrot cake wedding cake made by Libby's mother had been a hit. As Libby offered Jake a bite, she was amazed at the way her life just got better and better.

Jake had never looked more handsome in a white shirt, black rope tie, black jeans and tooled Western boots. She was wearing her mother's wedding clothes, an ivory silk blouse with a long ivory skirt with no train, and simple pumps. Jake had asked her to wear her hair down for the wedding, and she had, except for catching it back on the sides with silver clips her mother had given to her.

Cal Harris stood across the table from them with a glass of champagne in his hand.

"A toast to Jake and Libby, to destiny that brought them together and to Jake's good sense not to let Libby get away." There was laughter and applause from the guests. Libby knew how close they had come to not being there together, and she moved closer to Jake, reaching for his hand. She felt the gold band on his ring finger, the mate of hers that she wore with her engagement ring, a single small diamond set in gold that was a perfect fit.

Seth spoke up. "Friends and family. For their first dance together, I'm honored to present to you, Mr. and Mrs. Jake Bishop."

There was more applause, then Jake led Libby to the middle of the room where it had been cleared of furniture and rugs. On Valentine's Day, "Have Yourself a Merry Little Christmas" flowed out of the speakers. Libby stepped into Jake's arms, rested her cheek against his chest and danced to the only song she knew how to dance to, with the only man she ever wanted to dance with.

She drew back just enough to glance up at Jake, and the look in his eyes took her breath away. "I love you," she said.

"Thank you for loving me. I didn't make it easy, but you stuck it out." He leaned down and kissed her, then whispered, "I love you." Libby shifted, reaching to rest her hands on his shoulders as Jake drew her more tightly to him. "Kevin will never know how grateful I am that he ran when you crushed his feet."

She chuckled a bit breathlessly. "I'm glad he ran."

As the music came to an end, Jake leaned down to whisper in her ear. "I can't do this much longer."

She was confused. "Do what?"

He moved back as Seth came over to them. Jake gave him a hug, then stood back and asked him, "Do you know whatever happened to Moon Dance?"

"No," Seth said. "Why?"

"Just wondering." Jake tightened his hold on Libby's hand a bit before he looked back at her. "That was the horse I first rode around here." He never took his eyes off Libby. "Moon Dance."

She finally got it. "Really?"

"Yes, really," he said.

Libby spoke to Seth. "You know, we've done the cakes, had our toasts and had our dance. Is it rude if we leave now and leave you all to enjoy the barbeque?"

"No, not at all," he said, and came to kiss Libby on her cheek, then hug Jake again. "Go with my blessings, brother."

Libby and Jake took time to say goodbye to her parents and the guests, then finally crossed to where Sarge and Ben sat on the couch with Cal. "We're taking off," Jake said.

Ben stood and caught both of them in a group hug. "I never thought I'd see this day, but I'm so happy to be wrong."

Cal got up. "I'm not sure I ever believed in real love until now." He hugged Jake, then Libby. "I'm signing with Wicker Pines as head of their expanded physical therapy department and maybe work with the vets in their new veteran's aid section." He glanced over at Julia. "And I can be Sarge's in-home therapist and keep an eye on everything."

Jake smiled. "That sounds like a plan."

"I think so. Now, you two be safe and have fun wherever you go," he said, before he turned and headed in Julia's direction.

Sarge was looking up at Libby, then held out his hand to her. She took it without hesitating and could see a clarity in his eyes that made her day even better if that was possible. Since he'd come home two weeks ago, bringing Julia along as his caregiver, he'd been doing pretty well. "You look just like my Maggie did when we got married," he said. He glanced at Jake. "You love her, boy, and never stop, no matter what."

"I will, sir," he said. "I promise."

Libby bent to kiss Sarge on the cheek. "Thank you so much for being here for us. It means a lot to us."

"It was my honor, Liberty," he said.

"It was our honor having you here," Jake said as he bent down closer to Sarge. "I wouldn't be here if it weren't for you and Maggie. Thank you. I love you."

Sarge smiled up at Jake. "Oh, I love you, too, son."

Jake patted his shoulder, then stood and put his arm around Libby as Julia came over with Cal. "Are you two going to tell us where you're going on your honeymoon?" Julia asked.

Jake looked at Libby. "No, but it's a great place."

"Probably someplace with golden sand and palm trees," Cal said.

"No palm trees," Jake replied, and Libby laughed. "We'll let you know when we get

back," he said, and led Libby out of the room
into the entry. They hurried up the stairs,
changed out of their wedding clothes into
their jeans, T-shirts and boots in the master bedroom, then hurried back down to the
entry. They grabbed their jackets and didn't
look back as they stepped out into the cold
air of late afternoon.

"We did it," Jake said, reaching to hold on
to Libby's hand after they got in the truck and
drove west toward the highway. But a mile
before the blind curve, he turned off onto a
newly bladed road that led up to a set of new
gates that had been installed for the future
entrance to the camp.

The gates stood open, and he drove through
onto a road that had been cleared to make
easy access to the original mess hall and
bunkhouse. Jake jumped out and went to
close and lock the gates, then got back in the
truck.

"You think Pax will be okay staying at the
house with my parents?" Liberty asked as he
reached for her hand and drove up the newly
plowed road.

"Yes, and he'll get even fatter and happier."
Jake looked ahead and could see the old cabin

come into view where it sat snug and still covered in snow from a storm a week ago. Liberty had told him the cabin felt like home to her, and it was feeling that way to him, too.

He pulled the truck around to the back where he'd had the road crew clear it so the vehicles would be out of view. He had barely stopped when Liberty climbed out and looked back at him with her door open. "Come on," she said.

When he got out, she was there, reaching for his hand as they went around to the front of the house. The porch was cleared of snow, and he'd had two chairs put there for them to watch the next Christmas Moon.

"Perfect," Liberty said as they went up the stairs. "No one will ever know we're here." She opened the door, but before she could go inside, he swept her up into his arms.

"Not so fast," Jake said. "I've become a traditional sort of guy, as odd as that sounds, and I want to carry you over the threshold."

She giggled, and he loved the sound of it. "I'm all for that." She sobered just a bit as she put her arm around his neck. "I can't believe this is real. It's like a dream."

"Believe me, this is better than any dream,"

he said, and carried her inside. It hadn't changed much, except for clearing the dustcovers and freshening things up. The new electric heater he'd had installed—so they wouldn't have to light the potbelly stove and have the smoke give away the fact that they were in the cabin—had been turned on the night before. It was warm and homey and familiar and perfect.

Jake kicked the door shut, then put Liberty down so he could take off his jacket and boots. When he turned, she said, "I love this place," and he thought she might cry.

"Happy tears again?" he asked.

"You bet, beyond happy," she said as she took off her own jacket and boots.

As soon as he'd done the same, he turned and lifted her back into his arms.

He carried her into the bedroom. "You were right about not replacing the iron bed. It belongs here, and so does Maggie's quilt."

He kissed her, and he felt his heart soar. "I made a promise to Sarge to love you and never stop."

She grinned up at him. "You'd better keep your promises, Mr. Bishop."

"Keeping that promise is the easiest thing I'll ever do."

Liberty giggled, and Jake let the sweet sound surround him as he again bent to kiss his wife.

* * * * *

Get 4 FREE REWARDS!

We'll send you 2 FREE Books plus 2 FREE Mystery Gifts.

Love Inspired books feature uplifting stories where faith helps guide you through life's challenges and discover the promise of a new beginning.

FREE Value Over $20

THE 2020 CHRISTMAS ROMANCE COLLECTION!

'Tis the season for romance!
You're sure to fall in love with these tenderhearted love stories from some of your favorite bestselling authors!

YES! Please send me the first shipment of **The 2020 Christmas Romance Collection**. This collection begins with 1 FREE TRADE SIZE BOOK and 2 FREE gifts in the first shipment (approx. retail value of the gifts is $7.99 each). Along with my free book, I'll also get 2 additional mass-market paperback books. If I do not cancel, I will continue to receive three books a month for four additional months. My first four shipments will be billed at the discount price of $19.98 U.S./$25.98 CAN., plus $1.99 U.S./$3.99 CAN. for shipping and handling*. My fifth and final shipment will be billed at the discount price of $18.98 U.S./$23.98 CAN., plus $1.99 U.S./$3.99 CAN. for shipping and handling*. I understand that accepting the free books and gifts places me under no obligation to buy anything. I can always return a shipment and cancel at any time. My free books and gifts are mine to keep no matter what I decide.

☐ 260 HCN 5449   ☐ 460 HCN 5449

Name (please print)

Address   Apt. #

City   State/Province   Zip/Postal Code

Mail to the **Harlequin Reader Service:**
IN U.S.A.: P.O. Box 1341, Buffalo, NY. 14240-8531
IN CANADA: P.O. Box 603, Fort Erie, Ontario L2A 5X3

#359 BRIDE ON THE RUN
Butterfly Harbor Stories • by Anna J. Stewart

Monty Bettencourt's life is pretty great. He has a new boat, an expanding business...and a fleeing stowaway bride? Meanwhile, Sienna Fairchild has gone from walking down the aisle to trying not to fall overboard...or for her inadvertent rescuer!

#360 THE CHRISTMAS PROMISE
by Janice Carter

Ella Jacobs never forgot that her teenage crush, Ben Winters, abandoned her when she needed him most. Years later, can she reveal the truth behind what really happened that night, even if it means risking their love?

#361 HER HOMETOWN DETECTIVE
by Elizabeth Mowers

When Faith Fitzpatrick moves back home to open up a motorcycle repair shop, she's suspected of vandalizing nearby storefronts. Detective John "Tully" McTully is on the case, but has he met his match in the hard-edged newcomer?

#362 SECOND CHANCE CHRISTMAS
Turtleback Beach • by Rula Sinara

His brother's death drove former Navy SEAL Damon Woods to dedicate his life to ocean rescue. Now he faces a new challenge—Zuri Habib, the woman he rejected and aunt of a son he never knew he had.

HWCNM1220